Almost to Aspen ☆

FOSTER SANDERS

SPECIAL THANKS

Special thanks to Leila Jane Hewitt and John Gillespie for sharing their story. It needed to be told.

Also special thanks to Charlotte Hasty, Amanda Jackman, Pati Stapleton, James Dodd, Jr. and Mary Nelson for their support during the course of this journey to Aspen—and to talented Paul Neese for his cover art work.

Lastly, I thank my good friends that allowed me to use their names in this novel—you are trusting and adventurous souls.

PROLOGUE

Two assassins hoping to kill Leila Jane Hewitt had died in her bed, and her young fiancé had lost his life in an automobile accident trying to save her. She survived, but her life remained at a standstill. Tours of Ebenezer Forest had been suspended with no date set for reopening. Journalists from all over the world wanted to interview Leila. Every aspect of her heroic personal life had become a hot commodity.

Mark Mabry, Leila's love, had been buried at an emotionally charged and nationally televised funeral only a few days before. A number of reporters remained stationed directly across the street from her country estate.

The public had access to Ebenezer Forest's commercial telephone number, and the phone would not stop ringing. Leila and her best friend, Amanda Harrison, sat on the back porch talking to each other and listening to the messages as they rolled in. No calls had been answered at all.

Chapter 1

Brr""'ing, Brr""'ing, Brr""'ing. The Ebenezer Forest answering machine allowed lengthy responses.

A deep male voice began, "Miss Leila Hewitt, this is Powder White, calling you again. Powder is what everyone calls me—I know my name probably sounded fictitious when you heard it yesterday. My real name is William. I am calling from Aspen, Colorado. I've been watching the news, and seeing all the reporters around your home, and I want to invite you and whoever you want to bring—up to six people—to my private, very well-guarded estate in Aspen. I am sitting here with the sheriff of Pitkin County, Colorado. You can call him back at his office at 904-743-7433 and he will tell you he'll assign a deputy to ensure your safety if you would accept this invitation. From the news, it sounds like your life may still be in danger. I, and my many friends up here, have never seen a more courageous woman or a more special lady in our whole life—and I, uh, wanta help YOU, and I wanta meet YOU, I want to be your friend, and offer you a safe place to recover up here in Aspen. So whenever you are ready to accept this offer—please, please call me at 904-743-5555.

I am waiting for you to return my call, and I will remain waiting until you do. Here is the sheriff."

"Miss. Hewitt, this is Sheriff DeSalty from Pitkin County, Colorado. Powder White is a close friend of mine. If you accept his offer, I will see to it that you will be very safe here in Pitkin County. You have my word and my phone number." Pause.

"This is Powder again. I don't usually do things like this, but a lot of people come to Aspen to get lost for a while in the mountains. And they come to have a little time to heal—you know, to find a little peace and quiet. It sounds like you may need to get away for a while, and I want to help you, no strings attached. Just give me a call Miss Leila. Thanks." Click.

Leila looked over at Amanda, saying, "Have you ever heard of anything more ridiculous than that—calling a total stranger—can you imagine, going to the length of actually getting a sheriff to talk to me as a reference for his credibility?"

"Well," Amanda replied with a big laugh, "he sounded like a pretty nice feller to me. I would rather see you 'take a powder' in Aspen, Leila, than hang around here with all these scuzz-bucket media folks across the street." She laughed loudly, "And I've always wanted to go to Aspen. Call him back right now! I'll go with you!"

"You're getting crazier by the day," chuckled Leila.

*****

In the upstairs backroom of Jim's Restaurant & Bar in Aspen, Powder White looked around the poker table at his buddies with a big grin. They had all paused to hear Powder's phone call to the latest American superstar, Leila Hewitt. His fortune and nickname came from the Powder River Basin oil boom in Wyoming where his family owned the largest spread in the entire discovery area.

"What is your next move on the little ole lady?" asked Bud Holt, owner of a popular local athletic center.

Powder shrugged his shoulders, ran his right hand through his blondish-white hair, then turned toward the sheriff and said, "Thank you very much for your kind assistance, Sheriff. I have never laid my eyes on such a gorgeous gal in my whole life. I am going after Leila Hewitt like a mountain lion goes after a young doe!"

"My word, Powder, don't you think after all she has been through this Leila gal ought to be spared the likes of you," wryly questioned the salty and well known Aspen legend, John 'No Elk' Gillespie in his native Arkansas drawl. He picked up a deck of cards, looked over at Powder and added with a big smile, "That lady looks wa-ay too smart and strong-willed to buy into a pile of your baloney, Powder!" He started dealing the cards.

"They don't call you 'No Elk' Gillespie here in Aspen for nothin,' John," began Powder, "but it ought to be 'No D-e-a-r'! How long has it been since YOU had a woman?"

"It has been ten and a half years since my wife, Pati, died," replied John. "Are you in or out?" he asked Powder.

"I should not have asked that question. I apologize," said Powder. "I'm in."

Before the next poker hand had played out, a teaser news story appeared on TV Channel 7 in Colorado. Standing on the now famous Ebenezer Church Road across from Leila's house in

Ebenezer Forest was a Pensacola Channel 3 newscaster. He began,

> "As far as we have been able to find out, Leila Jane Hewitt has left her home only once a day to feed her animals since her groom-to-be, Mark Mabry, was buried in the Hewitt family cemetery in Ebenezer Forest near here. She has yet to make one single comment on the two men that intended to MURDER HER but died in her bed over a week ago in surely one of the most bizarre series of events in Florida Panhandle history. We are expecting her to come outside a little later this afternoon and feed these guineas and hopefully she will allow us an interview. Stay tuned!"

During the broadcast a live video of the guineas and a photo of Leila taken at Mark Mabry's funeral were shown.

The men playing poker at Jim's Restaurant in Aspen watched every second of the broadcast. When it was over Bud Holt asked, "She is something else--but what the heck is a guinea?"

"We have 'em back in Arkansas," replied John Gillespie.

"I will learn how to cook them if I have to," said Powder with a big smile on his face.

Bud leaned forward, saying, "To get next to that beautiful lady, Powder, you would probably bring in the finest chef from New York City to rotisserize a guinea or two."

Gillespie, looking at Powder, chided, "I predict you will not be able to 'mesmerize' Miss Leila--and I fully expect that if she ever meets you, she will give YOU the bird," he said laughingly.

Powder smirked at bit, raised his eyebrows as though he was thinking of his next move, and slowly replied, "We shall see."

Almost to Aspen

Chapter 2

James Watson, a lawyer during the week and a fisherman and heavy drinker on weekends, parked his banged up white Ford Ranger near the rear of his house in old downtown Destin, Florida. He left his rods and reels in the bed of his truck and entered the back screen door into his kitchen. Immediately noticing there was a message on his answering machine, he hit the play button.

"James, as soon as you get back from fishing, please call me. I have a Fort Walton hooker who wants to sign away her two young boys for adoption tonight," spoke a raspy voice. James instantly recognized the caller as his main private investigator, Pearlie Towns.

After pouring himself a strong vodka and grapefruit, James walked into the living room and sat down in the large recliner. He pulled out his cell phone. The tall, lean barrister never did anything fast--except fix himself the same exact drink at every opportunity. He dialed Pearlie's number and, when he answered, James got right to the point. "Hey, Pearl, can't this wait until morning?"

"Something is up, James--the whore needs to get out town fast--like tonight! I say pick up these children now, or she will be gone," urged Pearlie.

"Have you seen the kids? Tell me about them--how old are they?" asked James.

"Two white boys, ages four and two. I haven't seen them, but the hooker says they are healthy looking and nothing is wrong with them," reported Pearlie. "She has their birth certificates, and both show 'father unknown,'" he added.

"What is her name?" asked James, "And what did you tell her?"

"Her street name is 'Sweet Jaws' because she gives a killer BJ," started Pearlie. "Her real name is June Bradley. I told her the regular deal--you know, she can't sell her kids, she is only going to get a G-note 'loan' she probably won't have to pay back, yada yada. She says she has to dump the boys tonight."

"It is almost five o'clock, can you have 'em at my office at six-thirty?" asked James. "And Pearlie, this will be one and a half the regular amount for you--not double. I am going to try and keep the boys together."

"Why don't you place them separately instead of sticking it to me, James?" Pearlie whined.

"You are getting very greedy, Pearlie. Look how much you made last week on the doctor with the DUI. Go find yourself another drunken rich guy, and help me keep these brothers together," replied James, adding, "See you at six-thirty, and thanks, Pearlie."

*****

James Watson had been practicing law for ten years, and placing kids for private adoption was one of his only lucrative specialties. Nearly all of the kids he handled were placed before they were born. He had a list of affluent couples that wanted babies, and all would pay as much as they were asked to fork over. But James knew from experience that it was much tougher to place older kids--especially two of them to the same family.

He took a quick shower, freshened up his drink and immediately headed to his office. He knew he had to personally assemble the entire adoption package. All of the forms had been rapidly prepared by the time Pearlie and the new client arrived with her kids.

To James's surprise, June "Sweet Jaws" Bradley entered the law office carrying a third child, a baby. The two young boys were holding hands, almost clinging to each other. James greeted the mother and saw that the baby was dressed in pink. He asked June the children's names. She introduced him to Luke, the older boy, and little Jake. Neither boy looked at James. He stuck out his hand but there was no response or reaction whatsoever, even from the four-year-old.

June folded back the scarf partially covering the little girl's face and said, "This is Annette."

James asked Pearlie to stay in the waiting room with the two boys, then led June and her baby girl back to his office. He noted June's full name, official address and other personal information. June handed him the boys' birth certificates.

James then leaned back and asked, "Why are you doing this? Are you certain you want to abandon the boys?"

June was very pale and appeared distraught. Like her boys, she was reluctant to look James in the eye. She looked physically and mentally exhausted, and was only able to express herself very slowly.

"I can't do this anymore," she began with her head half raised. "I have tried, but three kids are just too many. And I need to get away from someone," she whispered, barely able to be heard.

"Are you okay? You know if you go through with this tonight, under the law you will have NO rights at all after this, and will never to be able to see your two boys again," he represented, knowing full well he was lying.

"I understand," June answered. "I have to do it."

"The boys look very attached to each other," said James. "And I think it would be best to keep them and Annette together. You don't want to split up your children, do you? It is not fair to them."

"I am NOT giving up Annette," replied June emotionally. "She is all I have."

James could tell that his suggestion was headed nowhere. He began obtaining all of the final information that he needed from June. He asked, and she maintained that she did not know the identity of the actual fathers of any of her three children. She refused to give any information as to where she was going or with whom. She did ask about the one thousand dollar loan she was expecting to receive, and he assured her it would be paid immediately after all the papers were signed.

James made the necessary copies after the papers were completely filled out. He then told June that the documents would be signed only after she told her children she would never see them again. He had learned from experience that if a parent

10

could get through that step, they were more likely in a state of mind to actually complete a permanent surrender. James did not tell June that in reality there was an interim period in which she might be able to change her mind.

James told June he was going to take her back to her two boys, and she was to tell them that she was going away forever and also that she loved them. But he was going to introduce them to a new mommy and a new daddy--and the two of them would be together with these new parents forever--and they would be very happy.

June looked up at attorney James Watson, with his belly half full of vodka and grapefruit, and into his bloodshot eyes, and asked, "Is that all true?"

"ABSOLUTELY," assured James.

He led her out of his office to see her sons for the last time. They seemed happy to see her come back to them again. June, Luke, Jake and Annette were then taken to a smaller office to say their farewells. The door was closed. They were alone together for about seven minutes. In the meantime, James wrote Pearlie a check that was to be his when June signed the papers.

When June led Luke and Jake out of the room, she bent over and kissed them both goodbye. The boys were wide-eyed but not crying. James sent Pearlie and the two boys back into the same room they had just exited and closed the door.

June, carrying Annette, followed James back to his office where she signed all of the papers. He gave her the promised check for one thousand dollars with the word "loan" typed in the lower left corner.

James then asked one more time, "Are you sure you will not allow Annette to stay with her brothers?" She said she was sure.

11

"Did you bring any suitcases with clothes or toys for the boys?" James asked.

"I didn't have time to do anything like that," she answered. "I was in a bad spot."

James led June back to his reception room and told her to wait. He returned to the office where the boys and Pearlie waited. He told Pearlie to take June and Annette wherever they were going--to their next destination in life.

Alone with the boys for the first time, James looked down at Luke and little Jake. Their young and pensive eyes drifted upward toward his.

James gave both boys a quick pat on the head and said, "Wait right here little fellows, until I turn out the lights."

Chapter 3

A chosen life of peace and quiet immersed in nature is rarely transformed into immense publicity and fame. Never in Leila's wildest dreams did she expect to fall in love with a younger man and watch him die on Ebenezer Road. She also never expected to shoot two men who would both end up dead in her bed.

Leila's life had reverted to what it was before she met Mark. Her first commitment was to God. It was followed by her commitment to her beloved Ebenezer Forest, with its precious animals and cherished flora. Preserving the glorious Choctawhatchee River Basin, which nourishes the wildlife habitat of her inherited and cherished family estate--including Hominy Creek and Ebenezer Church--were all part of her further commitment. She viewed all of her worldly possessions as gifts from her Almighty Lord. They were her charge and her fully accepted duty. They were once again Leila's absolute purpose for being on this earth and all she had left.

After Mark's death, Leila's faith assured her that everything that happened in her life was in God's plan for her. He had told her it was okay to share her life with Mark. She did so for as long as God would allow. Leila had witnessed enough in her life to know that death is a certain part of all lives. She believed in her heart that she was on earth for whatever purpose He directs. She would remain steadfast to her belief that her service to Him would be the priority of her existence.

*****

It was time for Leila to make a few decisions. She felt that with the ongoing clamor and manic public interest, she was a personal distraction to the normal functioning of Ebenezer Forest. Being bombarded with contact from the written and televised media, from movie producers, advertising interests and others, she had to do something to get Ebenezer Forest up and running again without all of the frenzy. At the same time her tremendous fame was attracting unbelievable numbers of groups desirous of scheduling a tour. She recognized the need to hire a manager for Ebenezer Forest. Her minister, Tom McGraw, had advised that she should get away for a while and allow the immense national interest in her life to abate.

In the late afternoon Leila, Amanda and Reverend McGraw were on the porch discussing who might make a good Ebenezer Forest manager among the people they knew or what process to undertake in finding such a person.

"Should it be a man or a woman?" asked Amanda.

"If you select a woman with all that has happened," began the Reverend, "I feel you will also need to hire a male security person. I don't expect the sheriff's office to keep a car out front for more than a month."

"Hell's bells! Brother McGraw," replied Amanda in a loud voice and pointing at Leila, "you didn't see what this fifty-six year old WOMAN sitting right here was able to do last week to those two filthy bastards who tried to kill her? A woman can do any darn thing a man can do!" There was a brief moment of quiet on the porch.

Brr"'ing, Brr"'ing, Brr"'ing rang the phone. The Reverend welcomed the interruption.

*****

A soft-spoken female voice began speaking very slowly, as though reading from notes.

"Hello, hello, my name is Mary Kate Nelson. I called yesterday but no one answered. After a lot of thought I think it is best that I just leave a message. This message is private for Ms. Leila Jane Hewitt."

Leila turned away from the phone and looked at both Amanda and Reverend McGraw. She made no motion of any kind. Accordingly, neither one moved or offered to leave. The message continued.

"I do not know if you know about me," began Mary Kate, "or if you have ever even heard my name. But I dated Mark Mabry for about a year several years ago. After he was injured at your house, I visited him at his home in Atlanta when he was recovering. He told me what happened that caused him to be arrested. He did not tell me very much about you. We spent one night together. After that, I moved to New York City--actually Westchester County. I have watched all of the news--every bit of it--about the men trying to kill you, and Mark dying in the wreck

15

the same night. I was devastated. I saw his funeral on live television and saw that you were devastated too. I cried so much. I still cry every day."

Mary Kate continued talking, but her voice was cracking and she was crying again. "You are such a brave person Ms. Leila--and I know you must be a very good person, or Mark would not have wanted to marry you." There was a rather long pause.

"I did not know whether I should tell you this or not. I am not telling you this to hurt you. I have prayed on it and believe you should know that I am going to have a baby in a couple of months. And I am certain that the baby is Mark's. There is no other possibility."

Leila let out a gasp and raised her hand to her mouth. Amanda began mumbling something unintelligible.

"Because you love him," said Mary Kate, "like I do, I thought that you should know that Mark will live on through his coming baby. I have not allowed my doctor to tell me whether it will be a boy or a girl. I do not want to know. I do not care as long as the baby is healthy. I am just thrilled," she added as her voice clearly strengthened.

There was another pause in Mary Kate's message. She continued, "Again, I did not tell you this to hurt you. I believe that you are entitled to know Mark will have a child in this world. I thank God for this gift. I am not asking you to call me, but if you would ever like to know more about our baby in the years to come, my phone number is 202-356-6999. I hope you receive this message in the spirit in which I share it. I am truly very sorry for your loss, and may God always be with you!" Click.

*****

No one on the porch moved for a full minute. There was complete silence. Leila stood up and looked briefly at Amanda and the Reverend, with tears now streaming down her cheeks.

"Would you both please excuse me. I need some time alone," Leila asked humbly, barely able to talk.

"Of course," they both replied.

Leila walked slowly back into the main house toward her bedroom. Before she had gotten totally out of hearing, Amanda looked at the Reverend and could be heard saying, "That cheatin' bastard!"

Reverend McGraw shook his head, stood up, put on his hat and slowly started for the back porch door. He partially turned and replied to Amanda as he exited, "God loves us all, Amanda, even the 'cheatin' bastards.'"

Almost to Aspen

Chapter 4

James Watson locked his law office door and walked the two boys toward his truck. Little Jake moved slowly, and James reached down to pick him up. A very strong stench of human waste stopped him cold and, instead of grabbing him around his bottom, he lifted little Jake up by his underarms. He set him on the ground when they arrived at the truck. James fetched an old rag from the truck's bed and told Luke to sit in the middle of the front seat. Then he placed the rag over the right side of the truck seat and lifted Jake upon it. He locked and shut the door. There was no talking.

By the time James walked around and took the driver's seat, the odor of little Jake's pants had overtaken the cab. He opened the windows automatically and started to drive the boys toward his house.

Halfway to his home, James saw an ice cream store ahead. "Would you boys like to stop and get an ice cream cone?" he asked.

Luke looked puzzled and replied, "What is that?"

"Ice cream, you know what that is, don't you?" James asked in dismay.

"No," replied Luke.

Little Jake made an indistinguishable couple of grunts. Luke looked up to James, "Jake is hungry."

"How do you know?" asked James.

"He just told me," Luke answered.

"I didn't hear him say anything," said James.

"He talks to me," responded Luke.

James wheeled into the ice cream store parking lot, and told Luke to watch his brother and not let him get out of the truck. Five minutes later he returned with two small chocolate cones and gave one to each boy. They both held the cones in their hand until Luke finally stuck out his tongue and slowly touched the ice cream atop the cone.

"Ow!" he exclaimed.

"It won't hurt you," assured James. Slowly Luke tried it again. Little Jake watched his brother and shortly he tried it himself. Soon both were enthusiastically "licking" their new experience, and both faces became quite brown.

When the threesome arrived at James's house, it was nearly dark. He led the boys into the back yard. They both immediately crouched down and started running their fingers through the grass.

James asked Luke. "Do you like to touch grass?"

"I have never touched it before," replied Luke.

"You never went outside and played in the grass?" an astonished James questioned.

"No," answered Luke as he and little Jake took a seat in the plush green growth, and began rubbing it with both of their hands.

James grabbed a garden hose and brought it over near the boys. He made little Jake stand up, and Luke started to pull his brother's pants down. Jake began to cry, and James quickly saw why. Much of the mess in little Jake's pants was caked rock solid. It had been there for days. James began to spray Jake with the hose.

The water in the hose was cold and the caked manure did not fall off fast. Jake was also cold, frightened and fighting back tears. He loudly made several of his grunting noises. Luke stood up, approached and started touching his brother to comfort him as much as he could without getting totally drenched himself. Finally, the excrement began to fall away.

When the cleansing was complete, James left the boys outside while he went into his house. He returned with towels. He dried them both, wrapped shivering little Jake, and brought them into his home. He realized he had no replacement clothes for either boy and knew they, especially Jake, were likely still very hungry.

"What have I gotten myself into?" James asked himself.

*****

The boys ate Sweet Sue's chicken and dumplings out of a can for supper and fell asleep early. "I need to act swiftly on this if I am going to make a good fee," James knew.

He recalled a local pastor asking him to please keep him in mind if he ever had any children for possible adoption. He went to his address book and looked up the phone number of Preacher Bob Belding at the popular Blue Walton Worship Center.

Brother Bob was very excited to get the call and, after a rather short few minutes' discussion, told James, "I will have you a wonderful adoptive couple by Monday morning, praise the Lord!"

James then called his widowed aunt, Sally Cox, and told her the situation. She had helped him on numerous other occasions in various times of need. After James committed to picking up all of the expenses, Aunt Sally agreed to receive the boys at 8 a.m. the next morning. She was very excited and also agreed to pick up some clothes for both of them at Wal-Mart the next day.

Aunt Sally committed to keeping the boys with her until they were placed in adoption. But she added that James would have to pick them up with twelve-hour notice if at any time they became "too much trouble"--or if she just changed her mind.

James figured this was the best he could do for now. He walked into his den, made himself another vodka and grapefruit juice and was soon asleep.

Chapter 5

After a sleepless night of completely reliving all of Mark's and her affirmations of mutual love, Leila remained numb with the knowledge that he was to be the father of a posthumous child being carried by Mary Kate Nelson.

"How much of what he professed to me was not true?" Leila repeatedly asked herself. "Or was Mary Kate's claim that Mark is the father of the coming child actually the truth?"

She wanted to believe that Mark was sincere toward her in every way, and she wanted to give him the benefit of every doubt. But, quite painfully, there was a significant uncertainty that she could not immediately dispel from her thoughts. After preparing her morning tea, she walked out to the porch and turned on the telephone answering machine that showed eight messages. It was only 8:10 in the morning.

The third message was from Mark's best friend, Jane Anderson.

"Good morning, Leila, this is Jane Anderson. I left Atlanta for Destin this morning, and I want to see if I can stop by around noon your time for a short visit. If it is okay with you, please get back with me as soon as possible. You have my cell phone number. Thank you." Leila turned off the answering machine immediately and dialed Jane's number.

Leila's call went to voicemail and she left a message. "Please do stop by, Jane, I would like that very much. I need to talk with you also." She returned to the main house to collect her thoughts.

Four hours later Jane turned down Ebenezer Church Road. As she drove down the shadowy lane, she couldn't help but remember how Mark repeatedly told her he was drawn to this graveled road and would explore it one day. "What an eerie combination of obsession and fate," she thought, as all of the bizarre later developments raced through her head.

There was a Walton County deputy parked in front of the Hewitt home place. Two local television stations' vans were across the road and their small crews were standing in the nearby shade. Jane had been around Leila enough to know there was concern in her voice message, and she knew that the news that she was bringing would not help the situation.

Jane's approach and entry into the Hewitt house was televised. She had become very recognizable in the Destin area. Every aspect of the Ebenezer Church Road saga was ongoing news. The death of both Deputy Tommy Tucker and T-Mex in Leila's bed, the oncoming trial of Sheriff Wayne Clark and Colonel Max Barnett, Mark's tragic death and Leila's national fame were not a series of events that would soon be back shelved by any form of news media.

The two women warmly hugged each other at the front door for the first time since Mark's funeral. Leila led Jane to the back porch, and after fully greeting each other Jane said she had a specific purpose for the visit.

"As you may have guessed, I am still dating F.B.I. agent Bob Kirk. He asked that I visit you and bring you up to date. The U.S. Attorney's Office in Pensacola has notified the Panhandle F.B.I. office that there will not be any indictment of Dr. Ty Tyson in the foreseeable future," said Jane. "Bob knows how close you and I are, and he wanted me to fully inform you of that fact. Because of this development, in his opinion, you are still in a situation dangerous for your safety."

"Heaven forbid!" gasped Leila. "I thought you told me that there is a very strong case against Dr. Tyson for his rape of me."

"It is very, very strong," replied Jane. "In fact, I think it is 99 per cent winnable. But, I am going to tell you this--between you and me. The United States Attorney in Washington, D.C. is not going to allow a Tyson indictment by the Pensacola office-- probably ever. And the local F.B.I. has been told by their national office to back off also!"

Leila hung her head downward and then looked back at Jane with total exasperation.

"What is wrong with our country--what have we become?" asked Leila dejectedly.

"Law enforcement has become absolutely political," Jane explained. "There is almost a civil war going on between the established crooks in Washington and law abiding people. If what I have told you is not enough, Walton County Sheriff Clark is about dead and Colonel Max Barnett is going to be eventually let off easy by the U.S. Attorney's office. Getting an indictment against Dr. Tyson in a Walton County court is not likely either unless we can get the rats out of power here. When is the last time you have heard of a big drug dealer arrested around here?"

"My gracious," Leila spoke resignedly.

"I want to recommend that you need to remain very observant and cautious about your personal safety," Jane added.

"So...wonderful! How am I going to be able to show a hundred folks around Ebenezer Forest every day and feel safe?" Leila asked Jane concernedly.

"There needs to be some real security here, Leila—someone besides yourself."

There was silence in the room. Jane broke the silence by asking "You wanted to discuss something with me, Leila?"

*****

Leila put her hand to her forehead in further exasperation. She hesitated, and then teardrops appeared in her eyes.

She proceeded very slowly, "I received a message yesterday from a Mary Kate Nelson. She wanted to inform me that she is pregnant with Mark's baby." Leila dropped her head toward her lap and began to weep.

Jane rose, walked over to Leila and draped her arms around her shoulders. She whispered softly, "I know."

"How do you know?" asked Leila, totally surprised.

"Charlie McBride told me at Mark's funeral that Mary Kate had called him." Jane thought to herself it should be Mark answering these questions to Leila. Then, after more thought, she added, "I don't personally know Mary Kate Nelson, and we don't know for sure if what she said is true."

"This is all so difficult," started Leila, now looking up at Jane, "to deal with this, particularly so soon after Mark's death. I can hardly think about any of this without feeling ill."

"Leila, how you feel is totally understandable. You have been through so much. Only time will ease the pain and give you the clarity of thought you need. You are strong--the strongest woman I have ever met--and you will come through all of this." She hugged Leila even harder.

*****

There was better news for Jane to share with Leila. "I haven't made this public yet, but Bob Kirk has asked me to marry him. And I accepted!" This brought the first smile of the day to Leila's lips.

"I am very happy for you Jane." Leila said. "How is that going to work out with your home and job in Atlanta?"

"I am vested in my retirement program with the Atlanta Police Department. Not fully, but there will be some retirement income down the road. Bob has a substantial family inheritance. We do not want to live in Pensacola. We both want to start fresh in the Destin area and raise a family here. He is planning to resign from the F.B. I. and intends to run for Walton County Sheriff in the next election. If he wins you will not have to worry about Dr. Ty Tyson. I plan to pursue a different career down here—I don't know what yet--until the babies start coming along."

"That is absolutely wonderful, Jane," exclaimed Leila. "Such great news! I am very happy for you and Bob. And I am particularly happy that your family will be living in this area."

As Leila walked Jane to the front door, she asked her, "When do you think you will be relocating?"

"I gave two weeks' resignation notice yesterday, and after that I will be staying at Mark and Charlie's place in Sandestin until Bob and I decide on a permanent home," Jane replied.

"I am totally exhausted, but there is something else on my mind," said Leila. "I will be willing to drive into Destin to meet you if you have time while you're here—or maybe you could stop by for a few minutes Sunday on your way back to Atlanta. Right now, I can hardly think straight."

"I know you are completely worn out, Leila. Call me when you feel stronger, or I will call you when I am ready to leave and we will make it happen," replied Jane. She proceeded to Destin with a significant amount of curiosity about what else Leila might want to discuss.

$\mathcal{C}hapter$ 6

At one p.m. Sunday, Attorney James Watson's phone rang, and it was Reverend Bob Belding of the Blue Walton Worship Center.

Brother Bob began, "We had a little problem here today after the eleven o'clock service. At the end of my morning message, I announced to the full congregation that I had two young boys God sent me to find a new home. The church was completely full today, and I invited any couple that had an interest in adopting the two boys to come up front after the service to discuss the opportunity. Well, James, I had no idea that there would be such interest. I believe it was eight couples that came forward and one single lady. I cannot remember ever seeing this woman before to the best that I can recall. I gathered everyone interested around me in a circle, and I started telling them about the boys. When I said their ages, four and two, the single woman started shouting. 'I know those boys!'"

Brother Bob continued, "She went on to say that one of the boys was her friend's son. The friend wants his son back now that he knows the mama disappeared this weekend. Well, you can certainly imagine that this caused a real big problem here, James. Everybody was very upset, including me."

"Oh, no," James replied disgustedly. "I thought you had a list of interested people. I can't believe you made an announcement to the entire church!" James well knew at that moment he had been much too brief in his discussion with and instructions to the Reverend Belding.

"I realize now that it was likely a mistake, but there is more," said Brother Bob. "About ten minutes ago, a man called the church office and talked to my secretary. He told her he was the father of the boy he claimed I was trying 'to peddle' this morning and he left me a number, demanding me to call him back today. He said his name is Rufus Jenkins." Brother Bob gave James the phone number.

Knowing he needed to defuse this situation, James made up a quick story.

"Since I talked to you, Brother Bob, I have been contacted by a nice out-of-town couple that wants to adopt these boys. It was a bad idea for me to think about keeping these boys locally. This area is way too small. You don't need to worry about this guy that called you. I will call him back this afternoon. You haven't done anything at all to worry about, but you should not take or return any calls from him, ever. I assure you he is not listed as the father on either boy's birth certificate. I would ask that you tell anyone that asks about this in the future that you have been advised by an attorney to have no comment."

"I sure don't like being accused of 'peddling children,' James-- what if the police contact me? What if Rufus Jenkins shows up here at the church?"

"I am going to call him right now," assured James. "I would appreciate you not giving anybody my name, even the police--but only them, if you have to. Don't worry--the mother has signed all of the required papers."

"Okay, I am going to follow your advice," said the Reverend, slowly and in a depressed tone. "I am going to pray for those two boys," he added as a clear afterthought.

*****

James knew he had to think this development through before he made the call. He thought back about how tired he was when he had contacted Reverend Bob Belding and about how many drinks he had consumed that day. He realized he should have vetted Brother Bob better on how to proceed and made sure he was fully advised to be discreet in his efforts.

It was also very clear to him now that the two boys should not be relocated in the Fort Walton-Destin area, for numerous reasons. He sure as hell did not want to return the call of Rufus Jenkins, whoever he was, but knew he was better prepared to handle it than Brother Bob.

James gave the call a few minutes of further thought, and then looked down at what he realized was a cell phone prefix. He started off by blocking the origin of his call, then punched in the number and hit the send button.

"HELLLLLO!" barked the male recipient.

"Who is speaking, please?" asked James respectfully.

"This is Rufus 'Odd Job' Jenkins--who in the shit is this?" was the reply.

"I am an attorney, asked by Reverend Bob Belding to return your call, sir," replied James.

"I want to know your FUCKIN' NAME, ASSHOLE--what is your FUCKIN' NAME?" Jenkins demanded.

James was quite taken back by what he was hearing. He replied in an obviously shaky tone. "I am handling a private adoption of a child that does not have your name listed as the father on his birth certificate. Every part of this adoption is confidential, including my name, sir."

"Let me tell you one thing, COCKSUCKER--LUKE is my boy, I don't give a shit what the birth certificate says, and I want your FUCKIN' NAME--I will beat your name out of that GOD-DAMNED preacher to find you if I have to. Do you hear me, COCKSUCKER?"

James Watson was now totally jarred by Jenkins' rant but was able to reply, "I am going to report this conversation and your threats to the sheriff's offices of Walton and Okaloosa Counties as soon as I hang up this phone, and you are hereby informed to stay off the premises of Blue Walton Worship Center."

"I HATE lawyers, you DIRTY SON OF A BITCH, and when I get ahold of you, I am going to BEAT YOUR ASS, YOU SORRY, SACK OF SHIT--------"

James Watson hung up the phone--both of his hands and lips were trembling, and his chest was so tight he could hardly breathe. He needed a drink.

*****

James Watson's best friend in the Walton County Sheriff's office was Terry Morgan. They had grown up together in Niceville. James knew Terry had enough seniority to be off on Sundays. After composing himself, he gave Terry a call.

"Of course I recognize that name. He is well known in Panhandle law enforcement simply as 'ODD JOB' Jenkins--and is one bad dude," started Terry. "He must have just gotten released from the state penitentiary. He was the main suspect in several murders, but there was never enough hard evidence to send him up. He walked into a bar and got into a fight one night in Valparaiso. He ended up slitting the other guy's throat with a broken bottle. Because it was a manslaughter case, and Okaloosa County didn't want to take a chance of him winning the trial on self- defense, they made him a deal for a four year sentence--just to get him off the streets. And yep, he probably just got out."

"He really sounds rehabilitated." replied James sarcastically.

"If you want to be safe, get an injunction against him going near the church or the preacher," offered Terry. "He has beaten the hell out of quite a few guys."

"Well, if something happens to me, you'll know who did it. Thanks, Terry."

Chapter 7

Around noon the same day, Leila was still a prisoner of her own fame. She did not feel comfortable walking alone past the half-dozen remaining news reporters and sheriff's patrol. Nor had she taken her usual morning stroll back to her beloved Ebenezer Church since Mark's funeral. She had prayed on the back porch earlier, as she did each morning, and now waited near her bedroom window for Amanda's daily visit.

"The Red Bay crowd missed you today. There was good attendance," started Amanda. "Every single person that approached me asked about you. I wish you could have attended. Please don't let these out-front stalkers interfere with your normal life!"

"I talked Friday with a shift chief from the sheriff's office," replied Leila, "and he said it is a public road, nothing they can do and I should appreciate the assigned deputy. I told him I do appreciate the deputy."

"You know the only reason the sheriff's office has helped you at all is that they would be stormed by the whole county and country, if they didn't," Amanda said. "I really think you need to get in your car and drive away, somewhere, anywhere, until the vultures leave. You can come stay at my house."

35

"I have to get the Ebenezer Forest tours going again soon--and reschedule all the ones that have been recently canceled. I have never had so many new calls." Leila picked up and showed Amanda a wad of phone messages. "Jane is coming by this afternoon at my request," she added, stopping short of sharing the news of Jane's engagement.

"Brother McGraw told me that unless I call him back after seeing you, he was going to stop by also. Is that okay?" Leila nodded her assent.

The two friends shared their usual tea. When finished, Leila surprised Amanda by asking, "Would you please walk back to the church with me now, dear? I hear it calling."

Amanda, shocked, yelled, "Are you serious? HELL, YES! That's the Leila I know—whoopee! I am going to walk out to my car and get my tennis shoes--I'll be riiigght back!"

*****

Leila slipped into a light blue, casual dress. "If I am going to be on Sunday television, I might as well look presentable," she mused to herself.

Amanda bounced back inside, walking shoes in her hand and a big smile on her face. "They are jumping out of their vans, Leila. They know something is happening!"

The guineas could be heard squawking in their pen across the street. Leila walked out to the back porch and filled a medium-sized bag full of corn.

When Leila returned, Amanda was standing in front of the main hallway mirror fixing her hair. "How do I look, honey?" She asked Leila. "I wish I could do something with this big butt," she added as she hit herself on the fanny with a loud slap.

Leila laughed. "C'mon we are going to walk it off! Are you ready?"

*****

Two local television stations were eager to get some additional, much-requested national video footage of Leila-- something other than her feeding the guineas. As she and Amanda walked toward the bird pen, the reporters noted that Leila was wearing a colorful dress for the first time since Mark's death and looked particularly relaxed and lovely.

"You look fabulous--can we get an interview today, please Leila?" A reporter pleaded.

There was no reply. She proceeded to the pen gate, opened it and went inside. She sprinkled about half the corn on the ground, left the pen, and spread the rest on the nearby outside ground for the un-penned male guineas to eat. The cameras remained rolling.

"Leila, do you feel safe in your house alone at night now that the two killers are dead," another reporter asked.

"You sorry skunk." Amanda mumbled at the questioner

The news crews scrambled when Leila and Amanda, rather than retreating back to her house, turned east on Ebenezer Church Road.

"They are going to the church road gate!" one of them guessed loudly. Two men with hand-held cameras raced ahead, and took a position on the far side of the entry. They turned and zoomed in as Leila and Amanda approached. The other reporters scurried alongside the women, still trying to get any kind of comment.

When Leila and Amanda stopped and opened the gate, all of the news personnel simultaneously begged if they could accompany them down Ebenezer Church Lane. Leila turned and announced, "Not today, thank you all. Ebenezer Forest will reopen to the public in the near future."

*****

Leila and Amanda walked briskly until rounding the first turn in the lane. Leila stopped, and then Amanda. "Let's really slow down and enjoy this walk," Leila suggested to Amanda. "It seems like it has been a long, long while."

As they eased along, the birds were chirping and the squirrels were barking, but not in an alarmed way--more like an enthusiastic welcome back to an old friend. A nature's serenade always warmed Leila's soul.

It was approaching mid-fall now, and the strongest aromas were from the evergreen magnolias. Leila stopped under each one as they passed to enjoy their lemony delight. The woods were opening up as the leaves fell, and twice in the first quarter mile she and Amanda saw fleeting glimpses of the white tails of deer as they pranced away in the distance.

As always, Hominy Creek could be heard from afar as they neared the refreshing stream. When it was reached, Leila thought back about the palomino mare pulling Mark's body back to her family church. The horse had not wanted to cross the wooden bridge. Leila and Amanda stopped atop it to watch the rock bass dart in the crystal clear water.

When Ebenezer Church came into its full splendid view, Leila stopped exactly where Mark was standing when she first noticed him watching her bathe nude in the church-side spring. She stared for a long while at the beloved place of worship where she had developed her love for her Creator as a young child. And she looked over at the Hewitt family cemetery where her mother, father, and Mark were buried.

Leila could feel her tears forming, and then dripping down her cheeks. But she was stronger now. She advanced side-by-side with Amanda, as they had all their lives, toward Ebenezer Church.

When they arrived at the church entry, Amanda whispered, "You go in, Leila dear, I prayed all morning. I will sit over here by the spring." Amanda had observed Leila's tears and believed she had some personal reconciliation to do with Mark.

It was over thirty minutes later that Leila exited the church and rejoined Amanda. Together they walked the short distance to the nearby cemetery and approached Leila's parents' resting place next to the still fresh dirt covering Mark Mabry's coffin.

Leila had prepared herself for this moment before she left the church. She had not prepared herself for the rather strong smell of rotting flesh that drifted into her nostrils from her right. She looked in that direction and could barely see the front legs of an animal partially obstructed from her view by a large live oak tree.

Leila walked around closer and saw the body of a large, half-devoured, decomposed raccoon. It apparently had been attacked and been dead for a couple of days.

Leila's attention was immediately directed to a movement directly above her. Clinging to a knothole on the same tree within an arm's reach, were two very young and famished baby coon pups. Leila raised her hands and lifted one, then the other, out of the tree. She carried the squealing pups over to the fresh spring.

"My gracious, they look near death!" Exclaimed Amanda as the young raccoons eagerly quenched their thirsts.

"I think we have reached them soon enough to save them," replied Leila with much more enthusiasm than before.

*****

The television crews could hear the coon pups' lively squeals as Leila and Amanda returned to the front gate of Ebenezer Church Lane. Leila stopped, and the film was rolling as she held the baby raccoons tightly up against her body.

The cameras were focused on the little saved twins squirming against Leila's blue dress as she watched them with her sparkling and captivating blue eyes. America was about to see what they had been waiting for since Mark's funeral. Leila Jane Hewitt was smiling again, and she was smiling broadly.

Her story of religious conviction and courage was billed by the media as larger-than-life. The heart-warming scene at Ebenezer Forest was shown again and again that evening across the country, exhilarating national audiences--and enjoyed no place more than in Aspen, Colorado.

Almost to Aspen

Chapter 8

Across Choctawhatchee Bay in Destin, James Watson was startled by a loud knock on his front door. Conversations earlier in the day with Brother Bob Belding, Rufus "Odd Job" Jenkins and Deputy Terry Morgan had left him very cautious at best. He went to the dining room window first and recognized the automobile out front as belonging to his Aunt Sally Cox.

He opened the front door and welcomed Aunt Sally and the two boys.

"I told you I was going to Wal-Mart. You are not going to believe what happened," Aunt Sally started. "The boys were with me, and we were waiting in the meat section for some chicken salad. Then this nasty-looking older couple comes walking into the store. They see the boys, and the old lady asks me are those June's boys?"

"Hold it, Aunt Sally," interrupted James. "The boys don't need to hear this."

Without saying anything else to the boys, James led them into his den, turned on the television and found a kids' channel. He told them to stay put and watch the program. He returned to the living room where Aunt Sally was waiting anxiously to continue.

"I didn't know what to say," she began. "When the old lady asked if they were June's boys, I was kinda scared and told her no. Then she hollered, 'YES, they are'--real loud! Luke did not like those people and grabbed me by the leg. Her yelling really scared me. I did not even wait for the chicken salad. I took the boys straight out to the parking lot. The old man followed us out to see what kind of car I was driving. So I went out of the parking lot the other way where he could not see my license plate. I am still scared, James. I don't know if I want to do this any longer!"

"Calm down, please, Aunt Sally. I hear you," urged James. "I am going to place these boys as soon as I possibly can, I promise you. I am having a few more problems than I expected, plus I have to be in court on another case in the morning. And besides, you promised me twenty-four hours' notice if you wanted to get out of this, and you know that is not enough time. I am asking you to please calm down and help me. I will try to get this done by the end of the week if I possibly can."

"All week, no way, Jamesie boy--a deal is a deal. The deal was twenty-four hour notice," Aunt Sally argued. "These boys ain't right--they talk to each other in some crazy language like they are from another planet. And Luke keeps asking me where are his new mama and daddy, like you promised him. I want them off my hands as soon as possible! Those two crazy creeps in the store scared the wits outta me!"

"Look, I will give you some more money to help me through this. I don't have anyone else to get help from. We are family and I need your help," relented James, actually begging.

"How much money?"

"A hundred dollars a day," James offered.

"That ain't much--and this is the last time," she declared.

*****

Before she left, James warned his aunt that it was best to stay home with the boys. He knew that with all that was developing he needed to find a taker for the boys, and needed to find someone soon. He called a lawyer friend in Panama City and another in Chipley. The one in Panama City said it would be tough to find anyone that would take two boys, and the lawyer in Chipley said he was too busy to get involved.

James did not know anyone else that he thought he could comfortably call on a Sunday. He decided to make a list of other possibilities that he would call after his court appearance the next day. After nearly thirty minutes, he had written down the names of only two other prospects to contact.

His phone rang, showing a return call from his attorney friend in Chipley. "Hey, James, I thought of this preacher way out in the country about halfway between you and me. He has a large church over there in Red Bay. I made a quick call to him. He said to have you call him, now if you want. His name is Reverend Tom McGraw."

Almost to Aspen

Chapter 9

Late in the afternoon, Leila was in the privacy of her backyard settling the rescued raccoon pups into one of two animal pens used for many years for this very purpose. The smaller, secure pen was the first stop. Later the pups would be moved to the larger one, which had an intentionally and cleverly designed escape hole to let healthier animals come and go as they please. This feature would make their re-introduction to their native wild more gradual and safe.

Putting food out for her young guests, Leila turned and noticed Jane Anderson walking across the lawn toward her. Jane gave a big wave as she neared, saying, "Amanda told me you were out here and that you have some adorable new boarders."

Leila finished topping off the animals' watering trough and left the enclosure to welcome Jane with a big hug.

"It will take about six weeks for the coon pups to safely venture out on their own," replied Leila. "Let's sit here under this sycamore. It is nice and shady." She pointed to two old metallic rockers placed there for this obvious purpose. "This old tree holds its leaves fairly tight until the fall, but when they fall, they all fall."

Leila briefly shared where she had found the young coons, and thanked Jane for stopping by at her request. "What I want to talk to you about, Jane, is--and I admit that the idea did not come to me until you told me of your engagement and your plans to move here soon. When I learned you will be looking for a new job, I had an idea. But rather than blurt it out then, I want you to know how serious I am--and I have now even slept on it."

Jane had a hint where this was going and was very much surprised. She had assumed Leila wanted to further discuss Mark's coming child, which had seemed to be really bothering her.

"With all of the attention I have been receiving, I have become a distraction to what I so dearly love, the operation of Ebenezer Forest," Leila shared. "I inherited this 8,000 acres and only 500 acres is now dedicated to the Forest. I would like to at least double its size, and I have other projects in mind. But I need someone to manage the business operations of Ebenezer Forest. Every major college forestry department in the Southeast, scout dens and environmental groups are all calling to reserve tours. You tell me I need to be cautious. What I think I really need, is you! I am offering you the position of operating manager of Ebenezer Forest." Leila said earnestly.

"I have hardly any experience in this field," responded Jane softly.

"I am not talking about you leading the tours," began Leila. "From a security standpoint, based on what you have told me, I don't see how I can safely resume that any time soon—and you would never have to do it either. I have a list of job applications from young foresters, and I am prepared to take one on now to handle that responsibility. Jane, I do not know what I would have done without you after I was raped and after Mark passed away. You are smart, and we could set up a new business plan for Ebenezer Forest in a week."

Jane shifted position in her chair and leaned forward.

"The forestry side of my property is very profitable, and I did not create Ebenezer Forest to make money. But to make it an improved educational facility for all ages, I am ready to add 'break even' modest operation fees. It is all about wildlife habitat, Jane. If we can attract more people to see what can and needs to be done to preserve our world's forests and bottomlands, then wildlife of every size and kind will be the beneficiary. This will be our goal."

Jane finally spoke. "This is all totally unexpected. I am surprised, but would like to think about it and discuss it with Bob. Would you please mind giving me a little time?"

"What I am suggesting to you," Leila continued, "is that a large part of it can be done from your home. And you will even be able to manage the business easily from there when you start your family."

Leila informed Jane a little more about how Clyde Branson, now with his son's help, kept all the roads and grounds in good shape. She revealed that all of the name plates on every tree in Ebenezer Forest were updated every summer by college students, mostly from Florida State and Auburn. She ended by saying, "I would be honored to have you join me, Jane. I am sure we can work out a very acceptable compensation."

Jane ended the conversation by saying she was most flattered by Leila's offer and would definitely consider it, letting her know within a week or so. She gave Leila a warm hug and headed back to Atlanta.

*****

Leila opened the back porch door and could hear Amanda and Reverend Tom McGraw talking in the living room. She called out from the kitchen, "Do either of you in there want any tea?"

"We beat you to it," shouted Amanda.

Leila prepared herself a glass and joined her two guests. "I am sorry I was so upset and walked out on you the other day, Brother McGraw. The news was very disturbing at the time," she said.

"All three of us were shocked, I assure you," replied the Reverend. "We missed you in church this morning, Leila."

"I'm sorry I wasn't there. Please forgive me." Leila responded. "I did do quite a bit of praying on the back porch."

"I am never happy on a Sunday, unless I share a prayer with you, dear Leila. Let's bow our heads and make me happy," he answered.

"Our Heavenly Father, ours is not to question why. All that happens is in YOUR great plan for us and is within Your total domain--not ours. We are here to humbly and reverently serve You, to not judge others and to not tarry in spreading Your word. For You and You only are the guiding light to our salvation. Please forgive us for our sins and trepidations. Please help us live better lives in your image. And please help us to help those in need. In Heaven's name, we pray. AMEN!"

"AMEN," both ladies answered.

The Reverend walked over and kissed his favorite congregation member on her forehead.

"Thank you, Brother Tom," Leila said softly.

"Amanda tells me you saved two little raccoons today," Brother Tom declared, looking at Leila with a broad grin on his face.

"That is just part of the job around here," answered Leila. "There are always going be animals to save. It is God's way."

"Speaking of needing saving," began Brother Tom, "I received an interesting call on the way over here. A lawyer from Destin has two young boys, ages four and two, left with him by a harlot. He is looking for a nice couple to take and adopt these boys. They were born and have lived in Fort Walton, but because Destin is so close, he needs to get them out of that immediate area along the coast. Do either one of you know of a good young couple or even a middle-aged couple that would want to take the boys in for adoption?"

"That's going to be extremely hard to find around here," replied Amanda. "Most couples that live up here in the country, young or old, don't make enough money to take in even one child, much less two at the same time."

"And the lawyer says his fee will be $7,500 dollars up front to cover the adoption legal work," said Brother Tom.

Leila sat quietly, sipping her tea.

"Sounds like an awfully high fee, like he's selling them kids. Is that $7,500 dollars each, or for just one?" Asked Amanda.

"I got the impression that the price was for both kids. And he said he wanted to find a couple that would take BOTH kids. He was really emphatic about that. And I forgot to tell you he told me that the boys were like animals. They only talk to each other in a weird language that no one else can understand. He described it as 'grunts' and said it did not look like the boys had ever had much interaction with adults at all," revealed Brother Tom.

"Heaven, forbid," Leila lamented, simply shaking her head.

The Reverend asked Amanda and Leila to let him know if they thought of anyone that might be interested in the adoption opportunity. They both said they would, and Brother Tom said his goodbyes and left.

"It has been a long day, Amanda," Leila sighed, "and I am very tired."

Amanda soon departed, tooting her horn at the watchful deputy and again at the persistent camera crew as she headed west on Ebenezer Road.

Chapter 10

Cocktail hour at Jim's Restaurant & Bar in Aspen starts at five p.m., and Powder White and his gang were never late. They always gathered in the same corner of the bar and rarely did anyone miss unless he was sick or out of town. The table was not reserved, but all of the other patrons knew whose spot it was.

Powder, Bud Holt and a couple of other regulars were talking about the coming ski season when the Sunday Night News cut to Walton County, Florida. About halfway through the broadcast Leila Hewitt was being shown holding two baby raccoons. The coon pups were trying to crawl up her pretty blue dress, and she was smiling ear-to-ear.

"There she is, Powder!" exclaimed Bud.

"TURN UP THE SOUND, PLEASE, NICK!" Powder shouted at the bartender.

The news report was underway:

"Leila Jane Hewitt, the new darling and heroine of America, took her first walk back to her family church and cemetery today where she recently buried her fiancé, Mark Mabry. He died racing to save her life. As you know by now if you own a television, Leila survived an attempted murder by two men--she shot both--and both died in her bed. She has still not allowed any interviews at all. But today she emerged out of her magnificent Ebenezer Forest with two baby raccoons that she had just rescued. It is easy to see that the young pups and Leila Hewitt are, at least for now, all quite happy!"

The camera closed in on Leila's beautiful face.

John "No Elk" Gillespie strolled down the bar toward his friends. He paused, watching as the news feature ended with some distant footage showing Leila inside an animal pen feeding the young raccoons.

"Well, has Miss Leila Hewitt accepted your offer yet, or even returned your call, Powder?" Gillespie asked.

"Time is not a critical factor in destiny," answered Powder.

John laughed and replied, "Neither is lust, you ole hound dog."

"I have been following this case pretty closely," chimed in local Aspen attorney Steve Wanninger. "A deputy sheriff AND a Mexican hit man, c'mon now. Why did those two particular guys want to kill Leila? They were probably following someone else's orders. The top two men in that sheriff's office have been indicted. I'll bet there is a really big reason why someone wants her dead, and she is not out of the woods just yet."

"You know, you are right, Steve. Sheriff DeSalty said the exact same thing. He pointed out to me that three murders occurred in the Destin area right before the attempt was made to kill Leila. He said it looked like all hell was breaking loose in Walton County, Florida. That is one of the main reasons he agreed to leave her that message for me the other afternoon," Powder informed his buddies.

"You don't really expect Leila to accept or even respond to you, do you Powder?" asked John "No Elk" Gillespie.

"I was hoping she would." Then Powder added, "You know, guys, Aspen Mountain is not going to open for another six weeks--until Thanksgiving weekend. I have never been to the Destin area. Would any of you fellows like to join me in the King Air, say on Thursday, on a little four- or five-day fishing trip down to the Florida Panhandle, my treat?"

Bud Holt immediately said he would go.

John "No Elk" Gillespie said he would like to make the trip. "But I know you are going to try and see that gal, and I do not want to be dragged into that folly. If we are really going to go fishing in the Gulf, count me in."

Powder laughed out loud and added, "We are going to go deep-sea fishing--at least twice--I promise you that. Now, I admit I will have something else on my mind while I am down there, but it sure doesn't involve you fellows."

Steve Wanninger declared, "Count me in if I can get a Thursday pre-trial conference rescheduled." He added he would let Powder know by ten a.m. the next day.

The friends then partook in a lively discussion about what would be the best way for Powder to meet and connect with the person of his interest, Miss Leila Jane Hewitt, without appearing to be an absolute fool. There did not seem to be any way around it.

However, John "No Elk" Gillespie came up with a grandiose plan everyone really liked. It would not be cheap, but Powder never was. The consensus on the idea was so high that all three of the friends agreed to accompany Powder on his first visit to Ebenezer Forest.

"No Elk" even stated, "This could really be a wonderful asset for Aspen."

After a few drinks Powder bellowed to the delight of his buddies, "How does the ole saying go? If Miss Mohammed won't come to the mountain, the mountain must come to Miss Mohammed!"

Chapter 11

Soon after Amanda and Reverend McGraw departed that Sunday evening, Leila tried to go to sleep. But her mind was fraught with a number of uncertainties which left her still wide awake after several hours in bed. She was at a crossroad of her life in many different ways and was well aware of it.

Her visit to Ebenezer Church earlier in the day had been comforting, but it lacked the satisfactory level of communication with God that she had been able to often achieve at earlier times. He had always been there for her, but now her life seemed spiraling out of control. She was literally feeling for the first time that without communication with Him she was alone in the world. Desperately seeking His direction, she decided that trying harder to connect with her Lord was more important than going to sleep.

She directed her thoughts back to when she had sought God's confirmation before committing herself to Mark Mabry. Recalling vividly the very personal encounter she previously had with Him about Mark, she fixed her mind on a total effort to recapture that prior experience of divine communication. Alone in a house of silence and shadows, she attempted to elevate her consciousness above her earthly self. But she felt weak and powerless to do so. Fifteen minutes passed.

Her efforts were not working. Leila turned and tossed, yet would not give up. "To receive His guidance, I need to cleanse my soul--to completely bare myself to Him and to myself."

In the next few minutes, she recognized and accepted that she had been selfish since Mark's death, far too absorbed with her own self-pity. She clearly recalled Reverend McGraw's prayer of yesterday, and also recognized that she had not been serving God enough. And she had been negligent in spreading His word. She remembered very well her preacher's last request of God, "Please help us help those in need." Leila made a direct confession to Him, "I can do better to live in YOUR image!"

Leila's intense effort to reconnect with God was interrupted by her recollection of what the Reverend had shared with her and Amanda, the sad plight of the two young boys. "What a tragic beginning in this world they must be having," she thought, comparing their life to her own blessed family experience. "I need to help Reverend Tom find a perfectly wonderful couple for these boys," she thought.

She tried again and again to personally commune with Him, but to what specific direction or for what express purpose, she did not clearly know. "I have total faith in you my Lord, please show me the way to serve You best," she prayed.

Without receiving conscious affirmation from Him of any kind, Leila eventually drifted slowly back into a light sleep as she pondered intently over ways she could possibly help find a suitable destination for the young abandoned brothers. And it would be the first thing she would address in the morning.

Chapter 12

The morning came quickly. Before daylight, Leila's mind was racing again. Her normal power of concentration was being repeatedly interrupted with unanswered questions. "I have complete gratitude for everything you have blessed me with, Lord," she tried to communicate. "How can I best serve YOU?" She tried very hard to receive His answer.

But at each attempt the dilemma of the two young boys overtook her thoughts. She contemplated every possible way she could assist in their placement into a good home, except one.

Her mind wandered, considering what it would have been like if as a young woman she had accepted the proposal of the young forester, Jude Jackman. Then she scolded herself for the futility of such thoughts.

"What would it have been like to have raised children?" She began to ask herself.

She visualized having sons or daughters with whom to share her beloved Ebenezer Forest. "We could have walked the deep, luscious forest together and fed the plentiful wildlife. I would have baptized them in our family church and prayed with them there every Sunday."

Sunlight finally began to reach Ebenezer Forest. Almost as if she had reached the dead end of a long, long road, it finally occurred to her what she had been experiencing. Each time she asked her Creator for direction, the plight of two young boys had entered and dominated her thoughts.

"Is THIS what YOU want me to do?" She asked Him almost hysterically.

"Am I too old, would it be fair to these children if someone my age took them in--and without a father figure? Why am I fighting the thought?"

"OH, MY DEAR GOD!" She exclaimed as the mere prospect of raising the two boys raced through her body like a powerful surge of current.

For a complete hour after dawn, Leila obsessed over every detail of what taking two young boys into her home would entail. Her very last thought before she rose from bed was "THANK YOU, GOD, I CAN DO THIS!"

*****

Two hours later, Reverend Tom McGraw was awakened from a sound sleep to answer a telephone call from an excited Leila Hewitt.

"Brother Tom, after a lot of thought, I have decided to offer myself as the sole adopting parent for the two boys that you told Amanda and me about. And I would like to ask you to set up a meeting as soon as possible with the attorney who is handling this. I hope you will accompany me to the meeting--as a support and my reference--please."

"What the heck, Leila," responded Brother Tom, totally astonished, "Aren't you kind of past the age to even think about something like this--and less than ten days after what you have been through? Are you okay, Leila?"

"How many times have you told me things happen for a reason, Brother Tom? I have been asking God for direction and, after a lot of prayer, I am very certain I have His blessing," Leila replied.

"Leila, you don't know what you are getting into. Raising one child without experience is hard enough, but two! Leila, please come over to Red Bay and see me today. Let's think this idea through."

Leila laughed aloud. "I have raised two bobcats together before--and four coyote pups--and many baby deer. And one young Florida black bear! Are you going to help me with this or not?"

"I think you may be entering into this prematurely, on the rebound. This is absolutely crazy, Leila. Please slow down," argued the Reverend.

"Time may be of the essence. I do not want to miss this opportunity. It may never come again. I think that raising two brothers together would be best for them--and good for me." Leila asserted. "I have the means, surely the time and plenty enough love in my heart to take this on. And they will be brought up in the church. Again, are you going to help me or not?"

"Shouldn't they have a father?" Asked Brother Tom in a weakening voice.

"With me they will have one in heaven--are you going to say He is not enough? And maybe an earthly one will come along later," she added as an afterthought.

There was a pause in the conversation.

"I have never asked you to do anything for me more important than this," Leila spoke slowly. "Brother Tom, please set up a meeting between me and the lawyer handling this adoption—today-- if you can."

There was another long pause.

"I'll do all that I can," the defeated Reverend McGraw assured.

Chapter 13

Four men had been previously indicted in Walton County on numerous drug and racketeering charges. Sheriff Wayne Clark had died over the weekend, thus joining two of his alleged accomplices, the murdered Roy and Ray Ashton. Only one indicted co-conspirator remained alive to await trial, Colonel Max Barnett.

As Chief Deputy Sheriff of Walton County, Barnett was cited with acts of public corruption, bribery, obstruction of justice, money laundering, tax violations and other criminal activity under the RICO statute exposing him to potential life imprisonment. He was not charged with crimes related to harboring illegal aliens and was not ever likely to be because he had successfully orchestrated the execution of the Ashton brothers. His involvement in the attempted murder of Leila Jane Hewitt was highly suspected but unproven.

Because of Barnett's high public visibility, he agreed to meet Dr. Ty Tyson at six a.m. at an out-of-town convenience store in Ebro on Monday morning. They met and left there in Tyson's car and proceeded north about five miles, then turned northwest toward the Choctawhatchee River. Both of their cell phones were left in Barnett's vehicle, batteries removed. Making a final turn down an improved dirt road, they approached a gate with a sign above it announcing Tomahawk Ranch. They had arrived at the secluded 1,000 acre hunting estate of Clarence Bectom Rogers, known in Destin as "Big Fuzz."

"Big Fuzz" was waiting on the front porch, and the two men followed him into his large hunting lodge.

"Y'all are damn sure no one was following you, right?" He asked.

"You betcha, 'Fuzz,'—where's breakfast?" inquired the doctor.

Fuzz threw a package of cinnamon rolls on a big wooden table, retrieved a gallon of milk, and they all sat down.

"With Sheriff Clark dying yesterday, what are you going to do, Max?" Inquired Big Fuzz.

"I am going to resign as colonel this afternoon, and your buddy Billy Munsey is going to be appointed by the governor as acting sheriff," replied Barnett. "Is your man Tall Tom Hopkins ready to go when the next election comes up?"

"Yes," answered "Fuzz," "the money is pretty much all in place, and the best billboards will be reserved for your man. There is only one name floating around as serious opposition, and it is an FBI agent by the name of Bob Kirk."

"We don't want any son of a bitch—like an FBI agent—being Sheriff of Walton County, or we will all end up in jail," warned Dr. Tyson.

"I'm already going to jail," growled Barnett. "By the way, 'Big Fuzz,' how do things look now for Doc and me in Pensacola?"

"You are going to be all right, Max, unless this bat-shit crazy new president gets rid of our boys in the Justice Department office, and right now he is only throwing out the top brass. Pensacola is gonna be told to cut you a deal—and they ain't gonna like it. There will be no trial, and you're gonna be offered a good deal. But don't tell your lawyer shit!" "Big Fuzz" poured himself another glass of milk before he continued.

"I will find a place for you when you get out of jail, Max, but we are going to have to back off on the Mexican labor business. The U.S. is deporting a hundred thousand illegals a month, mostly Mexicans, but not here in Florida yet. The concentration is in those states that the Democrats won. I want to cut our money-making operation to only those areas run by people we can really trust."

"What about me 'Big Fuzz'?" asked Dr. Tyson humbly.

"You will be all right, Doc, unless Bob Kirk is elected new Sheriff. The Pensacola office is handcuffed, but you better have 'roofied' your last piece of tail. We would all be a lot better off if you had not drug-raped Leila Hewitt. And by the way, I have got you down to raise $50,000 dollars for Tall Tom Hopkins' campaign. I will give you the names to use for the donations as soon as the Governor sets the election date."

"That is no problem. Thanks, 'Fuzz,'" responded the doctor. "I just received the second $100,000 from that big Rohypnol sale we made in South Florida, with one more payment to come."

"I am concerned that I might get linked to the Leila Hewitt case," interjected Max. "If by some chance this guy Kirk gets elected, Doc and I may have that to worry about."

"As hot a topic and as popular as she is, we can't possibly take Leila out right now," "Big Fuzz" explained. "We can count our blessings that Tommy Tucker and T-Mex are both dead, but we will definitely keep her elimination as an option. I have a couple of guys in mind who owe me some big favors."

"See you here in two weeks when deer season opens, Doc. I have a couple of fine gals from Vegas coming in to service my guests. Bring your black bag with you so we can dope them up. Every woman needs a good mood changer," chuckled "Big Fuzz" as the Walton County political powers parted.

Chapter 14

Reverend Tom McGraw finally received a return phone call from Attorney James Watson at two p.m. that afternoon. He told Watson nothing more than an older single lady had responded to the possibility of adopting little Luke and Jake, and she would like to meet and talk to him as soon as possible. The interested lady's name was not revealed.

With his Aunt Sally spooked by her experiences and James not having any other interested persons, he agreed to meet the preacher and the woman at his office in Destin a half hour after it closed. One adopting parent was not what he was hoping for. "But I need to move these kids--please let this person have enough money," he thought. After his secretary got the necessary adoption papers ready, the last thing James asked her to do was to make him a tall glass of vodka and grapefruit. He drank it swiftly and waited for the appointment.

On their drive to the attorney's office, the Reverend knew better than to try and talk Leila out of her intention--he was quite familiar with her resolve.

The closest he came was to suggest, "You do not know if the boys have any mental deficiencies or perhaps diseases. Maybe you should require them to be medically examined before making a final commitment."

"I could help them with those types of problems as well as anyone," she pointed out.

The Reverend decided it was better not to respond to her comment as they drove quietly toward Destin.

After a few more miles he broke the silence. "Certainly you will want to see the boys for yourself before you adopt them."

"Please pray for all of us," Leila asked simply.

*****

When James heard Reverend McGraw and Leila enter his waiting room, he waited a minute or so and then walked out to greet them. He did a double take when he saw Leila. He was expecting an older looking woman and certainly not one so attractive. She looked very familiar. When the Reverend introduced her by name, he recognized her immediately. All of Destin was familiar with Leila and her startling recent history.

Leading them back to his office, James quickly contemplated how he would handle disclosing the serious disturbance he had experienced with Rufus "Odd Job" Jenkins. His intention had been to say nothing to his adoptive client, but he knew Leila Hewitt was not a person from whom he should withhold any major information. "This could blow up on me, big time," he feared.

James started off by addressing one of his concerns, "Miss Hewitt, like everyone else around here, I am very aware from all of the television coverage of what you have been going through. Are you sure this is what you want to do--an adoption, a double adoption--so soon after everything that has happened to you recently?"

"I have thought and prayed about it. I do not have a family, and I am sure this is what I want to do," she declared.

"She will be able to see the children, won't she?" asked the Reverend, unable to control his concern that Leila might unknowingly be walking into a bad situation.

After what seemed like a long pause, James began, "Adopting a child, or children in this case, is not like test driving a car, Reverend. It is not like taking a bite out of a fancy desert before you decide if you want to pay for it. This is about DO YOU WANT TO RAISE these children? Do you really and truly want to be a parent? Because being a parent is FOREVER! No one gets a free look. But I have seen these boys, and even though there are no warranties, they appear to be in good health." This was his standard presentation when parents seeking to adopt wanted to see the children before making their final decision on whether or not to take them.

"I understand," Leila said.

"Well, could you tell her about these boys, please? She should at least have some information as to what they have been through so she can deal with it," asked the Reverend.

James did not want to lose this adoption. It appeared to him that Leila did not want to either. He looked directly into her eyes and said very slowly, "Miss Hewitt, are you ready to sign the papers to adopt these boys today?"

She shut her eyes, leaned her head back and looked upward. After a short while, she opened them and looked back into his steely eyes, and softly said, "Yes."

"Good! Let me tell you about the boys, Luke and Jake. As I told the Reverend here, they are four and two years old. You will see their birthdates on the papers you are going to sign in a few minutes. Again, they appear to be healthy. Their mother is a prostitute. She has left the area--for good. She does not know who the fathers are. The fathers are shown as 'unknown' on both birth certificates. Neither boy looks like he has had much experience with adults. They talk to each other with a language that others cannot understand. They are obviously behind other kids their age as to what they have learned, but both are very alert. They have not even been outdoors very much. They are very, very close to each other. I don't have much else I can add about these children."

James proceeded to tell Leila that he would file her petition to commence the private adoption proceedings the very next day. He would obtain a temporary custody order for her which would be good for one year. During that time the three of them would be visited by state child protection workers who would write reports about the children and their situation with Leila. If all went well, and he felt confident that it would, he would seek a final adoption order for her when the year passed. He said the fee would be $7,500.

As Leila reached for her purse, James added, "Each."

"I thought you told me the total cost would be $7,500," interjected the Reverend.

"You must not have understood," James answered coldly. "The fee is $7,500 now and $7,500 before I file for the permanent adoption order." Leila wrote the check.

James walked around to Leila and went through the adoption papers page by page as she executed each one. He explained that she would not actually see the mother's consent to the private adoption of her two sons, but assured her that it had been previously obtained. He also explained that the contents of an adoption suit were sealed by the court until the adopted children reached eighteen years of age. After that, the children would have a legal right to find out who their natural mother was and to seek her out if they chose to do so.

When the legal papers were completely signed, James shook Leila's hand and congratulated her for her decision. He then walked back around to his chair and said there was another important matter to discuss.

"These children were raised in Fort Walton," he began, "and they have spent some time, probably not much, in Destin. People that live in this Panhandle community may, on occasion, have seen these boys being packed around in both towns by their mother. This is a relatively small geographical area. I think it would be a very good idea to limit their exposure to Fort Walton and Destin as much as possible until they are old enough not to be easily recognized--so that you and they can enjoy a total break from their prior life. You can understand this, can't you?"

Leila nodded her head, yes.

"And I know you have appeared a lot on television lately, but I do not think it would be a very good idea to have these two boys shown, at all, for the same reason."

"I understand," replied Leila.

71

"There is one other thing you need to know. I recently made contact with a rather obnoxious character who was nosing around claiming to be the father of the older boy, Luke," began James, greatly minimizing his encounter with Rufus "Odd Job" Jenkins. "He is definitely not the legal father of Luke as he is not listed on Luke's birth certificate. And, as I said before, his mother told me she does not know who Luke's real father is. A blood test would probably show that this guy is not the father. But I want to tell you that this is a low-life type of guy, a filthy-talking person. He does not even know my name. All I told him was that I am a lawyer, and he had no legal rights at all. I also told him he would be in serious trouble if he caused any problems. Adoption records are sealed, and you will likely never hear from this man. But I am advising you to stay north of Choctawhatchee Bay as much as you can so that you and these boys can get off to a good private start."

Leila changed the subject. "How long will it take before the court allows me to receive the boys?"

"The papers will be filed in the morning, and I can bring them to your house in the early afternoon," replied James, already having her address in the paperwork.

"The press crews are getting much smaller, but there still may be some photographers in front of my house tomorrow afternoon. They are always gone by five o'clock. Can we make it around six? I have so many things to get for the boys," she asked excitedly.

"I will see you then," agreed James.

Chapter 15

The boys would arrive in less than three hours, and Leila knew she was already exhausted. She thought back over her hectic day.

She had gotten out of bed at six a. m. that morning, quickly made a list of everything she thought she possibly needed, and arrived at Wal-Mart within the hour. It was not the store of her choice, but she did not have time to go anywhere else. There she had filled her older model blue Oldsmobile with food, clothes, sheets and toys. After dropping all of that back at her house, she had gone across the bridge to the Sandestin area to find some type of small bed for Jake. When she found one that looked suitable, she had paid the vendor an extra fee to have it delivered to Ebenezer Road in the early afternoon.

On the way home, Leila received a call from Amanda. "Where the heck are you honey? I stopped by to see you. What is going on with you being out and about so early in the day?"

"I have some news for you, Amanda. I will be home in about twenty-five minutes if you want to come back." Leila had rarely done anything important in her life without Amanda knowing about it in advance. She expected Amanda to be in total shock after hearing what she was about to tell her.

"Some news--great! I love news," Amanda excitedly replied. "Where are we going?"

"Just come on by, honey," Leila answered. "You will see soon."

*****

Amanda was already in the driveway when Leila pulled in. For the very first time since Mark's death there was not a single news crew stationed across the street. Leila breathed a sigh of relief over their absence. Only the sheriff's deputy assigned to watch her home was present, and she waved to him for the second time that morning.

When the two friends entered the house, Amanda immediately saw the numerous bags of recently purchased items that Leila had left strewn on the large hallway floor. "My gracious," she exclaimed, "are we having a party?"

Before Leila could answer, Amanda picked up a bag of children's clothes and exclaimed, "What the heck is this all about?"

"You know those two boys that Brother Tom told us about the other day," Leila started.

"Don't tell me you are going to keep them here for a while," Amanda said in an amazed voice.

"No, Amanda, I am adopting both boys," Leila replied in a firm voice.

"WHAT! Oh, my GOD, Leila!" Amanda gasped, raising her hands to cover her mouth. "Tell me this is not really happening--

what have you done?" She raised both of her hands to her forehead in total disbelief.

The emotion of the moment was interrupted by the loud-ringing telephone on the back porch. Leila walked quickly toward it to better hear the message.

"Good morning, Leila. This is Acting Sheriff Billy Munsey. I am calling you this morning to discuss the deputy that Walton County has been providing to you and..." Leila hurried over and picked up the receiver.

"Yes, Sir, this is Leila. Yes, Sir. Yes, Sir, I understand. I want to thank you for providing what you did. Yes, Sir, you have a good day also." Click.

*****

When she returned to the hallway, Leila could see that Amanda was crying, more than gently. She approached and hugged her lifelong best friend.

"I had hoped you would be happy for me," Leila said softly.

Amanda collected herself for a minute and replied, "Leila you will be fifty-seven years old in a couple of months--this is just crazy. And so soon after what has happened--can't you see that you are doing this because Mark's girlfriend is having a baby?" Amanda started sobbing again. "Can't you see that you are not yourself yet, Leila? Please don't do this," she pleaded.

Leila never expected her to react so emotionally and hugged her harder. As she buried her face in Amanda's shoulder, she wondered for the first time if Mary Kate's pregnancy could have been a subconscious motive for what she was undertaking. The thought was very disturbing.

"It has already been done. The boys will be here late this afternoon," Leila whispered.

"You have actually ALREADY signed the papers--and all?"

"Yes, I have."

Amanda collapsed into a hallway chair. After a few minutes, and seeing Leila carrying the packages to their destination, she rose and helped the best she could. They worked together in silence.

*****

Shortly thereafter the phone rang again, Leila answered. It was Jane, and she had good news.

"I am very happy to tell you that Bob and I have discussed your offer. I am looking forward to joining the Ebenezer Forest team!"

"You do not know how wonderful it is to hear this, Jane. You just have no idea."

"When I informed the police department that I would be leaving, I found out that I had a lot of vacation time built up. I will be on paid vacation time for a whole month, so I can start any time you need me after this week."

"If you can start this coming Monday, that would be perfect. I really do need you as soon as possible," answered Leila.

"Charlie McBride is letting us stay at his place in Sandestin until after the election and perhaps even until we get settled elsewhere."

"Jane, I wanted to share with you that there is a new development in my life. I am adopting two young boys who desperately needed a new home."

"You are seriously thinking about it--that would be quite a surprise," replied Jane.

"I am not thinking about it--it's already done. They will be at my home tonight," revealed Leila.

"My word! That is quite a new development! You didn't say a thing about it Sunday when I was there," said Jane in a stunned voice. "How could this happen so quickly?"

"These children needed help--and--I was moved to help them," Leila responded awkwardly.

There was a pause, and Jane finally said, "They are very lucky boys--I can't wait to meet them."

"Thank you, very much," Leila replied earnestly, choosing not to reveal she was yet to meet them herself.

*****

Trying to nap before the boys' arrival, Leila continued to be troubled by Amanda's comments. The adoption had developed in three unbelievably short days. Her life seemed to be in constant acceleration since Mark Mabry had first appeared at her front door. She thought how simple and painless her life had been when solely centered upon Ebenezer Forest.

She could tell from their response that the two most important women in her life were quite taken back by her decision. "However, they were not here when I received HIS direction," she thought to herself.

Out front Ebenezer Road was quiet. There were no more gawkers. The deputies were gone as well, and they would not be coming back.

"I can do this--I can do this," she repeated to herself, until falling deeply asleep.

Chapter 16

James Watson picked up the Bradley-Hewitt adoption file at five p.m., locked up his law office and headed to his Aunt Sally's house. She had agreed to accompany him on the delivery of Luke and Jake to their new home.

After loading Luke and Jake and their few possessions into the back seat, the first half of the trip was very quiet and uneventful. The boys had no idea where they were going, and James decided he could not put off the revelation any longer.

He turned and talked as he drove. "We are taking you boys to your new home." There was no response. Little Jake was not known to have ever spoken, and Luke was a four-year-old of very few words.

"You are going to have a brand new mommy who is going to love you both very, very much," James began. "You are going to live in a nice, clean house with this mommy, and be happy forever and ever." There being still no response, and with none expected, James ended his speech.

But Luke soon spoke. "You told our mommy and us that we are going to get a new mommy and a new daddy. Are we going to get a new daddy?"

"Not today," answered James, "just a new mommy today."

Luke had shown no previous emotion at all to Aunt Sally or James, but he began to cry. Little Jake looked up at his older brother, and soon they were both bawling.

James, now agitated, drove a bit faster

"When will we get a daddy?" Luke said, still crying. There was no response from James.

"I want my mommy back!" Luke wailed, and Jake chimed in even more loudly.

Aunt Sally tried to stop the emotional meltdown. "You are soon going to have Thanksgiving and Christmas with your new mommy in your new house," she offered.

"What is that?" asked Luke between sobs.

"Thanksgiving, Christmas--haven't you heard of these holidays," she asked looking directly at Luke.

"No," he gasped.

"Your new mommy is a very nice and good person, and she is waiting for you two boys right now. You are going to both like her, and she will make you both really happy."

"I want a daddy too," persisted Luke sadly.

*****

There was still fairly good daylight as James turned down Ebenezer Church Road. Luke became attentive as the automobile slowly traveled down the graveled lane beneath the moss-covered oaks and magnolias. It was a very different from any other place he had ever seen before. Little Jake was too short to take it all in, but he could feel and hear the gravel and look upward toward the dark forest canopy as they passed beneath it.

When the four travelers finally arrived at the Hewitt home, a few guineas gave their usual welcoming yelps. The sounds caught the boys' interest, and they walked around where they could get a better look at the unusual birds. While Luke and Jake were distracted, James removed the executed temporary custody order from his file to give to Leila.

As they approached the house, Jake touched the various colored rose bushes that lined the walkway. Luke looked up at a tremendous gray-barked oak and was totally fascinated by its size.

They walked on across the large blocks of stone, girdled with monkey grass. The front door of the home opened, and Leila gracefully appeared with her stunningly beautiful face and smile. Her deep blue eyes were absolutely radiant in the setting sun. The two boys quietly stared at her with intense interest.

Leila stared back at Luke and Jake, totally entranced with the young, attractive boys who appeared to be looking at her with hopeful expectations. The reality of her decision was standing right before her. It was an unforgettable moment. All were frozen.

She then noticed that their eyes were red and damp with fresh tears. Leila was overcome with emotion. She bent down to lift them up, one by one, into her arms. She slowly hugged them as tightly as she possibly could without harm. And she gently kissed each one on their tender cheeks.

As each boy was placed back onto the ground, they both grabbed Leila's legs and held on as though they were finally safe at last. The boys' immediate clasp of her body melted Leila into a swooning and passionate state of joy, affection and commitment.

The stark contrast of Leila's warmth compared to the indifference of James and Aunt Sally made their quick departure almost unnoticed. And it would be the last time that Lucas or little Jake would ever see either one of them.

Leila showed the boys the entire house and later took them on a twilight tour of the yard. She let them feed the grateful squirrels as well as several doves and robins. They were then introduced to the coon pups. All four were thrilled and would soon become great friends.

Back inside, Leila fed Luke and Jake a wonderful home-cooked meal. She changed them into their new pajamas and retrieved her own favorite childhood book. She read it slowly to them, pointing out the features of each animal in every picture. They seemed to enjoy it so much that, to their delight, she chose another animal story.

Luke's and little Jake's new beds were not used that night, nor for many nights to come. Leila and her new children soon fell into much-needed slumber and peace.

Ebenezer Forest had a new tree, a family tree, and it began that forever special evening.

Chapter 17

Before ten o'clock the next morning Leila came to the full and stark realization that she needed help. Luke and Jake awoke before she did, and Jake had wet the bed. No big deal, but both were hungry again and Luke wanted to go outside and see the coon pups. She needed diapers and more sheets--and to start the oven.

The phone was ringing early, and she let it go to voice message except when Amanda called. She wanted to know when she could come over and see the boys. Leila answered, "Now."

The boys had to be fed first, and the guineas didn't like it. They were screaming across the street. Leila, knowing that the deputy sheriff was no longer out front, couldn't really tell if something or somebody else was aggravating the birds, or if they were annoyed by having no breakfast. She needed security for the boys and herself, and she was well aware of it.

At her first opportunity Leila retrieved a folder which containing the applications of over a dozen recent forestry graduates. All had responded after she requested Florida State and Auburn to post her job notice on their bulletin boards. Three top candidates were already identified, and she looked first to see which of those were available for immediate work. Atop the list was a young man by the name of Josh Snyder who, better yet, lived in nearby Niceville. Leila left her name and number with his mother. By lunch time Josh had called and was scheduled to come by later in the afternoon.

The guineas, coon pups, squirrels, birds and boys were all fed, in reverse order. Leila was able to return only a few calls before Amanda arrived. She successfully talked her friend into riding with all of them to nearby Freeport. Multiple necessities for Luke and Jake were needed that Leila's inexperience had caused her to overlook.

"I never dreamed something like this would ever happen to you, Leila!" exclaimed Amanda as they rode along. "Just call me Aunt Mandy," she offered as she rubbed Luke's head.

"'Something like'--you mean me and Jake?" asked Luke seriously.

"Yes, like you and Jake."

"Are we going to get our new daddy now?" Luke responded innocently.

Amanda and Leila were both taken aback by his question. But Amanda answered quickly.

"You can call me 'Uncle Mandy' if you want."

Leila turned and scowled at Amanda. She never knew what would come out of her friend's mouth.

"Your Aunt Mandy is silly, isn't she Luke?" Leila asked, suppressing her annoyance.

"Uh huh," he mumbled.

*****

Over fifteen hundred miles away, William "Powder" White was beginning a mid-morning breakfast at the Jerome Hotel in Aspen Colorado. A sizeable man, but not particularly overweight, he ordered a veggie omelet and looked at the enlarged map he had just picked up from an engineering office on Main Street.

The map showed his 3,500 acre mountainside forest near the end of Castle Creek Road, just eleven miles from where he was sitting. The approximately 600 acres he had directed to be highlighted included one of the few flat areas on the estate which gradually elevated almost a mile skyward through a beautiful draw. A large and lively year-round creek tumbled down through the parcel adding an appealing murmur. Powder was very pleased with the chosen tract.

Before his meal arrived, he was joined first and briefly by Sheriff DeSalty, who walked down the short two blocks from his office to deliver another piece of the plan.

"Here is your Honorary Deputy Sheriff's badge, Powder," he began laughingly. "What a man won't do to impress a woman!"

"Are you sure you don't want to go with us, Sheriff?"

"Too much going on, and I would love to. But if I left town with four bachelors, I would not have a wife when I got back."

"We plan on coming back Sunday, and I plan on bringing a good mess of fresh Gulf fish over to your place," promised Powder.

"What I really want to hear about is how your grand plan to meet this Hewitt lady works out," replied the Sheriff.

"Hey, all the guys and I have really gotten into it," he said as he showed the map to the Sheriff. "I'm going to do this project even if I strike out with Leila. It would be a nice attraction for this area."

"You have been most generous around here already. We all appreciate you very much, Powder," the sheriff spoke earnestly. "Good luck on your trip," he added before excusing himself to keep another appointment.

Attorney Steve Wanninger showed up a little late as usual. "I am very excited to be going," he said grabbing a chair.

"Great to have you along," started Powder. "Did you get a chance to work something up?"

Steve reached into his suit pocket and pulled out a folded document. "Before I put it into final form, I want you to read it."

Powder took a couple of minutes and then pointed to one paragraph on the second page. "I would add an all-purpose hold harmless acknowledgement to this paragraph. Other than that it looks fine. Good Job, Steve!"

"Thank you, Powder. What time should I be at the airport?"

"Six in the morning, and don't forget to bring a swimsuit. It is 86 degrees today in Destin."

*****

The same afternoon Leila interviewed and hired the young and impressive Josh Snyder as the first full-time forester of Ebenezer Forest. He was an eager twenty-three year old, was well-trained at Auburn University, and would start work Monday morning.

Before Josh departed, Leila took him and the boys on a stroll back to Hominy Creek. She became increasingly pleased with her new employee's knowledge and enthusiasm.

Luke and Jake were totally fascinated with the various trees and enthralling sounds of Ebenezer Forest.

Luke tried to chase a young, elusive rabbit, and little Jake almost fell off the bridge trying to touch the running water below. Leila carried him down the bank to experience the pleasure of the creek.

All three were thoroughly captivated by the powers of this special place as had been many prior visitors. Leila's boys and Josh were reluctant to depart Ebenezer Forest. But darkness was approaching, there and elsewhere.

Chapter 18

At seven-thirty p. m. on the same night, James Watson parked his Ford Ranger near the rear of his Destin home. Darkness had arrived. Nearing his back door, James reached into his left pocket for his house key and heard a brisk approach from behind him. But his reflexes were slow from several after work vodka and grapefruits, and it was too late.

The assailant grabbed him around the neck with a powerful left arm, and James felt a blade in the man's right hand gouge sharply into his neck. He was paralyzed with fear.

"Don't move mother-fucker or you are dead!"

With a lifelong history of violent crime, Rufus "Odd Job" Jenkins was criminally insane, but not dumb. He was not yet ready to kill James--until he got all the information he wanted from his victim.

"Where is my son, Luke Jenkins?" He demanded.

James Watson was not ready for death--but he was now aware that he had been attacked by "Odd Job" and realized instantly he was unlikely to survive. He did not utter a sound.

"Do you hear me, you slimy bastard? I am going to kill you if you do not tell me right now!" He eased the knife just a bit deeper into James's neck.

Now in progressive, traumatic shock, James was unable to speak.

"Odd Job" increased the pressure of his left arm around his victim's neck to the point that James was becoming breathless. Within twenty seconds he was gasping for air and beginning to fall limp.

Minutes passed, and James's next awareness was the feeling of severe pain between his legs. "Odd Job" was holding him down on his kitchen floor and was lightly slapping his face to bring him back into consciousness.

James dimly comprehended that "Odd Job" was holding his severed testicle sac in his face. The realization was horrific. Each time he tried to make a sound, he was violently pounded.

"Tell me where my boy Luke is, or you will die," "Odd Job" kept savagely demanding.

Soon after, James began to talk in detail. The complete, rare truth flowed from the lawyer's lips as he was being viciously tortured to death. He was forced to repeat his answers several times for verification as he was bleeding to death.

When there was nothing else to learn, "Odd Job" leisurely, but not neatly, slit Attorney James Watson's throat wide open.

He stood up, took off his bloody gloves and casually washed his hands. He pulled new gloves from his pocket and put them on. Next he located a bloodless shirt from within the house.

Finally, "Odd Job" exited through the back door and ambled off into the devil's darkness.

Chapter 19

The King Air lifted off from Aspen's Sarty Field right on schedule. Because of the time zone difference and the necessity of a refueling stop, the four friends chose Dallas as their choice for lunch. It would be a day of travel and checking into and relaxing at the Sandestin Hilton on the east side of Destin.

All of the visitors were amazed by the beauty of the crystal white sand and clear turquoise water along the Florida Panhandle's coast. "I need to buy a place down here for the spring and fall," commented Powder.

During dinner Thursday night at the famous Tuscany Italian Bistro in Destin, Powder and his three guests laughed heartily at the humor of their Leila-inspired, cross-country adventure. Powder tried to persuade them from ever mentioning their escapade in the Aspen area if his plan to romance Leila did not work out. He obtained no commitment at all from his friends on this attempt.

Their intended plan was to stop by Ebenezer Forest Friday morning without an appointment. Nothing else was firmly scheduled for that day in case a problem was encountered in obtaining an audience with Leila.

A private boat had been chartered for a full day fishing trip on Saturday. Powder was not going to join John Gillespie, Steve Wanninger, and Bud Holt on the Saturday fishing excursion. He was hoping he might have further opportunities with Leila. No one had any idea that she was now the fully obligated mother of two young boys.

It was agreed that if any two guys still wanted to fish again Sunday, the return trip would be delayed until late afternoon to accommodate another half day fishing venture.

Upon their return to the hotel lobby lounge, the four men caught a local ten p.m. newscast describing the gruesome, bloody murder of Destin attorney, James Watson. The story included the description that the victim was castrated before being killed. Still fewer than three weeks since the death of two men in Leila Hewitt's bed made national headline news, the visitors' interest was more than keen.

"Man, that killer must be a violent son-of-a-gun for him to have cut the lawyer's nuts off," commented Powder.

"They didn't tell me about that risk of the legal profession when I was in law school," quipped Steve Wanninger.

"Best you had better not piss off any of your clients--like me," laughed Powder.

"I never heard of Destin, Florida until the Hewitt story erupted," remarked Bud Holt. "This place is starting to sound like lower Chicago."

"I would not be surprised at all if it turns out the dead man is Leila Hewitt's lawyer," replied Steve dryly.

"Leila may not like lawyers and could be the killer herself. Maybe you ought to stay here in the hotel tomorrow, Steve," Bud joked.

"You guys best not make too much fun of Miss Leila," warned Powder. "You may be talking about my next wife."

"Heaven forbid," opined John "No Elk" Gillespie.

Chapter 20

The disturbing media reports of James Watson's gruesome murder gave rise to several citizens' calls to the Walton County Sheriff's Office. The first was from Reverend Bob Belding of the Blue Walton Worship center. He left his number with an operator and received a return call from a shift supervisor at nine a.m. Friday morning. Brother Bob gave him a brief account of how James Watson had returned a call for him to an irate "Rufus Jenkins." He submitted that Jenkins should be a suspect in Watson's death.

Watson's personal friend in the Walton County Sheriff's office, Terry Morgan, was accompanying his wife on a medical treatment matter in Birmingham, Alabama. But after hearing the news of Watson's murder, he called in to his office to alert the captain of the possible involvement of Rufus "Odd Job" Jenkins.

Meanwhile, in a run-down area of neighboring Okaloosa County, an apartment dweller reported an incessant barking dog at an apartment occupied by private investigator Pearlie Towns. After gaining entry to Towns's unit, a Fort Walton city policeman discovered that Towns had been killed by a single bullet to his right temple. He had been dead for approximately three days.

No connection was made between the deaths of private investigator Pearlie Towns and attorney James Watson.

In Walton and Okaloosa Counties one of the few things that move more slowly than the sheriffs' offices are those of their respective county judges. It would be at least a week before a search warrant would even be considered for issuance toward Rufus "Odd Job" Jenkins.

To complicate matters, Watson had been slain in Walton County, and Jenkins' last known address was in Okaloosa County. With "Odd Job" recently released from prison and because his Shalimar attorney had been much sharper than his prosecutors, he had completed his full sentence of a flat four-year incarceration as negotiated in his manslaughter plea. Thus not subject to probation at all after release because of the way that his sentence was worded, he was free to change addresses without contacting anyone. There was little surprise when "Odd Job's" location was not known when the two jurisdictions finally got together late Friday afternoon to seek him out for questioning. The two counties' lawmen would not learn until Monday that there was insufficient probable cause for any judge to issue a warrant for his arrest.

*****

Leila's pastor, Reverend Tom McGraw, was also startled when learning that Leila's adoption attorney had been brutally slain. He well remembered the reference James Watson made about an unnamed, angry man James had had contact with claiming to be

Luke's father. He also remembered that James had stated that this person did not even know his name. This recall eased the Reverend's concern somewhat. He was soon distracted, and the thought was not acted upon then.

But at his first extended afternoon break, the possible connection of Watson's death with his favorite parishioner's adoptions began to bother Reverend McGraw again. He decided to call the sheriff's office to share his concern. He was referred to same shift supervisor that had been contacted by Reverend Bob Belding.

When told that he was the second pastor of the day with a similar message, the Reverend felt an immediate sick feeling in his stomach that his dear friend Leila may have walked into a "hell's trap."

"Oh, dear God, please let this not be true."

Reverend McGraw knew that the facts discussed with the supervisor were not enough to prove anything. He also realized that no certainty of danger for Leila and her two children had been clearly indicated. Yet sometimes Karma can grab one by the throat--and the good Reverend felt grabbed. He was terrified for her. He envisioned a dark serpent of Hades positioning itself around Leila's neck, ready to squeeze.

Chapter 21

The four Colorado friends traveled north across Choctawhatchee Bay and followed directions to Ebenezer Church Road. Turning down the shaded lane, they passed beneath some of the largest hardwood trees in the South. They proceeded slowly to enjoy the impressive splendor. The oak leaves were nearly ready to drop and their brilliant orange, yellow and dark red colors were majestic and picturesque. They briefly came to a complete stop to admire a gigantic magnolia tree. Its unique aroma was easily smelled through their now open windows.

"I can see why this place is so popular to visit," admired John "No Elk" Gillespie. "I feel like I am in a world from the past."

"These trees are easily a couple of hundred years old," guessed Bud Holt.

"There are the famous guinea pens, fellows," began Steve Wanninger as they approached Leila's home. "Let me get a picture." He took several.

Pulling into the driveway behind Leila's old blue Oldsmobile, the group left their vehicle and huddled for a brief time before approaching the house. Powder wanted to do all of the talking.

*****

Leila had not watched any news broadcasts in the last twenty-four hours and was totally oblivious to James Watson's violent death. Cars full of curious folks were commonly traveling down Ebenezer Road since the shootings. They almost always turned around across the street from her house in the empty spaces adjacent to the bird pens. She had been carefully heeding Jane's advice to be vigilant, particularly since the sheriff's office had recalled the security deputies.

Sitting on the living room floor showing animal picture cards to the boys, she heard a car door shut on her side of the street. She quickly rose to peek out a front window. She was able to get a good look at the four men while they were talking on her front lawn. From appearances only, she was not alarmed. Nonetheless when they all walked across the porch, and one of them used the brass door knocker, she guardedly opened the still-chained front door.

"May I help you, gentlemen?" she asked politely, peering through the crack.

Powder was thunder-bolted by Leila's beauty, especially her gorgeous blues eyes that were even brighter in person than when he had seen them on television. He finally spoke with a nervous yet seemingly sincere voice.

"Miss Hewitt, my name is William White. We apologize for not making an appointment, but we have traveled a long way to pay our respects to you and to ask for your permission and support for a project to honor what you have done here in the Florida Panhandle. All four of us have a deep interest in and love of wildlife--and we understand the importance of wildlife habitat. We ask to have just a little of your valuable time. Would you allow that, please?"

Leila did not yet recognize she was being addressed by "Powder" White, the same fellow that flirtatiously offered her a safe haven in Aspen. But influenced by the speaker's declaration of interest in her lifetime passion, she opened the door and allowed the four men to enter her home. She did not know how long this would take and chose, unlike her usual custom, not to offer the visitors morning tea.

"Come in please, for a few minutes," she allowed.

All four men were stunned at their blonde-haired hostess's unbelievable attractiveness. They were not prepared for her extraordinary allure. Each awkwardly introduced themselves.

Before William could begin to speak, both of Leila's boys unexpectedly entered the room. Little Jake made a straight run to John Gillespie's legs, and Luke stopped right beside him. John patted them both on their heads and kneeled down to their height.

William looked surprised, and asked Leila, "Are you babysitting?"

"No, these are my children, Luke and Jake."

William was surprised but went forward with his presentation. "Miss Hewitt."

"Please, all of you gentlemen may call me Leila."

"Leila," he started again. "We all learned for the first time on television about what you have created here in Florida. It is unique, wonderful and direly needed in America. Our forests are being destroyed every day. So many of America's young people have absolutely no access to observe the beauty of nature and its wildlife, much less understand the importance of wildlife habitat for the survival of our animals, forests and humankind." He stopped to clear his throat.

"Watching what you have recently been through," William continued, "people all over the world are now totally familiar with Ebenezer Forest. We came here today to tell you we believe it may be in God's plan to replicate what you have done here. It would be of such huge benefit to our country! I cannot wait to walk and see all of your forest. It is our idea to create in other places what you have started right here in Walton County. I would like to personally develop the very first model of Ebenezer Forest in the hope others will follow with similar wildlife habitats springing up all over the country, from the Atlantic to the Pacific. Think what this could do for our precious national wildlife and wildlife habitat!"

Leila was listening intently to every word.

"Attorney Steve Wanninger here has prepared documents, and we have brought you a copy. Of course this is offered just as a starting point of discussion. You will have no financial obligation, no financial risk at all. All we ask you to please consider doing is just to allow similar habitat conservation programs, donated by other people like me. They will all be totally independent but will be called 'Approved Leila Jane Hewitt Ebenezer Forests.'"

He showed Leila his map.

"I am from Wyoming, but this is a map of a tract of land I own in Pitkin County, Colorado." He pointed out the highlighted area. "This is 600 acres that I am willing to donate and totally fund as the very first Leila Jane Hewitt approved

Ebenezer Forest for all of the people who visit it in our world-famous Aspen, Colorado."

All four men looked expectantly at Leila, clearly awaiting her response.

She did not respond at all for a few long seconds. She squinted, as if thinking hard, then slowly asked, "Are you the one and same man who called me several times under the name 'Powder' White?"

The three men behind him broke into big smiles.

William looked more than a little sheepish, and answered with his own increasingly large grin. "William 'Powder' White, Leila, my dear, very PLEASED to finally meet you!"

Chapter 22

The visitors from Aspen were so pleasant and apparently committed to the proposed Ebenezer Forest project that Leila decided to invite them to her back porch for tea and a longer visit. All four men were very encouraged with Leila's amused, but definitely interested, reaction to Powder's presentation. They followed her, along with Luke and Jake, down the large hall to the rear of her home.

While Leila prepared their tea, Powder walked over to the breakfast table and again spread his map showing the tract he had selected. Everyone was soon served, and Leila was shown several dozen large colored photographs of the property's very impressive terrain and watershed. The conversation was light, and Leila felt very comfortable with her guests.

She was particularly impressed when John "No Elk" Gillespie talked without notes about a number of animals she was not familiar with that could be found in Powder's future Ebenezer Forest. After naming some of the better-known Colorado mammals, he added, "And of course, there are some more challenging to see residents such as shrews, ermine, ferrets, pocket gophers, jumping mice, marmots, white-tailed antelope squirrels, western vole and others."

"Wow," Leila said, "I always love to be introduced to creatures of God I have never met before."

*****

"Hellooo, Leila." bellowed the familiar voice of Reverend Tom McGraw as he unexpectedly appeared at the side door of the back porch. He knew there was someone else in Leila's house, having seen the strange vehicle out front. Observing several visitors with her, he spoke from outside with an abnormal and concerned voice. "Everything okay back here?"

"Yes, come in please, Brother Tom," responded Leila. She immediately noticed his very anxious look and observed his face was much redder than usual.

"I wanted to stop by and make sure you are all right after the news about James Watson," he said without thinking. He looked over and saw Luke and Jake for the first time, then scanned the room assessing the strangers in a troubled way. It never occurred to him that Leila was still unaware of the fate of her attorney.

Leila had no idea what her pastor was referring to. But seeing how upset he was, she knew she did not want her two sons to hear the details. She turned to her guests and asked, "Would you please excuse me for a few minutes?" She led Reverend Tom back outside and out of hearing distance.

As soon as they departed, having recognized Watson's name from the newscast they all had watched the night before, Steve Wanninger whispered to his three buddies, "By damn, the dead attorney really is--or was--Leila's lawyer!"

Immediately foreseeing what could soon develop, John Gillespie said, "I'm taking these two boys to the front of the house."

*****

Before Leila and her pastor returned to the back porch, there was someone at the front door. John opened it and a very pretty, dark-haired woman introduced herself as Jane Anderson.

Jane noticed the two boys and addressed them first. "Oh, how adorable. What is your name?" she asked the oldest.

"My name is Luke, my brother doesn't talk--his name is Jake."

Jane smiled at both boys and turned to the stranger and asked, "Who are you, Sir?"

"I am John Gillespie, just a visitor. You may have arrived at an inconvenient time," he replied very politely.

"And why is that, John? I am a close friend of Leila and a new employee of Ebenezer Forest. Where is Leila?" She asked in a compelling tone.

"She is in the back of the house, addressing a personal issue," he replied.

"Well then, you stay here with these boys," Jane ordered as she immediately headed toward the back porch.

When she arrived and saw three strange men and no Leila, she was not inclined to exchange pleasantries.

"Where is Leila?" She demanded.

Powder pointed at the side door and said, "Out there with her preacher."

Jane never slowed down and continued straight outside.

The men from Colorado knew they had walked into an uncomfortable and developing situation.

"Should we leave?" asked Bud Holt.

"No, we are going to stay and help, if they let us," replied Powder. "You two come over here and sit at this table by me."

He, Bud and Steve were at a complete loss as to how the two boys had entered the picture. They had recently read she had never married, and there was never a reference to children whatsoever in any article or televised newscast. They recalled it was often mentioned that she lived alone and was alone the night Leila shot the two men that had died in her bed. They were in total agreement that Leila's unsurpassed beauty and grace made their entire adventure worthwhile, regardless of whatever was to follow.

It was another ten minutes before Leila, Reverend Tom and Jane returned to the back porch.

*****

Leila was understandably upset to hear that her adoption attorney was savagely killed. Aside from her personal regard for his life, she worried about how it would affect her adoption proceedings.

Jane was calmer than Reverend Tom, with his unapologetic, deep fear for Leila and the boys' safety. Although normally very collected, he could not abandon his chilling premonition that they were all in the line of fire of a madman. He insisted that he had never before experienced such a strong omen. He was finally able to extract a promise from Leila that she would stay on highest alert to safeguard herself and her sons.

Jane pointed out that she was technically still an employee of the Atlanta Police Department. She offered to spend the rest of the weekend, while she still had some police power, finding out as much as she could from local authorities about James Watson's death.

Before they went back inside, Reverend Tom led the two ladies in a heartfelt prayer.

*****

Leila had informed Brother Tom and Jane outside that her Colorado visitors were well intentioned. Consequently the four men received much more regard when everyone soon mixed together. They all shared a little more information about themselves. The Coloradans more fully discussed their reason for the visit from Aspen. Jane agreed that the proposed Ebenezer Forest satellite project was a most intriguing idea.

Leila also revealed to Powder alone, when she had the first opportunity, that she had adopted Luke and Jake only earlier in the week. She was vague in the details. Powder had plenty of questions, but respectfully asked none.

Later, Powder received his sought-after invitation from Leila for a tour of her estate the next morning. John Gillespie asked if he could join them, adding, "I would much rather see Ebenezer Forest than go fishing."

Whether from a lack of plans or pure interest, Leila surprised herself by also agreeing that she and her boys would accompany Powder and John after the tour to lunch at any place of her choice.

Leila eventually almost had to ask her guests to leave. Brother Tom and Jane were able to spend a little more time with Luke and Jake while Leila walked her new Aspen friends around her side yard back to their vehicle.

When all were gone and her two sons were settled, she finally had a chance to rest. She realized the day had left her with a better feeling than had most of the solitary ones in her recent past. Leila had a lot to think about. But the gruesome murder of James Watson and its possible connection to her own family were frightfully foremost in her thoughts.

Chapter 23

Powder and John "No Elk" Gillespie arrived back at Ebenezer Forest at nine-thirty a. m. Saturday morning. Leila had the boys ready and waiting for them on the front porch. Wearing matched camouflaged shirts she had purchased earlier in the week, Luke and Jake were dressed for the occasion. Jake's shirt was one of the smallest sizes sold in the store, and it swallowed him up. The two boys were extremely excited to be going on their second excursion into Ebenezer Forest. As Leila watched them run over to greet their two new Aspen friends, she realized that she could not alone give them the full parental experience that God intended.

She handed John a large ice bag full of water and snacks, and they all followed her around to the smaller of her two barns. Arriving first, she reached down and grabbed the handle of the old-style barn door and pulled it upward as high as she could reach. It was high enough for all to walk inside. Watching as Leila unplugged the electric charger from an old golf cart, they all moved out of the way as she backed it outside. Powder pulled the heavy door back to the ground.

"I rarely use ole Jenny here, but I wanted to start the tour at the end of Ebenezer Road on the Choctawhatchee River. The boys have yet to see it, and it is the very heart and lifeblood of our entire forest."

She positioned John in the middle of the back seat with a boy on each side. "They didn't make seat belts when Jenny was born, so I am counting on you, Mr. Gillespie to hold them tight."

"Yes, Ma'am, you can count on it," he replied cheerfully.

Leila steered Jenny over to Ebenezer Road and turned to the East. There was nothing but deep forest between her house and the graveled cul de sac at the road's end. The electric cart was almost soundless as it eased along. Approaching a long, narrow meadow that her property manager had recently planted in winter wheat, they slowed to watch several large deer and their young fawns grazing on the fresh growth. The boys were thrilled with the sighting. With his new knowledge of animals, Luke shouted, "Deer, deer, deer," as he pointed them out to his little brother.

When the road ended, the winding trail was barely wide enough for Leila to ease the golf cart toward the river. Leila soon saw the tremendous and familiar Florida maple tree appear where her last intimate moments with Mark Mabry had been spent. She could feel a lump forming in her throat. But she pulled up to the exact spot she had visited all of her life, and then stopped.

On this high bluff, the clean and unspoiled waterway could be easily viewed in both directions. Her young sons were fascinated by the fast-flowing river.

"This part of my family estate was left out of the Ebenezer Forest designation because of the depth and swiftness of the Choctawhatchee River. With many very young boys and girls coming to visit the wildlife in the river's overflow bottomland, it was the safe thing to do," Leila explained. "We are going to now head north from here and eventually enter Ebenezer Forest from its far side."

The trail meandered along the river bank with fairly thick woods beside it. After making a turn to the west and traveling about a quarter of a mile, the entry into Ebenezer Forest was quite stark.

Leila explained that most of the entire 500 acres had been under-brushed at her direction many years before. This left numerous large trees more visible from greater distances. The rich soil beneath their canopy had sprung back with lush, varied and colorful vegetation. There were some exceptions made to the under-brushing, leaving thicker growth along the ridges in some areas.

"On other parts of these ridges, to allow dense growth for wildlife food and cover, years ago I clear-cut a number of carefully placed patches along every ridge. I planted these small areas with plants like knockout roses, native blackberries and raspberries, feather reed grass, and a whole lot of honeysuckles which the deer really love," she explained. Both men were totally entranced by this beautiful woman who was sharing her amazing knowledge with them.

They stopped for a while to leisurely walk beneath the tall umbrella of trees. At each different type they read its popular and scientific name, the latter of which included its genus and species. The small, harmless and metallic sign on each one had been carefully placed by Leila or student helpers.

Proceeding past the northern line of Ebenezer Forest, Leila drove several hundred more yards. They came upon a more than thirty acre soybean field that was far removed from the sight of usual visitors to Ebenezer Forest. "This is one my best 'kept from the public secrets,'" she began. "Of course the acorns would argue differently, but this field helps explain why most of my visitors remark how unusually pudgy my deer and other game are."

From there they continued until arriving at her beloved Ebenezer Church. Both men were already familiar with its exterior appearance, its adjacent clear-water spring and her family cemetery. They had been watching on live television when Leila threw herself onto Mark's casket at the end of his funeral service.

Leila led the whole group inside her family church. Her visitors vividly remembered reading about how in this room she had so unforgettably lost her composure.

She never entered her family church without prayer. Both men kneeled in the row behind Leila, Luke and Jake as she prayed aloud. Afterward, Leila took her sons to the rear restroom, and Powder and John went outside to wait near the spring. They were overwhelmed.

"Leila is like an angel," said Powder in awe. "She has to be one of the purest and most special people on earth."

"I feel like you, Powder. Being here, with her, is such a moving experience. I feel as if I am in a trance just watching her," John answered. He paused and continued, "Do you think she is going to talk to us about the murder of her attorney?"

"She is as strong and interesting a woman as I have ever imagined. I don't know. I just don't know if we should broach it," Powder replied.

Soon, Leila and the boys returned to complete the tour. Following a slow ride back to her home, they were all ready for lunch.

Chapter 24

That same morning, Jane placed a call to the Walton County Sheriff's office and asked to speak to supervisor Mike Rainey. Reverend Tom had informed her that Rainey was the officer he had spoken to about a very agitated and unknown person that attorney James Watson had mentioned when talking to him and Leila at their first appointment. The Reverend had also told Jane that Officer Rainey had already received a similar call from another minister concerning the Watson murder case.

Deputy Rainey was out for the weekend, but Jane was able to get the dispatcher to give her his cell number after stating she was calling on behalf of the Atlanta Police Department about an extremely urgent matter. Rainey answered on the second ring.

After identifying herself as a police officer, and claiming to have been referred to him by another department, she started off by saying, "I know you talked to Reverend Tom McGraw about the James Watson case, and I am aware you also talked to the other preacher. We have information that this case very likely involves a series of ongoing murders." She then directed him point blank, "Give me the full name of the prime suspect."

Unaware that Jane had no clue of any part of the suspect's name, the officer replied, "I believe his whole name is Rufus 'Odd Job' Jenkins."

"What is your next step?" Jane quickly fired back.

"I don't know if the Chief has put anyone in charge of this case yet or not, but we are going to meet on it Monday afternoon. 'Odd Job's' last known address is in Okaloosa County, and we tried to get them to pick him up for questioning, but he's skipped or just moved. We don't know yet."

"What is the strongest thing you have on him?' Jane kept firing.

"Our captain told me that one of our officers, Terry Morgan, called in to report that he received a call from Watson last week, and Watson was afraid of 'Odd Job' because he claimed to be the father of a kid Watson was placing for adoption. I think Morgan will be back to work Monday, too. That is all I really know."

"That is all you know about this guy, 'Odd Job'?" Jane pressed.

"Naw, everybody in four counties knows that he is one bad dude, really crazy and dangerous, a life-long criminal. He just got out of jail for manslaughter."

"What is the situation with the forensics?"

"All I know is there were no fingerprints--nothing. Who else is 'Odd Job' supposed to have murdered?" Rainey asked.

"He is just a suspect now, but I will keep you informed. Thank you very much for the information, Officer Rainey."

"What is your name again, Ma'am?" Rainey asked.

"Jane Anderson, Sir, thanks again. I am sure we will meet."

She hung up realizing that the situation was much worse than she could have ever imagined. She opened her laptop and searched Jenkins' name. She learned he had been sentenced in

Okaloosa County, and she wanted to see his full pre-sentence report. But it was Saturday and her first day of work at Ebenezer Forest would start Monday morning.

She could not wait until then to further alert Leila. She had to do it today, and it needed to be done in person, immediately.

Jane called Leila at noon, twelve-thirty and one-thirty. No answer. She was unaware that the Colorado guests were treating Leila and her boys to lunch. She decided to go straight to Ebenezer Forest Road and check on their safety.

*****

Leila selected Nick's Seafood House on the north bank of Choctawhatchee Bay as her choice for lunch. It was located on Highway 20, between Freeport and Niceville, thirty minutes from her home. The group made the trip in Powder's leased vehicle, leaving her automobile in front her home. In the hurry to leave, she also forgot her cell phone.

When Jane showed up to check on Leila, she was very disturbed to find no activity at all. She walked the yard, looked in the windows and decided to wait on the porch.

Meanwhile Leila and her new friends were enjoying a panoramic view of the bay and a wonderful seafood feast. The boys were totally unfamiliar with such an experience and ate heartily enough to really splash up their camouflaged shirts. Eating out was a rare activity for Leila. With her new family and friends, it had so far been one of her better days since Mark's death.

As the meal continued, Leila realized that she and the boys felt at ease with Powder and John. She found both men most enjoyable. Powder was charming, spirited and humorous. John chose his words more carefully, but was confident, smart and rather mysterious. When Powder referred to his close friend as "No Elk," Leila had to hear the history. Powder related that John had been hunting for years without ever returning with an elk. John simply grinned and said, "Maybe this year."

Before leaving the restaurant, Powder expressed how impressed he was with Ebenezer Forest and how it inspired him even more to go forward with his Aspen plan. He was very sincere.

"Leila," he began, "I want to again ask you to accept my invitation to visit Aspen--which includes Luke and Jake. And I am talking about in the near future. I will send my plane to fly you all up any time you want. I would like for it to be soon, before the selected parcel gets so covered with snow that you will not really be able to see it."

Looking straight into Powder's blue eyes, Leila replied, "I will consider accepting your invitation, Powder, but it cannot be in the next couple of weeks because Jane and a new young forester are starting to work on Monday."

"Does that mean you are seriously considering allowing me to say that my project may become an 'Approved Leila Jane Hewitt Ebenezer Forest'?"

Leila paused, smiled and answered with a twinkle in her eye, "Well, you should know, Powder, if the boys and I get on that plane, you are making real progress."

Powder slapped John on his shoulder, and they both smiled broadly. "That's what I'm talking about—now we're getting somewhere!" Powder exclaimed.

When Leila saw their genuine and enthusiastic reactions, she felt even stronger that she was moving in the right direction. She agreed that after returning to her home, they would check the Ebenezer Forest calendar to select a date when a trip to Aspen could possibly be scheduled.

*****

Leila and her guests were surprised to see Jane waiting in a chair on the front porch. As they joined her at the front door, Leila noticed her furrowed brow and serious expression. Greeting each other with a hug, Leila said, "Come on in with us to the back, Jane. We have one quick thing to do."

Jane knew what she had to discuss should not be said in front of the boys. "I need to have a brief word with you, Leila. Would you please let Powder and John take the boys to the back for just a few minutes?"

With those words, all three adults knew something of concern had developed. Leila and her guests complied.

It was over twenty minutes before Jane departed, and Leila walked slowly down her central hall to rejoin her guests and children. She walked over and slowly hugged Luke and then Jake. She looked at Powder and John, and they easily observed that she had been crying.

In an emotional voice she asked, "John, would you please take the boys out to the coon pup pen for a while?" He gathered them in a light and encouraging way, but even they could sense their mother's somber mood.

When they were alone, Leila revealed to Powder all of the details Jane had told her about her attorney's murder and what was known of the only suspect. She said that even though it was not certain the suspect was Watson's killer, he claimed to be Luke's father and had a history of violence. "No one knows his whereabouts, but he has let it be known that he is looking for Luke."

Leila began to tear up as she spoke. Powder approached her, pulled a handkerchief from his back pocket and gently dabbed her eyes. He was very drawn to her and wanted to hug her, but did not dare.

"Leila, please come to Aspen until all of this passes," he said softly. "You and the boys will be very safe there. I will see to it."

The thought of something happening to Luke was more than she could handle. The situation was getting the better of her. She leaned forward into Powder's arms and began to weep. He held her against his chest until she finally pulled away.

Collecting herself, she spoke quietly, "Powder, I am sorry you walked into all of this. Are you sure you want us to come to Aspen?" She looked up at him with pained eyes.

"I have never wanted anything more in all of my life," he answered.

The depth of his reply unsettled Leila. She was not ready, not nearly ready, for his intensity. After a long pause, she asked, "Will you respect me and my children?"

"Yes, I promise you--I will."

Chapter 25

Rufus "Odd Job" Jenkins pulled his borrowed vehicle into a trailer park in Lynn Haven, Florida. His first cousin Jay Chidister was expecting him. They grew up together in the slums of Fort Walton and both were criminals--and killers. There is as big a difference between killers as there is between members of any other profession. Some are good and some are bad. The smart killers make a lot of money, and the sloppy ones spend more time in jail.

Jay was unusually smart and had never been incarcerated. His talents were recognized at an early age by the biggest gangster in the Panhandle, C. B. "Big Fuzz" Rogers. Drugs, running scores of illegal Mexican workers into the Panhandle workforce and brokering deals with corrupt politicians were the more profitable activities of his clique. Troublemakers were always surfacing that needed elimination, and that was one of Jay's specialties. But he rarely ever pulled the proverbial trigger himself, unless it absolutely had to be perfectly executed.

On one occasion, seven or eight years before, Jay let his dumbass cousin kill a Mexican trouble-maker to help him pick up a few extra dollars. "Odd Job" really slopped it up and, if not for "Big Fuzz's" help back then, he would have been prosecuted and sent to jail for life. Instead "Odd Job" was never charged.

"Odd Job" had contacted Jay the day before to say "I need a little help." Jay told him where he was now living and what time to arrive. He did not really want to associate with his dangerous and unpredictable cousin, but was hopeful his prison time had calmed him down a bit.

When opening the front door, Jay questioned, "Whose phone did you use to call me?"

"I always remember your rule, Jay--I ain't stupid. It wasn't mine."

"Good, what's up?"

"I know you heard through the family that I just got out of jail. It was a long four years. I wanted to see my boy..."

Jay interrupted. "Here we go again. You don't even know if that kid is yours. 'Sweet Jaws' tricked every guy with twenty bucks in Okaloosa County. Okay, go on, what happened?"

"I know he is mine. And June disappeared when she heard I was gittin' out. At first I thought she had just run away. But I found out she was going to give Luke away, and I found the bastard lawyer she was using to give him away." He hung his head.

"Aw, shit, 'Odd Job.' Don't tell me it was you that killed that lawyer in Destin?"

"Odd Job" would not look up.

When he finally did he added, "And I had to kill a man in June's complex to get the lawyer's name."

"Whose phone did you use to call me, 'Odd Job'?"

"Our cousin Dottie's."

"What does she know?"

"Nothin."

Jay shook his head disgustedly. He recalled vivid memories of his cousin being sexually abused as a young boy, his countless social explosions and fights, arrests, the manslaughter and now this.

"That woman who shot them two men trying to kill her, over by Red Bay--you know, the purty one who was all over the television. She has my boy Luke," "Odd Job" said dejectedly.

Jay sat up straight and became more acutely interested. "You mean to tell me Leila Jane Hewitt has the boy, Luke, living with her right now?" He was totally shocked.

"That's what the lawyer told me after I cut his nuts off," replied "Odd Job."

"Odd Job" was unaware that Jay had provided hit-man Jorge "T-Mex" Espinosa to Walton County Sheriff Colonel Max Barnett and "Big Fuzz" Rogers so he could kill Leila Hewitt for them. And he did not know that Jay was now personally supervising all work that was done at "Big Fuzz's" hunting estate located directly across the river from Ebenezer Forest.

Most importantly Jay had heard from "Big Fuzz" the previous day that the Feds might not be as finished with Dr. Ty Tyson as they had hoped. Ideas began flashing though his head about possibly using "Odd Job" to eliminate Leila.

"Whose car is that outside," Jay asked.

"It belongs to a friend of mine, Debbie Day, and I have to get it back to her before noon."

"C'mon, and let's get this over with right now--you HAVE to disappear. I am going to follow you back to her house. And dammit, do not get too far ahead of me. Here is fifty dollars. Tell her I was not home, and act mad about it. Call a taxi and have them drop you off at the bus station on Perry Avenue. And stand outside until you see me park down the street, then walk down and get in. And do not use your phone ever again!"

"I don't think I need to run, Jay. How are the police gonna know it was me? I wore gloves and was real careful."

"Even if that is true and the police aren't looking for you right now, 'Odd Job,' it is always a good idea to let any case settle down. You have a lot better chance of not going straight back to prison if you vanish for a while. Do you want to take my advice or not?"

"Yeah," he drawled, looking downward again.

*****

When "Odd Job" climbed into Jay's car almost an hour later, Jay smashed up his cousin's cell phone and threw what was left of it into the first dumpster they passed.

He also took possession of "Odd Job's" gun. He had serious questions about "Odd Job" being reliable enough to pull off a successful, unsolved murder of Leila Hewitt. But it was a possibility. He decided to talk to "Big Fuzz" soon to discuss the various opportunities that "Odd Job's" situation presented.

"I might be able to make some money off this dumbass cousin of mine after all," Jay thought.

Chapter 26

Leila spent all day Sunday with her two boys on Ebenezer Road. She would have preferred taking them to church, but felt too threatened to consider it. She could hardly believe it actually felt necessary to keep her shotgun handy. Even though she was now living in fear in her own home, not once did she second guess any of the decisions she had made about adopting Luke and Jake. However, she was quite frustrated that there was absolutely nothing she could do about her present situation but remain vigilant.

Powder called around noon to say goodbye just before he and his guests departed for Aspen. He reiterated his invitation for Leila and the boys to be his guests in Colorado until things settled down. She replied that she would consider it, but reminded him she had much to accomplish before she could accept his kind offer.

Amanda called after church, and Leila filled her in about the recent developments concerning her lawyer's death. Amanda offered, "Bring the boys and hide out at my house until the danger is over. I'll stay up every night on guard while you all sleep. Please come, Leila. You are just sitting ducks over there on Ebenezer Road!"

"I never want to be run out of my own house," Leila replied as she warmly hugged her dear friend.

*****

Her property caretaker, Clyde Branson, arrived first thing Monday morning. Leila had already dressed and fed the boys. She asked Clyde to join her in welcoming Josh Snyder, who arrived next, and then Jane Anderson.

When everyone was assembled on the back porch, Leila slowly went over the huge map of her estate that she had hung for that purpose. She passed out a list of duties that Clyde completed every week, showing his planned schedule, weather permitting. She also acknowledged to her new employees that she considered Clyde's entire family as part of her team, as many of them helped their dad whenever needed.

She had prepared a list of duties for Josh, which almost exclusively included Ebenezer Forest. The most important of those duties would be to lead the group tours that were heavily scheduled for next spring and summer. His other responsibilities primarily involved tree, shrub and grass maintenance while keeping a keen eye on the health of all animals, as much as possible.

Jane was provided the Ebenezer Forest calendar she would manage, together with handling the accounts receivable and payable. Jane would also assume all wage and withholding responsibilities. Leila announced Jane's other major assignment would be the area of marketing.

She also informed her team that public interest in Ebenezer Forest was at an all-time high after the recent intensive publicity. She then requested all three of her assistants to exchange phone numbers, and excused Clyde and Jane so that she could take a quick tour with Josh to familiarize him with her entire family property.

When they returned, Leila and Jane spent the rest of the morning updating the website, which included Jane being able to access the whole commercial operation from her own computer. Predictably, they were interrupted a few times by the boys, yet they were becoming much more accustomed to their new surroundings.

The more work Leila delegated, the more relaxed she became. She was beginning to realize, for the first time, the tremendous pressure and responsibilities she had been shouldering almost alone.

"I should have done this a long time ago," she mused to herself. Then she looked at her sons and thought, "There are a lot of things I should have done a long time ago."

*****

After Jane and Leila ate lunch with the boys, Leila put them down for an afternoon nap. Jane had something else she wanted to discuss.

"Bob suggested I should inform you of new developments occurring in the U. S. Justice Department in Washington. There are major changes going to be made in the Pensacola office," she began. "And this is something he picked up from one of his former F.B.I. buddies in just the last week. That old group of shady insiders, who so confidently thought they were going to survive in the department and be able to continue the same game of 'buddy politics,' is being busted out by our new President."

"You mean the swamp is really being drained?" asked Leila.

"The core gang in Pensacola calling the shots over the Panhandle was apparently fired last week. There will be no more sweet deals like the one Colonel Max Barnett was about to receive. In fact, the deal he was going to get is not going to happen, and he may end up with around a ten year sentence."

"Wonderful," exclaimed Leila.

"And, happily, this is very bad news for Panhandle drug dealers, since their industry will now be much more heavily targeted," Jane added.

"The way this affects you," Jane continued more solemnly, "is the case that was being pigeon-holed against Dr. Ty Tyson is now wide open again, and you will likely be contacted in the near future about appearing before a Grand Jury."

"Oh, my--I cannot believe it--I have mixed emotions. With all of this other stuff that has been happening, I have so much to deal with," Leila replied woefully.

She had always been hopeful that Dr. Ty Tyson would be prosecuted. Now, with her children endangered by a vicious killer, she felt daunted by the thought of a long legal proceeding ahead of her.

After more thought, Leila asked, "What you are trying to tell me? Is my life--and maybe Luke's and Jake's too--in danger from two directions?"

"I know, Leila, I almost did not want to tell you."

"Do you really think there is a chance of another attempt on my life by Tyson's crowd?" she asked in a discouraged tone.

"Bob says you need to be very cautious. With your permission, I would like to offer to work here with you more than we have talked about--and less out of my own home for now."

"With Bob's campaign kicking off, I hate to see you do that, Jane. Maybe I will accept Powder's offer to visit Aspen."

"I am certainly not asking you to do that for me, Leila," Jane said sincerely. "But honestly, with everything that is going on, you should at least consider hiring additional personal security, particularly at night."

"My multiple enemies are probably sad I only have one life for them to take," Leila said with a slight smile. "They are just going to have to deal with it."

Almost to Aspen

Chapter 27

Jay Chidister decided to place "Odd Job" in a unit at the rear of his trailer park that was normally occupied by undocumented Mexicans. It was one of a large block of trailers leased under the name of a nonexistent business and was already equipped with essential living necessities and a television. He gave "Odd Job" the phone number of a specific cab driver and the code name to use to get free travel around the Lynn Haven-Panama City area. His last words were "I will check on you every morning and before I go to bed every night, but don't walk up to my trailer, and stay the hell out of trouble."

The following day, Jay was the first to arrive for a meeting at "Big Fuzz's" Tomahawk Ranch. Colonel Max Barnett and Dr. Ty Tyson drove in together after going through their usual procedures to make sure they were not being followed. "Big Fuzz" was still on his phone outside when they finally pulled up, and it was a few minutes before he joined the others inside his lodge.

"Sorry, I'm running behind, fellows. I was just talking to Laurie Ward in D.C., and it is as bad as we heard. She says your lawyer does not even know it yet, Max, but you are not going to get the deal he thought was worked out."

"Son of a bitch," the Colonel barked, "to hell with that! I was told last week it was a sure thing!"

"We all thought it was," replied "Big Fuzz," "but today Laurie says your deal was completely worthless because it was never taken into a Pensacola courtroom and put on the record."

"Hot dammit, I'm looking at some serious jail time. I'm the only defendant still living, and it looks like they want to hang everything on me," he moaned.

"Big Fuzz" took a long, slow sip of his coffee and looked over at Dr. Tyson. "Pensacola was also told to go ahead and present everything they have against you to a Grand Jury, Doc. They think they have enough evidence to connect you with the Ashton brothers' date-rape drug operation and nail you as a major player. They want to really jam it up your butt with your using the same exact substance to rape the Hewitt gal."

"Damn, can't we get some help from somebody up there in Washington? Two senators got laid on that boat out of Bar Harbor Restaurant in Destin, and both of them are still in office!" whined Dr. Tyson.

"Yeah, but the 'Big Man' is not in the White House anymore and our boys are not going to be able to survive like they thought they would with this new prick in office." replied "Big Fuzz." "In fact, many have already received their walking papers, according to Laurie."

"My lawyer in Tallahassee told me from the beginning that if Leila was out of the picture, I would have very little jail-time exposure at all--then Tommy Tucker and 'T-Mex' had to go and screw everything up. Can't we take another stab at her?" pleaded Dr. Tyson.

"Jay here has some interesting news for us to think about," said "Big Fuzz." Everyone turned to look at Jay who had sat in on many meetings with this crowd before but never had much to say.

"Well," Jay began, "here is the deal, guys. My crazy-ass cousin, 'Odd Job,' just got out of prison and has already knocked off the lawyer that was killed in Destin this week, and another guy in Fort Walton before that. The reason he killed both guys is that he wants is to find this boy--who he thinks is his son. And the dead lawyer had already turned the kid over to--GET THIS--Leila Hewitt! So, if we are able to kill her right now, 'Odd Job' will be the natural suspect. We can kill Leila and let him get blamed and bury him somewhere where he will never be found. Or we could just sic him on her and let the hide go with the hair. Either way I think 'Cuz' may need to be waxed after she is taken out."

"I know that dumb piece of shit," started the Colonel. "He's not smart enough to do anything right. Jay, I'd say you find somebody better than 'Odd Job' or 'T-Mex' to pull it off without a hitch this time, or you do it yourself. I know you can handle it, either way. Then we could all do your family a great big favor and burn up that idiot son-of-a-bitch cousin of yours."

"Preferably before the new sheriff is elected," urged Colonel Barnett. "If we can get Tall Tom Hopkins elected, no problem, Doc, and no one else will ever be charged. But it will be a whole different story if Bob Kirk is elected."

It was decided that "Big Fuzz" would sleep on it, and make the final call on the details of Leila's murder.

Almost to Aspen

Chapter 28

Later in the week Jane Anderson asked Leila if her fiancé, Bob Kirk, could join them for a late lunch at Ebenezer Forest. Leila fed the boys early and put them down for a nap before he arrived.

"Have you gotten your sheriff's race shaping up, Bob?" Leila asked.

"I am going to have to work really hard to get elected. It will be the 'good ole local country boys' from north Walton County versus the south end out-of-towners. I am hoping to be able to convince some of the DeFuniak crowd to support me, but I can see already that will be a challenge."

"I have never been involved in politics," Leila began. "My family has always asked Brother McGraw if we had a question. Well, now that I think of it, he usually lets us know who he likes. Have you talked to him?" Leila asked.

"Not yet, but I will soon. If you have any other names of people that may be influential, particularly up here north of the Bay, I would really appreciate it. The main reason I wanted to visit with you is to discuss the new developments in Pensacola."

"Yes, Leila, we don't want you to think Bob is stopping by to ask you to get involved in his election," Jane interrupted. "We are primarily concerned about your safety."

"Well, I thank both of you, but before we get into that, I insist on doing this. I want to be one of the first donors of your campaign." She reached into her purse and pulled out a check that she had written before his arrival. She handed it to Bob. "It isn't much. But I am not aware of my parents ever making a contribution to a political candidate—and I have not either. I know that your opponent was handpicked by Sheriff Clark and his buddies. And I also know firsthand we need to stop all of this horrible crime still going on in Walton County!"

Bob looked at the one thousand dollar contribution and thanked Leila profusely before continuing.

"Everyone in the F.B.I. office in Pensacola is thrilled that they are no longer going to be shackled by a group of bad guys in the Justice Department in D.C. protecting certain people in the Panhandle. It looked at first like the bad guys were going to survive the presidential transition. But everything happened fast, and they are now out, which includes a few bad eggs in the Pensacola office." Leila was listening intently.

'There is a solid belief in my old office that the mob running drugs and illegal immigrants around here is part of a dangerous, nationwide syndicate. The new push against these criminals is a double-edged sword for you, Leila. They may end up in jail, but you are surely going to be drawn into the prosecutorial process. Why? Dr. Tyson is believed to be an integral part of this criminal group. The fact that there has already been an attempt on your life reinforces what the F.B.I. believes about him. The crime he personally committed on you, being directly connected to his involvement in the national distribution of the same date-rape drug, exposes him to a much lengthier penalty. And he may, to help himself either before or after conviction, turn on his buddies."

When Bob paused, Jane added, "Leila, I finally received a return call from the Interim Sheriff Billy Munsey while you and the boys were at the supermarket this morning. He said that 'Odd Job' Jenkins was a suspect, but only a suspect. There was no real evidence at all to justify a warrant for his arrest. He admitted that his office does not know 'Odd Job's' whereabouts. They are not going to distribute his photo to the news agencies or issue an all-points bulletin for him to be picked up—even for questioning. When I argued with him, he insisted that a couple of 'Odd Job's' phone calls are insufficient evidence, no matter who the suspect is. I think he is wrong and told him so."

"How did the conversation end?" Bob Kirk asked his fiancée since he had not had the chance to discuss this conversation with her.

"He said that both Walton and Okaloosa counties' law enforcement agencies had been alerted to be on the lookout for Jenkins and that he expected him to turn up eventually."

Bob shook his head disgustedly and heatedly commented, "What a pathetic effort on his part! It amplifies what I stopped by to express to you, Leila, which is you need to be on high alert for yourself and the boys. Jane says she has told you the same thing already. You should definitely not be going to places like the supermarket or anywhere else with or without the boys. And I hate to put it to you this way, but there is a real possibility that you are in danger from more than one source."

Bob and Jane both looked at Leila for a response.

"What do you think I should do, Bob?"

"At the very minimum, I advise you immediately hire a security guard--or a bodyguard--call it what you want. You do not even have a security system, which only gives you limited protection while you are at home."

"Until they locate this 'Odd Job' character you could always consider Powder White's offer," Jane suggested.

"Heavens, I don't even really know the man. And I am surely not at all thrilled with the personal interest in me that he is showing--not now after what I have been through."

"Amanda tells me that he even had the Aspen area sheriff call to vouch for him," replied Jane.

"Does that really mean anything? He may be Sheriff Wayne Clark reincarnated for all we know," Leila replied. "Powder seemed kind of all right, I guess. He has called me to talk, twice, since he returned to Aspen. And both times he encouraged me to come and stay a while."

"Give me his full name and I will call a good friend at the Bureau to have him and his sheriff totally checked out within twenty-four hours," offered Bob.

After Bob departed and Jane went back to work, Leila walked into the room where Luke and Jake were napping and stood above them for long while. "I cannot let anything happen to these boys," she told herself.

She went to her own bedroom to rest for a few minutes. Shutting her eyes, she tried to imagine herself and her sons going to Aspen. It would be her first trip, but she had seen many pictures of the area in books and on television. She recalled watching how cold it appeared during World Cup Skiing events over the years.

"I don't even own any of the clothes I, or the boys, will need." And it seemed terribly far away from her beloved Ebenezer Forest.

Almost to Aspen

Chapter 29

As the King Air glided toward touchdown at Aspen's Sarty Field, Leila watched the plane fall below the mountaintops into the world famous Roaring Fork Valley. She had read that the locals also call it Aspen Valley. The highest part of her Northwest Florida homeland being only 300 feet or so above sea level, she was awestruck by the stark elevation and contrast of this Rocky Mountain area. This was Leila's first visit out West, and she had studied the history of the Aspen area as much as time allowed before the trip.

"Those mountains over there are called Elk Mountains," she pointed out to the boys only a minute before landing. "I showed you pictures of elk and moose, remember? We are going to see some real live ones soon." Both boys' eyes were wide open and watching.

Luke and Jake saw and recognized Powder waving to them in the terminal before Leila did. He joined them as the passenger unloading line slowly reached the public area. He was sporting a huge smile and gave Leila a hearty hug. He acknowledged the boys and turned back to Leila.

"Welcome to Aspen," Powder began. "Here, these are for Luke and Jake." He placed a green Aspen cap on each boy's head. Then he reached into a bag on the nearby bench and pulled out a dozen red roses for Leila. "This is for the prettiest lady in Colorado!" Leila blushed as other passengers watched with interest.

After everyone was loaded into Powder's large SUV, they headed south toward town and turned west on Castle Creek Road. They then traveled alongside the bubbly Castle Creek, which was a lively addition to the beautiful mountainous landscape. Powder pointed out the impressive estates of several movie and sports stars as they passed them by. Castle Creek Valley began to narrow as they approached its end. Powder turned into a most impressive stone entrance. The automatic gate opened upon signal, and they continued another 400 yards up a winding road until a massive lodge came into view.

"My gracious," Leila thought to herself observing that the structure was like those she had only seen in photos from Scandinavia. Highlighted by huge glass windows and walls of exquisite rock, it exceeded all of her expectations. "What a fabulous lodge," she exclaimed.

Inside she and the boys were shown to one of several fabulous two-bedroom guest suites. Even though they were introduced to his resident chef, Powder said, "Be ready in thirty minutes. We still have a couple of hours to go before dark, and I want you to see Aspen--and we will have dinner there tonight. "

*****

After an exciting but abbreviated tour of Aspen, Powder escorted Leila, Luke and Jake into the upstairs section of his favorite hangout, Jim's Restaurant & Bar. The town had few secrets and a large number of the diners that evening were expecting her. Their reaction was as if Jennifer Anniston had arrived. It seemed as though everyone was familiar with Leila and her recent fame. The locals were trying either to shake her hand or take her picture. Powder, one of Aspen's bigger than life residents himself, had done a poor job of keeping quiet his intention to court the now nationally recognized beauty and gunslinger.

Leila had no idea what she was walking into and had never experienced anything like it in her entire life. Powder was not rude or discourteous to her, but Leila felt entirely showcased. The most conspicuous table was reserved for them. The Sheriff was already present and waiting at the next table with his wife and another couple. The owner came by to greet Leila and have his picture taken with her. Leila respectfully declined. She noticed Powder took him aside and whispered some kind of explanation to him.

Powder had a glass of wine, and another, before the menu was ever presented. Leila ordered water as her sole beverage and, being health conscious, insisted that her two sons follow her lead. The dinner took over three hours. By the time it ended, both boys' heads had begun to droop with exhaustion. Leila felt totally out of place and began to question the entire trip.

When the dinner was mercifully over, and they were back at Powder's lodge, Leila could hardly wait to shut the door to her quarters. She was still disturbed that everything had been happening so fast since Mark's funeral. She considered buying commercial airline tickets home as soon as possible. The thought was dismissed after recalling her reasons for making the trip--her concern for the safety of her boys and herself. "I will make the best of it," she finally resolved. "And I will try to help with Powder's plan to develop an Ebenezer Forest in Aspen."

*****

"Big Fuzz" Rogers, as one of the top mobsters in Florida, had a number of contacts around the country he utilized for various crime syndicate purposes. One particular hired killer he had used before was an Aspen resident.

Mike "Ace" Tingle picked up the phone after dining alone in Jim's Restaurant & Bar and called "Big Fuzz" Rogers in Destin.

"What are you calling me for at midnight, 'Ace'?"

"Guess who just rolled into Aspen."

"I give up," replied "Big Fuzz."

"That pretty gal--the one that your local boys bungled up her murder--Leila Hewitt."

"You are kidding me. What would she be doing in Aspen?"

"She is here as the guest of a high roller from Wyoming and has two kids with her."

"How much would you charge to kill her," asked "Big Fuzz" curiously.

"$250,000 as usual. Any time you get tired of fuckin' around, give me a call."

"Big Fuzz" chuckled, "You are too expensive and I already have somebody ready to go. But keep an eye on her, 'Ace'--I will let you know if I ever need you. And thanks for the head's up."

Chapter 30

"Odd Job" Jenkins walked out of his trailer and got into his cousin Jay Chidister's car. He was carrying a bag containing all of his few possessions, which he was instructed to bring. He only knew that he would be gone for a while to work at an undisclosed location.

"Where you taking me, Jay?" he asked.

"I am doing some work north of Ebro and thought you might like a change of scenery and to pick up a little cash." He did not reveal that "Big Fuzz" and he had decided two days before that "Odd Job" would be easy to manipulate into taking Leila's life. His name had not been mentioned once in the news in connection with the murder of attorney James Watson. That fact was important in their decision because if "Odd Job" was caught in the act of murdering Leila, he had an independent motive that would not be traced to his cousin Jay. The plan was to give him the opportunity but never to outright instruct him to commit the crime. The scheme also included that if "Odd Job" did not get caught in the act he would mysteriously vanish forever.

"Big Fuzz" had called Jay two hours earlier to say he had learned the night before that Leila was in Aspen with her two sons. He and Jay decided to immediately hire "Odd Job" to work on the barn construction project underway at Tomahawk Ranch. They reasoned that if "Odd Job's" murder of Leila ever backfired, his employment would provide an answer to potential questions relating to his presence in the area. They believed this would further remove them from any involvement in a murderous scheme.

Although he was the top dog in procuring illegal immigrants into the Florida Panhandle, "Big Fuzz" was smart enough to hire lawful workers on his own jobs. When Jay and "Odd Job" arrived, a crew was busy framing a barn located only a hundred yards from the ranch's main lodge. Jay drove past the job site a full quarter mile further into the woods and stopped at a group of hunting dog pens. A bluff overlooking the Choctawhatchee River could be seen from that location.

Jay pointed to a small camper trailer and directed, "You will bunk here. Drop your stuff off inside, and then let me show you what your responsibilities will be."

"That is a nice little trailer, with television and all--thank you, Cuz," "Odd Job" said as he rejoined Jay.

There were six separate dog pens, but only three were occupied. Male and female walker deer hounds were separated into two pens, and the third contained about a dozen beagles. "You are to feed the dogs and clean the pens daily," Jay instructed.

They returned to the barn construction site where Jay also assigned his cousin to clean up the worksite each day after the carpenters and crew left. He then took him inside "Big Fuzz's" lodge and showed him a huge map of Tomahawk Ranch. At "Big Fuzz's" computer, he pulled up the entire vicinity on Google Earth.

"This is where your son Luke is living," Jay baited "Odd Job" as he scanned across the Choctawhatchee River to focus on Leila's house on Ebenezer Road. "This is Leila Hewitt's place, and over here is the famous Ebenezer Church--see, it is almost directly across the river from the dog pens, only a few minutes' walk to the west." "Odd Job" was absorbing every detail. "And the trail from the church goes southwest almost straight to Leila and Luke's home."

Jay had been carrying "Odd Job's" pistol in his back pocket. He pulled it out and returned it to him, saying, "Keep this in the trailer at all times and never bring it up to the front of this property with you. If you shoot anybody, make damn sure you kill 'em.'" From a bag he retrieved the gun's bullets and handed them to his cousin.

"I saw on the news that Leila is visiting in Colorado right now and Luke is with her," Jay continued. "I don't know when they will be back across the river. There is probably no one over at her place now. But you are never, ever, gonna get possession of that boy of yours or be able to keep him until Leila is dead, or better yet, just suddenly disappears. If her body is not found, no one will ever be charged with killing her."

Jay drove "Odd Job" back to the dog pen area and then walked him over to the riverbank. He pointed to a winding trail which meandered down to a very short wooden dock. Atop it was a ten foot bateau. Jay noted, "There are two paddles under the boat. If you ever want to take a little float trip sometime after work, be careful."

The two men walked back to the trailer. "I will see you in the morning," Jay said as he prepared to leave. "Stay out of trouble."

Almost to Aspen

Chapter 31

The invigorating magic of Aspen will captivate even a strained soul. After a restless night of recalling her ongoing concerns and the unwelcome attention she had received the night before, Leila slid open her glass bedroom door and stepped out onto the chilly wooden deck that afforded her an incredible view. The dry air and altitude seemed to take her breath away. But as she deeply inhaled, a blast of pure oxygen dashed into her lungs with an exhilarating impact. She followed with a half dozen more deep inhalations. There was no pollution or thickness to the air, just the feel of cool cleanliness. It seemed to purify her eyes and her thoughts. She took a moment to acknowledge her gratitude to Him and was ready to face the day with her sons with new vigor.

Powder had left at daylight to fly up to Wyoming to take care of a one-day business necessity at his office there. He asked John Gillespie to take Leila and the boys into Aspen for lunch and then on a ski-lift ride up Aspen Mountain. "No Elk" was happy to oblige.

John parked his auto a few blocks away from the intended restaurant to give his guests the opportunity to experience a walk through downtown Aspen and Wagner Park.

For every visitor to the area a stroll through Aspen is an unforgettable experience. Beautiful plants and trees between wide brick walkways are totally refreshing. The colorful shops, unique smells from ice cream and hot dog stands, and friendly smiles from everyone will turn even a scrooge into a pleasant friend. Watching locals walk their dogs in every direction, the boys did not know which way to turn or pet. They were thrilled.

John had selected the popular Mezzaluna Restaurant and they were soon seated. The toasty fireplace in the corner added to an absolutely wonderful atmosphere. After ordering, the boys eagerly began to color their wildlife-laden placemats. It gave Leila and John their first real opportunity to have a conversation.

"So how do you know so much about animals?" Leila questioned. Having observed he was not much of a volunteer conversationalist, she realized she was broaching the only significant topic she had ever heard him address.

"I was raised in the Arkansas woods, where there were more animals than people," he said slowly looking straight at Leila, as a half-smile appeared on his face. She knew from his response that this was not going to be easy.

"So did you go to animal college?" she teased.

John laughed out loud. "Yes, I graduated from the University of Arkansas with all of the other Razorbacks."

Leila noticed how appealingly handsome John was, particularly with a full smile. He was tall, thin and about her age. His blue eyes had an attractive twinkle, and his thick brown hair was graying at the temples. She had found him extremely nice looking from the first time she met him. But it was the kind of thing she would never have admitted to herself, until now.

Leila thought about ceasing her interrogation, but elected to proceed. "What kind of work did you do?"

"My family was similar to yours. We had a large tract of land that my sister, Becky, and I inherited, but our dad also ran a very successful lumber mill. After he died, it was sold along with most of the land. We kept only the prettiest two hundred acres, which Becky and I divided.

"Family, kids--come on, I want to hear it all!" Leila encouraged in a smiling, cheery tone.

John's face became more serious, and he paused for a few, long seconds. "I lost my only wife, the love of my life, about ten years ago to brain cancer. Her name was Pati. She was never able to have children. I worked twenty years as a school teacher, retired and moved here, after she passed away."

"I am sorry to hear of your loss, John," Leila said earnestly. "God's plan is not for us to necessarily understand."

There was a pause, and to change the subject Leila asked, "What do you like to do most out here in Colorado, John?"

He thought for a moment. "I like to do fourteeners."

"What on earth is that?"

"Climb to the top of mountains that are over fourteen thousand feet elevation."

"Do you do it alone?"

"So far, I have."

"What is it like?

"I've seen some of the most surreal and majestic views on the planet," he answered slowly, staring straight into Leila's eyes.

"That sounds thrilling," Leila replied, impressed by his passionate description and delivery.

"Maybe you could join me one day," he suggested.

"That's an adventure I have never considered." She hesitated. Recognizing his sincerity, she smiled and added, "Maybe."

*****

At the foot of Ajax Mountain, Luke decided that he would ride the ski lift with John. Leila and Jake went first, and he looked back several times to make sure his big brother was still following. When the mid-mountain restaurant and lookout facility was reached, the boys quickly ran to each other to rejoin hands. Leila was happy to recall that just a couple of weeks before they would not even trust a minute of separation from each other without emotional squalls.

As they all stood on the overlook, John repeated the names of all visible mountains until Luke could recall each one. Even little Jake looked like he understood the distinctions, but was still not verbalizing anything. A strong wind was blowing at their new elevation, and it was soon necessary to take the youngsters inside.

Leila and John sat next to each other in comfortable lounge chairs and chatted while the boys chose smaller children's seats near the large windows. They did not seem to tire from looking at the vast panorama of the Elk Mountains.

"Powder asked if I had an interest in managing 'Ebenezer Forest in Aspen,'" John told Leila to her surprise.

"That would be wonderful," Leila exclaimed, truly excited.

"The main concern I have is that Powder's tract does not have nearly the variety of trees that you have marked for identification on your place. It may not be as much of an educational attraction for tourists," he added.

"One of the new features I have in mind at home is to add a waterfowl park," started Leila. "Many various birds and ducks use the Choctawhatchee River as their flyway. I think it will be a great addition for my property. I was looking carefully at Powder's creek, particularly where it broadens out in several areas, and I think it is a perfect place to add several huge screen enclosures for ducks and geese to be added as extra attractions up here."

"That is a tremendous idea, Leila," replied John.

"So, are you going to take Powder's offer or not?" asked Leila curiously.

John paused. He looked into her lovely blue eyes intently but differently than he ever had before. He spoke slowly, with a look and tone she never expected, "I would Leila, but only if I could work closely with you."

His words were few, but she could not mistake the way he spoke them and the way he was still looking at her. She tried to hide the sudden lump in her throat. Emotionally moved, as never anticipated, she wanted to hide how he made her feel, but did not answer quickly enough.

"I would like that," was all she could roll off her lips--but it was true and she knew it.

Looking silently at each other, Leila finally smiled--then John smiled, and they went down the mountain.

Almost to Aspen

Chapter 32

Rufus "Odd Job" Jenkins watched as the barn-building crew working on the Tomahawk Ranch packed up and left for the day. It was four o'clock p.m. Within minutes he had returned to his trailer, picked up his pistol and hurried over to the Choctawhatchee River. Having been told that Leila and Luke were in Colorado, he thought it would be a perfect time to check out Ebenezer Forest. There was no question in his mind if he was going to acquire his son, only when and how.

Paddling across the river, "Odd Job" relived his delusions. "I know Luke will be very happy when we are together soon. Luke used to whisper my name when I was in prison. We talked every night while the other prisoners slept. I promised to never let him be sexually used like I was. Until I have my Luke, life is not worth living."

His disturbed thoughts continued to consume him as he reached the western bank. "I don't trust Jay or nobody else. He was stupid to show me where Luke lives. When I have Luke, he and I will disappear," he planned. "Nothin' or nobody will keep Luke and me apart. This time, nothin!"

In reality "Odd Job" had never seen Luke in person, only in a single picture. It had been sent to him by Luke's mother, June

"Sweet Jaws" Bradley, a year before he was released from prison. She had heard that "Odd Job's" uncle had willed him some money which she claimed she desperately needed.

*****

He scrambled up the far bank knowing that if he walked due west toward the setting sun he would hit a main road. When he came upon it, he turned south. He wanted to make certain he knew the way to Leila's house and also to find a place nearby where he could hide when she returned with Luke.

Walking at a fast pace, the last thing "Odd Job" expected to encounter late in the afternoon in the deep woods was another person. But that was exactly what happened when he and another man rounded a corner from opposite directions just north of Hominy Creek. Both men stopped dead in their tracks.

"Odd Job," a heavy-set man with a big neck, huge arms and ugly face, in the past had scared a Green Beret. The young forester, smooth-faced Josh Snyder, shocked, stared back at him.

Josh had been warned by Jane to be on the alert for anything or anyone unusual. He well knew he was face-to-face with "unusual." And he was terrified.

"I am lost," "Odd Job" spoke first. Noticing a canteen around the young man's neck, he asked, "Could I please have a sip of your water? I've been walking for hours."

Josh made the biggest mistake of his life. He approached "Odd Job," taking the canteen from his shoulder and opening it as he neared. When he was close enough, "Odd Job" lunged at

Josh and, once his big paws grabbed hold, easily slammed the young man to the ground.

"Don't move boy, or I'll break your fuckin' neck." "Odd Job" snatched the knife hanging from Josh's belt while holding him one-handedly to the ground. Next he untied a rope that was also attached to Josh's belt. Then he pulled the belt off Josh's pants.

"Please don't hurt me," Josh begged.

"Odd Job" was not taking a chance of being placed anywhere near Ebenezer Forest. He did not want to kill Josh where they were. He could not leave him there and knew his body would be hard to carry back to the river--or anywhere else. He had an idea.

He cut part of the rope and tied Josh's hands behind him. Taking the belt and wrapping it tightly around the young man's neck, he then tied the rest of the rope to the belt. He made sure everything else was picked up off the ground.

He ordered his prisoner to stand up and start walking in front of him without turning around. They proceeded--a man walking a man, on a leash.

"Odd Job" had marked the exact spot where he had first hit the main road. He told Josh to turn there and keep moving with the sun to their backs.

When the riverbank finally came into view, Josh begged again. "Please don't drown me, Sir. I promise I won't tell anyone we ever met, please.

"Shut up, you little turd--do you know who I am?"

"No sir," he lied, having a good idea "Odd Job" was exactly the evil person Jane had cautioned him about.

"Odd Job" made Josh sit in the front of the flat-bottomed boat, facing forward. He paddled across the waterway and walked Josh up the steep, winding stairs to the dog area. He placed him into an empty pen.

Each enclosure had a two-by-four stud in the center of it for roof support. The roof was too low for either man to stand. Josh's hands were retied behind the pen's heavy wooden centerpiece. While this was going on, the dogs were barking as though they had full recognition of the inhumane tragedy before them.

When his captor felt Josh was adequately secured, he walked behind him with a loose piece of lumber. Using his best judgment, "Odd Job" savagely smashed Josh in the head hard enough to knock him out cold, but not powerfully enough to kill him.

Overhead, dark thunder clouds began to rumble.

Chapter 33

Jane Anderson turned off Ebenezer Road into Leila's driveway around nine a.m. the next morning. She saw Josh Snyder's vehicle parked across the street and assumed he was already at work. Entering Leila's home by the back porch door, she walked over and activated the telephone message recorder. There were two calls from Steve Snyder wanting to know why his son had not returned home last night and if he had reported to work. Jane called him back immediately.

Josh resided in his parent's home and had a girlfriend living in Alabama. Mr. Snyder said he had spoken to the girlfriend, but she had not been contacted by Josh. Mr. Snyder said he was leaving in minutes and would be at Ebenezer Forest in less than an hour.

Jane, new to the area, knew very few people she could call for assistance. She reached her fiancé, Bob, who told her to call the sheriff's office immediately. A single deputy showed up shortly before Mr. Snyder arrived. The deputy made a report and left after saying, "If Josh doesn't show up all day, call us again in the morning."

Mr. Snyder was visibly shaken, and Jane offered to get the golf cart out so they could ride the property together. It had rained most of the night. The property's roads were sloshy, and the cart became stuck in the mud twice. But they found not one sign of his son.

Around eleven a.m. they returned to Leila's house to allow Mr. Snyder to call a number of his friends and relatives. By two p.m. three sets of two-person teams were on the property looking for Josh, using cattle horns and other noisemakers hopefully to give Josh direction if he were lost. Josh's mother was helping by e-mailing photos of her son to all of the local television stations which had agreed to use them on the evening news.

As early as three p.m. various news and television reporters were arriving on the scene to gather in the familiar spot across from Leila's home. Several were asking to interview Leila. In a very short while, Josh's disappearance had attracted a large group of supporters and press representatives, with more on the way.

Conspicuously missing all afternoon was the sheriff's office. Before five p.m., future candidate for sheriff, Bob Kirk, arrived and passionately asked, "Where is the Walton County Sheriff's office?"

*****

Earlier the same day, across the river and less than two miles away, Jay Chidister had shown up at Tomahawk Ranch an hour after daybreak. A half crew of carpenters was busy at work on the new barn, and "Odd Job" had yet to make an appearance. Jay chatted for a few minutes and continued on past the main lodge to the dog pen area.

He could see "Odd Job" standing outside his trailer and looking in his direction as he approached.

"What's going on, Cuz?" he asked. "You are not working today?"

"I got a little problem, Jay."

"One of them dogs bite you?"

"Naw, when you told me that Leila gal was out of town, I went over there yesterday after everybody left here just to look around."

"Oh, shit, what happened? Did somebody see you?"

"Yeah," mumbled "Odd Job" in a low tone.

"Well, what happened?"

"I ran into a guy, and he got a good look at me, Jay."

"Hot dammit, 'Odd Job,' how close was he?"

"Odd Job" did not answer.

"Son-of-a-bitch, you ain't hard to describe. He is gonna pick you out of some pictures, and they will be looking for you everywhere! What a stupid screw up."

"He ain't gonna pick me out of nothin, Jay--I ain't stupid."

"Crap, tell me what happened--what did you do?"

"Odd Job" again did not answer. He simply stared at the ground. Then he slowly raised his head and motioned Jay to follow him. When he got halfway around to the rear side of the dog pens, "Odd Job" stopped. He raised his finger to his mouth to make Jay remain quiet and pointed to a cage.

Jay walked closer and saw a human form, motionless and tied in a seated position in the middle of the dog pen floor. The person had a bag over his head, and Jay could see blood on the shirt below. He was dumbstruck. He shook his head in disbelief and disgust.

"Is he dead?" He finally asked "Odd Job" in a whisper.

"No, he was movin' just a little while ago."

Jay motioned "Odd Job" to follow him around to the front of the pens. He was shaking. Not because he was inexperienced, but because he well knew the possible consequences of what his cousin had done.

Jay knew "Big Fuzz" would explode if he found out this had happened on Tomahawk Ranch. He now fully realized that "Odd Job" was far more deranged than he had ever expected.

"Let me think about this for a few minutes," he told "Odd Job." It did not take him long to make a decision.

Following Jay's instructions, "Odd Job" removed Josh from the dog pen.

"Where are you taking me?" Josh weakly asked.

"Shut your mouth," growled "Odd Job" as he led him into the woods. Jay stayed at the trailer.

With the bag still over his head, Josh was pulled by the rope approximately 300 yards into the deep woods. Not a word was spoken by either man as they walked.

In a dense thicket "Odd Job" wrapped a towel around his pistol and pushed Josh's face down upon the wet ground. "Please don't kill me, Mister. I beg you, please don't."

BAM! A single muffled shot exploded the back of the young forester's skull. He would never be seen again.

Afterward, "Odd Job" waited by the dog pens until Jay returned from the lodge with several implements for his cousin to use in chopping the victim into a thousand pieces—to soon become only silent remnants of the Choctawhatchee River lore.

Chapter 34

Totally unaware of events unfolding in Florida, Leila was wide awake an hour before daybreak. Her mind was immovably fixed on her experience with John the day before. She never saw the attraction coming and was trying to explain it to herself, but was having difficulty.

At first she tried to deny that anything at all had happened. "They were just ordinary words," she thought. "And just smiles."

"I did feel really touched for a minute," she tried to rationalize. "Maybe just a minute or two."

"Did I slip into some kind of trance because I miss the love I had with Mark?" she asked herself. Her mind recalled the way she had felt when Mark had kissed her. She tried not to think about Mark. "I have to go forward. Maybe it wasn't about missing Mark, just a momentary weakness because I simply miss closeness and affection."

She wondered briefly if John had any real interest in her sons. "Is he possibly more like Powder than he appears?" She rejected the thought. "Powder has shown only ordinary interest in Luke and Jake--certainly not like John. From the beginning John has seemed to have a real interest in them. Am I vulnerable to John because I know Luke and Jake are so fond of him? Or because I know in my heart they really want to have a father?"

She recalled John's interest in the outdoors and in animals and plants. "Half of America likes one or more of those things," she thought. "His growing up on a forested property as I was, is just pure coincidence," she considered.

She dismissed the fact that she and John had both lost the love of their life because of death. "But that's likely not a factor in my reaction, since I only found out about his loss yesterday."

Unable to come up with a concrete explanation to herself of why she was so moved the afternoon before, she decided she would clear her head for about fifteen minutes and then start afresh, conceding her attraction to John "No Elk" Gillespie. She shut her eyes and attempted to flush everything out of her thoughts. She laughed at herself when she realized it was what she always did when she wanted to talk to God. But she could not even go two minutes without thinking of those special moments of yesterday.

She interpreted the way he looked at her as a true connection. The way he spoke to her, so slowly with his voice cracking, admitting, "I would Leila, but only if I could work closely with you." Twelve words--she counted them. "Twelve simple words and he grabbed my heart," she thought. She smiled, remembering her embarrassing inability to speak.

"I cannot clear my mind for fifteen minutes," she confessed to herself.

"He is handsome, fit, intelligent, kind, sensitive and humorous," she stopped and smiled at herself yet again. "Why am I always so cautious? Has God sent me an open door?" She decided to ponder her last question thoroughly. And she did until she fell asleep.

When she awoke before breakfast her thoughts returned to John. "I should be counting all my blessings. I have a new interest. I am staying in Powder's fabulous estate in Aspen. Being here, I don't have to worry about my boys."

Recognizing she had been obsessing about John "No Elk" Gillespie, she again confessed to herself, "I like my thoughts. I never expected my fifties to be like this. Things could be a lot worse."

Almost to Aspen

Chapter 35

Shortly after noon, Leila and Powder were waiting for John to join them at a scheduled meeting to discuss the Aspen Ebenezer Forest project. Powder had already asked Leila if she thought John would be a good manager of the project. She did not mention that John had told her the day before that Power had already asked him if would accept the position. Of course she had agreed.

Powder also asked Leila if she would be his date for the evening. He thought he had a sitter lined up, but if she were unavailable, he would ask John to stay with the boys.

Leila did not want to accept his invitation at all. The last thing she wanted was to be paraded around Aspen again. And she did not want John to be relegated as a babysitter for her and Powder. She replied with the best response she could think of at the moment, "Why don't we take the boys and John, so that I don't have to leave them, and we can celebrate John's acceptance to head your project?"

"I was hoping you and I could have some time together, just the two of us," he explained slowly.

Leila was concerned that the whole project might possibly become threatened by her interest in John. She decided to face the issue head on, right then.

"Powder," she began slowly, "you know I have been through a lot over the last six weeks and I do not want to lead you on in any way. I feel that if this project is to work we need to put it first and maintain a professional relationship with each other." She realized as she spoke that she was talking herself into a position that she did not really want to take—certainly not with John. She would have to handle that aspect later.

She continued from a different angle. "If John is to head up the project, and I do think he is the perfect person for the job, he should not be treated by you or me as a babysitter. He is a sharp, experienced person we should treat as a professional, which he certainly is."

Powder was stung by Leila's rejection of his proposed date, yet realized she was right in regard to his friend John. "You make a good point, Leila. I will suggest to John that we all go out together tonight."

*****

John gave Leila a quick hug upon his arrival before turning to firmly shake Powder's hand. After they were all seated, he looked squarely at Leila with his warm, sensuous eyes. His gaze made her want to be held in his arms.

As the three talked, she appreciated John's always humble demeanor, but noted he was fixed on her like never before. She returned his attention. There was no mistaking it--their chemistry had survived the night.

The meeting had been going for only ten minutes when Leila received a text from Jane.

"Please call me as soon as you can. I need to inform you of a situation. Thanks."

She excused herself and called Jane immediately.

Jane was clearly upset and spoke rapidly. "Leila, Josh is missing and it does not look good. His car was left in front of your house overnight, and no one has heard from him. His father is here and says this is totally out of character. A search of your property is underway as we speak!"

"Oh, gracious," Leila gasped. "Dear God, I pray he has not been harmed." She felt immediately responsible for having left the innocent young man exposed to possible danger.

"There is nothing you can do right now, Leila. I will call you before I leave here this afternoon and sooner if anything develops."

Leila hung up the phone and buried her face in her hands. She cried as she prayed for Josh's safety. She walked into a hallway bathroom to collect herself. However, as soon as she walked back into the room with John and Powder, she was again unable to control the emotional stress arising from Jane's call. She began to sob.

The men rushed to console her, and she fell into the arms of both.

*****

Leila waited in her suite for Jane's next call. The night out in Aspen had been canceled. She watched as Luke and Jake sat before a television set in a nearby corner of the room. They had become the most important thing in her tumultuous life. And she was all that they had. All three had developed a deep love for each other, and it had only been weeks. She realized the magnitude of her responsibility to them. "I will never expose them to evil," she pledged.

She considered that she had not met her responsibilities to young Josh Snyder. "Under the circumstances of the current dangers, should I have allowed anyone to work at Ebenezer Forest? Probably not," she suspected. She thought about the danger presented by Dr. Ty Tyson and his criminal gang. She had no idea how many were in his mysterious crowd or who they were. "Are they the reason Josh is missing? Or is the person who killed James Watson behind Josh's disappearance?" she mulled these questions without any possibility of a quick answer.

For the first time in her life she started to doubt whether she could ever again live safely with her sons in her beloved Ebenezer Forest. She went over and over in her mind the series of events that led to her hiding on a mountainside in Colorado.

"My dear GOD, please help me make the right decisions on the difficult choices I see coming," she prayed. "And please help me be strong and ready for whatever obstacles are ahead."

*****

When Jane finally called, there was no good news about Josh's fate. They had no way of knowing there never would be.

Walton County Acting Sheriff Billy Munsey had called late in the afternoon to inform Jane that he had scheduled a number of activities for the coming morning. There would be three dozen volunteer deputies prepared to walk the entire Hewitt property beginning at seven-thirty a.m. At the same time two scent dog teams would start working the main roads and the Choctawhatchee riverbank to see if they could pick up Josh's trail. Jane had already arranged for Mr. Snyder to bring multiple personal items belonging to Josh in the hope of helping the dog teams in their work. The sheriff's flotilla would start at daylight working the riverbanks in search of Josh.

"The press is building up their intensity to find out where you are Leila," Jane reported. "And just as a matter of public relations, I would advise you to come home as soon as you can," she added, "until we can get some answers. I would also advise that you not subject the boys to this kind of situation. We do not know where this story is headed."

"I understand and agree with both of your suggestions. I will be home as soon as I can. Until then I would appreciate that you please continue working out of my house until we know more. Is that possible for you?"

"Of course it is," Jane replied. "Josh's disappearance is absolutely tragic. I pray there is some explanation and he is still alive. But if he is deceased I hope it was accidental and he wasn't tortured or something--and he was not killed by someone trying to harm the boys or you."

"Are you going to be safe?"

"I promise you, Leila. I am well armed."

"Great. And thank you, Jane. You are an absolute Godsend."

Chapter 36

Before the boys fell asleep, Powder knocked on Leila's suite door to tell her that the Aspen press had called him and wanted an interview with her. "I told them you had no comment," he assured. "Apparently it is all over town that you are staying here at Powder Mountain."

"Oh no, here we go again, but thank you, Powder." she replied.

After making sure the boys could not hear her, she said, "Powder, with Josh missing, I have to get back home as soon as possible. Can I pay you to have your plane fly me back?"

"No indeed. You tell me when you want to leave and I will have my plane ready. Do you want me to go with you?"

"I appreciate your kind offer, Powder, but I need to go alone. And I know I should not expose the boys to any part of this situation."

"With all of the publicity you had a month ago, you surely know this is already front page national news."

Leila just shook her head in acknowledgment. "The first thing I am going to do in the morning is to try and find someone reliable up here to take care of Luke and John. If I cannot find anybody I am comfortable with, I am going to ask my best friend

Amanda to come up or my pastor Brother Tom to recommend someone from back home to fly up here until I get back. I will be gone just a few days no matter what."

"How can I help you?" Powder asked.

"Maybe John knows someone in town I can hire. Please give me his phone number. I'll call him in a short while--the boys will be asleep soon."

Powder gave her the number and offered, "If I can do anything else, just buzz me. Otherwise, I will see you at breakfast."

*****

Twenty minutes later John answered Leila's call on the first ring. His first words were, "I was wishing you would call."

She was taken aback at first, but then asked, "How did you know it was me?"

"I didn't think you had my number—just saw your area code."

"Why didn't you call me?" Leila asked.

"Because I didn't want to press you, like everybody else does. But I think of you often.

Leila found herself beginning to breathe harder. She had hoped it would be like this. "We hardly know each other," she deflected softly.

"When we looked at each other on Ajax Mountain, I felt like I had known you for a long time."

There was silence, and then Leila whispered, "I feel the same way, John." She could hardly believe her own directness.

"You have to go back home, don't you?"

"Yes. But I should not take Luke and Jake with me under the circumstances."

"I know," he replied. "I will take good care of them."

Leila was overwhelmed that she had not even asked him. She took a deep breath in relief and joy. "I will not be gone long," she assured, already missing not just her boys.

"I hope not," he answered

"What should I tell Powder?"

"Just tell him I can pick you and the boys up in the morning at his place so you can see where I live before you leave town. Then the three of us will bring you back to Powder Mountain. Everything will be fine."

"I don't know what to say, John. I am so grateful."

"You don't have to say anything."

"Will you let me hug you tomorrow, when we get to your place?" Leila asked.

"It will be my first hug in over ten years, so please make it a good one," he replied laughing.

"I promise."

Almost to Aspen

Chapter 37

The lead story on a Panhandle television station early the next morning was that a young man had disappeared from Ebenezer Forest. "Big Fuzz" saw it and immediately texted Jay Chidister, "I want you to meet me somewhere in an hour. Get back with me as soon as you get this message."

"Anywhere you say, 'Fuzz,'" was the quick reply.

Texting was not the usual manner of contact by his boss and never at this early hour. Jay knew what likely prompted the urgency, and he did not look forward to the meeting. Fully expecting to be reamed out or worse for not already calling "Big Fuzz," he had hardly slept since discovering what "Odd Job" had done the day before. He well knew it was a big problem for himself and the man he was headed to meet.

"Big Fuzz" was already at the designated Donut Café in Inlet Beach when Jay arrived. Walking in like a nervous cat, he joined his boss in a private corner. He was unshaven and his eyes were bloodshot. He looked like hell, which was not his normal presentation.

Already knowing the answer, "Big Fuzz" started, "Tell me 'Odd Job' didn't have anything to do with that forester disappearing from Ebenezer Forest."

Jay had been wrestling with how to tell "Big Fuzz" what had happened from the moment he stumbled on the situation at the dog pens. It was not "Odd Job" he was concerned about, but himself. What happened was bad enough, but Jay knew that if "Big Fuzz" found out the actual killing had occurred on Tomahawk Ranch, at Jay's direction, he would go ballistic. He, more than anyone, was well aware of "Big Fuzz's" history of eliminating any people or obstacles that were problematical to him. Jay had decided it was best to skew the facts a bit.

"I hate to tell you, but 'Odd Job' did take the man out. But the good news is that there will never be a problem—EVER. I promise you, 'Big Fuzz'—I took care of it. End of story."

"Tell me the mother-fuckin' story!" demanded "Big Fuzz," already in a rage and staring at Jay with a furrowed brow and crimson face.

Jay was not going to tell the whole story to "Big Fuzz." He had made that final decision on his drive to the café. He believed to do so might be signing his own death warrant, and he was not going to sign it.

"Listen to me, 'Big Fuzz,' I have never let you down and I never will. The man's body will not ever be found. I am one hundred per cent positive. 'Odd Job' made a stupid mistake—on his own. But I have totally taken care of it. It does not and will not ever affect you. If you want me to kill my cousin, I will gladly kill that dumb bastard—for free!"

"Big Fuzz" still wanted to hear the story. "Just tell me what happened, Jay," he asked in a cooler voice, trying to hide his

182

growing rage toward Jay, who had never refused any question of his before this moment.

Jay knew he could not do it. "You know nothing about this, 'Big Fuzz.' You do not need to. It can never be connected to you. You could pass any lie detector test. I am not telling you FOR YOUR OWN GOOD. I would die for you."

It was not the place to press Jay further, and "Big Fuzz" feigned to back off a bit, but was inwardly fuming. "If you are so certain this will never become a problem for us, why did you just ask me if I wanted you to kill 'Odd Job'?"

Jay immediately realized that his logic was imperfect. After a short and somewhat telling pause he replied, "To show that I would do anything for you, 'Big Fuzz.'"

Still concealing his rage, "Big Fuzz" said, "We need to get that crazy bastard off my ranch."

"The carpenter's crew will be finished in two weeks," began Jay. "They all know 'Odd Job.' He is the one-man cleanup crew and, if we pull him out now, it might look like it was done for a reason we are not supposed to know anything about. I suggest that you stay away from the ranch until all the workers, including 'Odd Job,' are gone. You have zero exposure! I will spend all of my time out at the ranch to make you feel better."

"I never should have let the psycho near my property. I'll decide what to do with him later. But for the time being, he is your responsibility. No more screw-ups, Jay. Do you understand me?"

"Yes, Sir, I completely understand. Thank you."

Chapter 38

As Leila soared south above the clouds, she occupied her mind with how her life was still spiraling in multiple directions. Ebenezer Forest was her world, almost her only world, until the boys came into her life. She knew the decision to adopt them was made in profound haste, but she attributed her choice as a gift from God rather that a reaction to the loss of Mark.

She wanted very much to share her beloved forest with her new sons, and it would remain her top priority. She wanted them to know the beauty of life that she had experienced in God's outdoor wonderland. It was her hope that one day they would be a part of the tradition of sharing Ebenezer Forest with others who might not otherwise have such a wonderful opportunity.

The inability to bring Luke and Jake home with her had upset Leila. They were her charge. It was the first time she would not be in their close reach, and if something happened to them she could not quickly come to their side. But she was comforted with her memories from the morning. The boys were always happy to see John. He had clearly become the primary male figure in their life, and he seemed to be truly attached to them. Her thoughts drifted back to John.

John's home was far more comfortable than Leila expected. She considered that he may have understated his means, not that it was important to her. "His humility is so attractive," she thought.

She recalled pleasantly how he had shown the boys the room they would be staying in with its view of a ski-lift on Aspen Mountain. They loved it. When they were all returning to the living room, she had glanced into John's bedroom as they passed. She noticed a picture of a woman on the table next to his bed. "That must be Pati," she thought.

Although he had hugged Leila upon first picking them all up, there was really no opportunity for any other exchange of intimacy. The boys had been nearby every moment. She did not know whether to respect his gentlemanly forbearance or to be downright disappointed.

Powder had been waiting for her to return to his home so that he could take her to the airport. She knew that there would be no occasion once there to express her deep thanks or feelings to John.

She smiled to herself and thought, "I can't believe I did that," recalling herself placing her hand high on John's thigh as they turned down Castle Creek Road. But she was happy she had left it there until arriving at Powder Mountain. She shut her eyes now, treasuring the exact moment John had put his hand on top of hers and squeezed tenderly. She imagined him caressing and touching her whole body the same way.

"We have never really kissed," she lamented as she dreamed of how pleasurable it would be, as the airplane thrust in and out of pockets of warming air.

*****

Amanda awaited Leila at the Panama City airport. They waved at each other at the same time and were soon on their way to Ebenezer Forest.

As soon as they were in the car alone, Amanda blurted out, "Thank God you were out of town! If some monster has killed that poor boy, he would probably have killed you too if you had been at home."

"If that is what happened maybe I could have saved him if I had been here," Leila replied. "I feel so terrible--and responsible. I pray though that he is still alive."

"I have been praying for him too, but please, don't ever blame yourself, Leila. We don't even know yet what has really happened."

After they thoroughly discussed the tragic disappearance of Josh, Amanda eventually changed the subject.

"Are you the same girl I grew up with?" she began. "A year ago, everything was like it always had been. And now it seems like your life is a giant thunderstorm, with bolts of lightning striking every few minutes. I worry and pray every night that one of them will not hit you!"

"I know what you mean, dear. Sometimes, if I didn't have such faith in God, I might suspect I am having some really bad luck."

"I think somehow you have got yourself on a nasty rollercoaster ride," Amanda replied, "and we have to somehow get your skinny ass off of it!"

187

Leila laughed. Amanda always made her laugh, and she loved her very much.

*****

There was no humor on Ebenezer Road when Leila and Amanda arrived at her family home. A full press corps was set up across the street. They were all in the vicinity of her guinea pen, and the guineas seemed much more aggravated than usual. The cameras were rolling as Leila and Amanda exited the vehicle. They could hear numerous shout-outs from reporters.

"Can we have an interview, Leila?"

"Are people still trying to harm you, Leila?"

"Have you adopted two children, Leila? Where are they?"

The last question startled her. It was totally unexpected. The press dragging Luke and Jake into mainstream media was the very last thing she wanted.

Jane and Josh's mother and father were on the front porch awaiting her arrival. Cameras zoomed in to closely capture Leila warmly embracing the distraught couple she had never met. Leila could not control her tears. The emotion of the scene would be spread across the country that evening on national television.

But before they could all proceed inside, a man in a dark black suit walked up on the porch and tapped Leila on the shoulder to get her attention. When she turned around, he handed her a bundle of papers from the Federal District Court in Pensacola. It was a subpoena for her to appear in nine days before the same

Grand Jury that had previously indicted four men from Walton County for various racketeering and other charges.

Only one of the indicted four men was still alive, Colonel Max Barnett who was formerly of the Walton County Sheriff's Office. The Sheriff had died of natural causes, and the other two subjects were victims of unresolved murders.

Several members of the press recognized the federal marshal serving Leila. Her wide-eyed reception of the subpoena was also clearly captured on camera. The service of the subpoena to Leila sparked the commencement of a second national story.

But the news report with the biggest consequences for Leila and her family would not appear until the following morning.

Almost to Aspen

Chapter 39

Leila's pastor, Reverend Tom McGraw, called Leila shortly after eight a.m. He asked if she had the time to meet with him as soon as possible. She invited him to come right over and knew from the tone of his voice that he was going to bring some concerning news.

Jane was back at work before the pastor arrived. With everything that was happening, Leila needed her more than ever. Jane had assured Leila she was committed to her for the long term. With Josh missing, the tours of Ebenezer Forest had come to a complete halt. They concurred that it was too soon to consider a replacement for Josh. Even though they hoped there would be a positive resolution to his disappearance, they feared the worst. They would decide later, after a respectful amount of time, when to reopen Ebenezer Forest to visitors.

Reverend Tom was carrying a newspaper with him when he was welcomed into Leila's home. Leila knew there would be the normal courtesies before it was opened, but she also knew he always carried a Bible to her home, never a newspaper.

Leila invited Jane to sit in with them, and as always Reverend Tom began with his usual prayer. After the "amens," he told Leila how much he loved her and how everyone at Red Bay

Church was praying for young Josh Snyder. He then cleared his throat and said, "I wanted to stop by and bring something to your attention that you need to be aware of and to discuss it with you." He finally opened the paper. It was a copy of the morning edition of the Fort Walton News-Daily.

A huge picture of Leila and the Snyders facing each other on her porch dominated the front page. The main headline read

LEILA HEWITT RETURNS TO EBENEZER FOREST
TO MEET JOSH SNYDER'S FAMILY

Below that was a side story entitled

RACKETEERING INVESTIGATION REOPENS
WITH LEILA HEWITT SET TO APPEAR BEFORE
GRAND JURY

But it was the third headline and story that hit Leila the hardest.

HAS LEILA HEWITT, "THE GRAND HEROINE OF
EBENEZER FOREST," ADOPTED TWO SONS?

Confirmed reports from Aspen, Colorado are that Leila Jane Hewitt, noticeably absent from Ebenezer Forest since the mysterious disappearance of her employee, Josh Snyder, has been spotted and photographed in the past week in the popular ski resort with two young boys. Sources in Aspen say she has adopted these boys after the recent dramatic shootings on her Walton County estate. In that nationally reported incident two men ended up dead in Hewitt's bed the same night that her fiancé was killed in an auto accident racing to assist her. Hewitt's appearance in Aspen has reportedly caused quite a stir in the area.

Hewitt and her two boys are reported to have been the guests of well-known Aspen playboy William "Powder" White. The two boys did not appear with Ms. Hewitt yesterday afternoon when she arrived back at her Ebenezer Forest estate.

Leila was at a total loss for words. She shook her head and grimaced in total exasperation.

Jane spoke first, "I detest the press--they have no consideration for anyone."

Reverend Tom said, "I am really alarmed by this article. Since your attorney was killed I have been greatly concerned about the safety of you and your boys. This only makes it worse."

"I am very thankful they are not here now," Leila expressed.

"And you do not need to be spending any nights out here alone," replied Jane.

"Nothing has developed on James Watson's death, and I still fear it was related to the adoption," warned Reverend Tom.

"Leila, there are many rumors going around that alarm me. I think you would be safer in Aspen with your sons," Jane declared.

"I have no intention of staying away from them until my Grand Jury appearance," Leila began. "I am going to buy my own ticket and return to Aspen the day after tomorrow."

*****

Two hours after Reverend Tom had departed, Leila and Jane were still on the rear porch canceling tours and attending to other matters. In the midst of deciding how to best support the Snyder family, who were still holding on to fading hope, the porch phone rang. As they had already done several times that morning, they let the call go to voice mail--this time to hear a woman with a very slangy and squirrelly voice:

"Leila Hewitt, this is, uh, my name is June Bradley. I been told you have Luke and Jake--they are my sons. I appreciate you takin' care of 'em for a while, I really do. Buuut, I have changed my mind about givin' 'em up for adoption. I talked to a laaw'yer and he tells me I can git 'em back, and that is what I am gonna do. I don't want to cause you any big trouble or anything. So I would like to just come and pick 'em up as soon as possible. Sooo, if you would call me back at 850-992-9898, uh, I would really appreciate it. Thank you." Click.

Leila was stunned and instantly broke into tears. Jane ran over and tried to console her to no avail. "OH, NO, GOD! PLEASE, NO!" Leila begged desperately.

It would be hours before she could again talk sensibly with Jane.

Chapter 40

The content of the message from the boys' mother was devastating enough, but the fact that she sounded impaired made the call more disturbing. The mere thought of having to return Luke and Jake back into the hands of June Bradley left Leila physically ill. She would feel even worse later when she discovered June's street name was "Sweet Jaws."

By mid-afternoon Jane was able to help Leila sufficiently regain her composure to take some much-needed proactive action. She had yet to hire a lawyer to replace the deceased James Watson. Jane insisted to do so was priority number one, and added, "Whoever you hire should be damn good."

After an hour of calling around and receiving the same recommendation from several people, Leila and Jane agreed on calling attorney Rusty Lucas. He was an older gentleman who was well connected in Walton County. He was expensive, even before Jane named who his client would be. Leila had little choice but to hire one of the best attorneys. She had no objection to Jane giving him the reason for the call and the complete background he needed to address the issues.

Once up to date, Attorney Lucas asked to speak to Leila. "Ms. Hewitt, it is an honor to be asked to represent you. Do you want to hire me as your legal counsel as of this moment?"

"Yes, Sir, I do."

"My retainer for handling the adoption through completion is $20,000 dollars, plus all costs. I will charge you hourly, against that retainer, in the amount of $400 dollars per hour. I will advise you when the retainer limit is reached. Is that agreeable?"

"Yes, Sir, it is."

"This fee that I am quoting will not cover any appellate proceedings. That would have to be renegotiated. Is that agreeable?"

"Yes, Sir, it is."

"I am going to put an investigator on this woman, June Bradley, today. I will need you to come by my office in the morning to sign the employment contract with me, to sign a document for me to enroll as your attorney of record and to sign a document to exclusively authorize me to speak for you publicly. Can you do that?"

"Yes, Sir."

"I have two major pieces of advice for you now--and I require that my clients agree to both. Number one, you will not speak to anyone about the facts of this case, but me. And number two, you will keep my office aware of your location at all times. That means notifying my office every time you change locations. Do you agree with both of these requirements?"

"Yes, Sir, I do."

When the conversation was over, Leila and Jane felt much better having accomplished the retention of the new attorney.

They had no earthly idea that the main client and closest friend of attorney Rusty Lucas was none other than Clarence Bectom "Big Fuzz" Rogers, the "King Rat" of Destin.

Almost to Aspen

Chapter 41

On the way to her new attorney's office the next morning, Leila received a call from Jane to tell her to contact an individual who had called her from the Florida Department of Children and Family Services. Leila did so immediately and was told that the Department wanted to schedule a meeting for a home investigation as part of her pending petition for adoption. She advised the caller she was leaving the state that afternoon to return to Colorado and would return home in about a week with the boys. The woman she conversed with was not the person who would actually perform the investigation, but she said she would pass on the message.

Leila was not able to meet her new attorney, yet the requested papers he wanted signed were ready for her signature. His secretary asked for Leila's retainer check, and she obliged. She returned to her home and soon departed to catch her commercial flight to Aspen.

Leila waited to tell John she was returning to Aspen until only minutes before her plane left Panama City. "I don't know how late the plane will arrive. Would it be okay if I stayed at your townhouse tonight?" She asked politely.

"You know it is, Leila. I would like that very much."

"I haven't told Powder I am returning yet. Please let me tell him tomorrow."

"That is probably best--we can talk about that tonight. The three of us cannot wait to see you," he replied.

It was after dark when the plane landed, and John, Luke and Jake were waiting at the terminal. The boys ran ahead to wrap their arms around Leila as she showered them with kisses. When John approached, Leila met him with a warm, lengthy hug. She felt a joy that had been missing since she had left the boys with him.

Then John surprised Leila by stooping down beside little Jake to whisper, "Tell your mommy what I taught you to say."

Jake looked up at Leila with excitement in his eyes, then back at John, and back at Leila.

"C'mon, Jake--say it. C'mon, Jake," urged John.

"Hi, Mommy," he finally said with a big smile.

"OH, GREAT GOD," she exclaimed as she fell to her knees to squeeze Jake tightly. She had never heard him try to speak before and had wondered if he ever would. She held him against her breasts as hard as she safely could. "I love you SO much." She then reached out and drew Luke into her embrace, "I love you both, very, very much!"

She finally looked up at John with glistening tears of happiness and did not have to say a word. It was a special moment.

*****

John had a pot of what he called "turkey soup" ready to warm when they returned to his home. They sat and ate at a table "like a family," Leila thought. It was almost enough to take her mind off the alarming developments she had left behind in Walton County. She did not know how much of it John had learned from the media. She watched him kindly and gently relate to her sons. It gave her a warm and stirring surge of contentment.

"How can I have this tremendous attraction toward him when we have hardly talked," she wondered to herself.

But that evening when the boys were asleep, Leila and John had their chance. Sitting five feet apart, they were alone at last. She inquired how the boys had been in her absence. They had done well, except he felt it necessary to share one incident.

"The first night of their stay, as I was putting them to bed, Luke asked, 'Are you going to be our daddy tonight?' I did not know how to answer. I thought about it for a second and said, 'I am your friend and will make sure you and little Jake are safe tonight.'"

"There is no telling what my boys have been through."

"There's more," John added. "After my response Luke said, 'Our last mommy told us almost every night we were going to have a new daddy—and we did.'"

He noticed droplets appearing in the corners of Leila's eyes. "That tore me up," John admitted. "I wrestled with telling you-- but I thought you should know."

"I was afraid they, particularly Luke, might have memories like that," Leila shared sadly. "I certainly do not want to question them and stir up past memories." She paused for a moment. "Do you think the boys need counseling?"

"I thought about that, but I would rather see their bad memories replaced with love and positive experience than submit them to a paid-by-the-hour psychologist," he replied.

As the conversation went on, mostly on other topics, it grew late. During a rare moment of silence, John broached a topic that he had been waiting to address. Powder had invited him and the boys over the day before to his estate for lunch. John said Powder had made a big point to tell him "You had agreed that the three of us need to keep our relationships strictly professional with each other if Ebenezer Forest in Aspen is going to work." He looked anxiously into Leila's eyes awaiting her response.

His serious question caught Leila off guard, and she hesitated for a bit. "Powder was pressing me toward dating him, and I said something close to that. But I don't remember including your name."

She paused for a long moment, and then coyly added, "Are you seeking an exemption?"

John broke into a large smile.

"It could be problematical for the project if I exempted you," she added flirtatiously.

"I would like to keep the plan alive," he started, "but let me be clear--I want the exemption."

He rose from his chair and stood erect. He took a slow step halfway to her and stopped, intensely gazing into her sparkling eyes.

She surprised him by also rising to her feet, eyes fixed on him, with a sensuous and gorgeous smile.

"What are you doing?" she asked.

"What are YOU doing?" he replied as he took another step, now within reach of her.

"If you are finally about to kiss me," she spoke with a grin, "I am going to stand up and take it like a woman!"

And they passionately submitted themselves into each other's arms and hearts.

*****

Leila was totally exhausted when John kissed her goodnight at the guest bedroom door. There had been hundreds of kisses. Neither one of them could quench their thirst for the other. It was natural and powerful. Their powerful exchange of affection left her in dreamy and trusting exhilaration with the new man in her life. Facing the certain perils ahead seemed more manageable now.

Almost to Aspen

Chapter 42

Powder was not around when John dropped off Leila and her sons back at Powder Hill the next morning. When he returned to his home around noon he was surprised to learn from Leila that she had spent the night at John's place. "I cannot believe you didn't give me a call," he said, appearing to feel slighted.

"I did not know how late my plane would be arriving, and I was anxious to see the boys," Leila explained.

"You never have to fly commercial, Leila. I would have sent the King Air to pick you up."

"You have been very kind. I didn't want to put you out any more than I already have."

"You would never be putting me out. You are all my special guests."

"I have to be back down in Florida on Monday for my Grand Jury appearance. You probably know all about that. John said it was front page news here in Aspen."

"Yes, and I am disappointed that you are now getting so much attention here in Aspen. I was hoping it would be a much quieter environment for all of you."

Leila bristled as she remembered the large first night reception that was waiting for her at Jim's Restaurant and did not reply.

Powder added, "I am going to reserve the plane for you and the boys' trip back on Sunday. Do you want me to go with you?"

"Thank you Powder, but John has already offered to go with us if I take the boys. Luke and Jake are really becoming attached to him. I may not want to take them back with me just yet, unless I absolutely have to. I am still undecided."

"I am getting jealous of John," Powder admitted.

"I hope that whatever happens, your and John's friendship will never be affected," Leila replied boldly. After a telling moment of complete silence, she added, "And our project will continue."

Powder was totally blindsided, and visibly shaken. The big fish in Aspen was being scaled by the most alluring woman he had ever met. "Am I reading you right?" he finally asked.

Leila had not discussed this disclosure with John at all, but she never avoided the truth. "If you are reading that I have feelings for John, you are right--I do."

"Wow!" He finally replied. "I didn't expect this."

"Neither of us did either."

"Are you planning on staying at his place from now on," asked Powder in a forced, but not vindictive tone.

"Not unless you would like us to--we are not there yet. I just wanted to be totally honest with you. But if you want us to leave, I completely understand."

"Absolutely not," he said rebounding, but still clearly stung. "You are all safer here, and I think I understand all of the other considerations involved."

"Thank you so much. I sincerely appreciate your kindness. And Powder, I really love the plan you have for Ebenezer Forest in Aspen. It is going to be such a wonderful attraction!"

*****

Leila and the boys spent every night at Powder Mountain as she waited to hear from the Florida Department of Children and Family Services. After her talk with Powder, Leila had noticed that he seemed less comfortable around her. He was courteous and friendly, but certainly different. The next day he said he had to take care of some business in Wyoming and would be gone through the weekend. He still insisted on making his plane available on Sunday for her trip south and remained ostensibly enthusiastic about the Ebenezer Forest project in Aspen.

On Saturday, John picked up Leila and her sons for lunch and afterwards took them on an afternoon excursion around Aspen valley. He was very familiar with all of the interesting local trails and remote scenery not normally accessed by visitors to the area. Scenic vistas, waterfalls and wildlife sightings thrilled his three guests. There was plentiful snow already on the ground, and it was a treat for all. In a few more weeks many of the vantage points, John pointed out, would be inaccessible except by snowmobiles. Loving the outdoors as she did, Leila was exhilarated watching her boys enjoy the day. And she found herself more and more drawn to this strong, quiet man from Arkansas.

Later, with the boys taking afternoon naps, Leila and John sat by an open fire and shared stories of their prior lives. And they shared themselves by nestling into the other's arms, with deep adventurous caresses and exploration. She was mesmerized by his sensuous kisses and slender, chiseled body. The mere taste of his moist and earthy tongue plunged her into quivering rapture.

There were no questions in her mind of age or other differences. They were from the same generation and background. There would never be any looking back. She knew from his slow, gentle moans that he shared her titillation. She could feel him stiffen from her very touch, which increased her own desire.

But when she told him of her commitment to God and to herself of sexual abstinence until marriage, he replied in a whisper, "I am familiar with First Corinthians 7:2."

Leila was not totally surprised but quite pleased." I am happy you know scripture. Are you willing to accept that love should be perfected in HIS way?" She asked.

"Well, let me put it to you this way. If marriage is the cure, do you have any philosophical objections to being cured one day?" He playfully responded.

She gazed back at him with an adoring twinkle in her sparkling blue eyes. "Not at all," she answered, barely able to breathe.

On Sunday, it was time for Leila to return to the Panhandle to honor the subpoena she had received. She had still never been contacted by the Florida investigator assigned to make a report on her pending adoptions, and she decided to leave the boys in Aspen. She was so happy that John again insisted that he keep them. She felt they were in an extremely safe environment with him, and it gave them an opportunity to spend more time with their favorite male--which was something she very much wanted to do herself.

Chapter 43

Before she left Aspen, John had confided in Leila that he and Powder "had a talk" about his and her new relationship. John would only disclose that his and Powder's friendship and the project had survived, for now. Hearing this, Leila was more comfortable than ever with the project they were all involved in together.

Back in the Panhandle for the Grand Jury appearance, Leila met Jane early Monday morning. Jane had agreed to drive her to the Federal Courthouse in Pensacola. The trip took over an hour.

The subpoena required her to appear before nine a.m., and they arrived about a half hour early. Parking 150 yards away, Leila saw the waiting press corps filming a tall, gray haired and dark-suited man who had arrived before them. He was accompanied by what appeared to be two lawyers. She recognized the tall man as her prior assailant, Dr. Ty Tyson.

The ladies stopped to ask a policeman parked near them if there were any other entrances into the building ahead. They were told there were none. Their only approach was past awaiting reporters, to the sound of rolling cameras and clicking snapshots. A number of other non-press onlookers had gathered along the shaded walkway. The Pensacola community had never seen Leila in person, and many were curious for a glimpse of the slim, well-curved legend. Images of Leila, accompanied by the similarly appealing Jane Anderson, also made great fodder for nationwide audiences.

Once inside, they were directed to a wide downstairs hallway where two marshals were keeping the subpoenaed witnesses apart. Leila and Jane speculated from the demeanor of those present that, in addition to Dr. Tyson, there were at least two other witnesses present.

When Leila and Jane were courteously seated on opposite ends of the hallway from Dr. Tyson, Leila whispered, "Tyson doesn't even have the guts to look in this direction."

Finally, around ten a.m., one of the other witnesses was the first person escorted into the jury room. Jane guessed, based on his dress and the fact that he was not accompanied by a lawyer, he was an F.B.I. agent. He testified for over two hours and was finally discharged shortly after noon. When he departed, two federal prosecutors came over and introduced themselves to Leila and Jane. One of them began to explain the situation.

"Unfortunately, things are moving much slower inside today than we had anticipated. We want to call one more federal agent after lunch, and then Dr. Tyson. We want all of them to be called before you testify. It is important to our presentation. We are going to have to unfortunately excuse you until nine a.m. again tomorrow. Several of the jury members have obligations later this afternoon, and the delay cannot be helped. I promise, Ms. Hewitt, you will be called first thing in the morning. Thank you very much for your understanding."

*****

As Leila and Jane exited the courthouse, the crowd outside was larger than when they had arrived in the morning. It was well leaked that the unsolved murders of the Ashton brothers and Daisy Dodd, as well as the two men sent to kill Leila who had died in her bed, were all connected to this Grand Jury investigation underway inside the federal building. Grand Jury proceedings are supposedly secret in America, but the mere assertion of that had become a farce. The news crews present were even aware of the Leila-Dr. Tyson connection, and they were looking for any reason to let the story fly. The rumor that attorney James Watson's death in Destin was connected to Leila Hewitt's adoptions had "legs" too and was beginning to circulate. The Panhandle was spellbound by the ongoing scandals, and all of Northwest Florida was willing to roll in the mud of the story until there were answers.

The shouts from the crowd were especially offensive to Leila.

"Where are your new kids, Leila? Why are you hiding them?"

"Did you nail Dr. Tyson today?"

"Was that young guy killed at your place your new lover?"

This whole bucket of tar had become boiling and turbulent. It had exposed an unending quagmire of evil, corruption and murder. The only bright spot in the entire dark and dismal gloom was Leila Jane Hewitt.

As she walked through the disturbing swarm, she looked over to the right. Off from the others, stood a tall, skinny, dirty and bearded man. He looked as if he had recently slept under a bridge or in a garbage can. He was holding a clean white piece of cardboard that was about three feet square, and on it he had scribbled a question that was very legible:

LEILA

WILL YOU

MARRY ME?

She couldn't miss it, and would not soon forget it—neither would the millions of viewers across the country that would see the man and his sign repeatedly on their television screens that night. It all made Leila very, very sad.

Chapter 44

It had been just over a week since June "Sweet Jaws" Bradley had called Leila and declared she had changed her mind about the adoption, wanting Luke and Jake to be returned to her. She was staying in Cantonment, Florida with a disabled older woman. June shopped for her during the day, and the old lady watched June's baby girl, Annette, while she whored at night. June's physical and mental condition had taken a sharp downward turn since leaving Fort Walton. Practically all of the money that she and the older woman got their hands on went for either food or illegal drugs. Their preferred substance of abuse was methamphetamine, which "Sweet Jaws" would orally ingest before she worked the streets at night.

June's main periods of lucidity were in the afternoon. She had first called Leila at that time of day during one of her better moments. She had actually talked to two attorneys about representing her to reclaim the boys. She didn't have the funds to retain the first one. The second one was a female attorney employed by a pro bono group. The latter had summarily dismissed June after about five minutes of observing her twitching eyes and rampant paranoia. "You need to get medical help as soon as you can," the lawyer advised.

Leila's circus-like reception at the federal building in Pensacola was carefully watched that night by June, who was already very angry that Leila had not returned her call. She had become totally obsessed with regaining Luke and Jake, oftentimes experiencing delusions of how it was going to be when she would surely get them back. With growing rage she watched Leila being glorified on several channels. When it was time for her to go to work, she fetched a small plastic bag and consumed the light brown powder that would jumpstart her into her usual evening of dark connections.

*****

Less than fifty miles away, Doctor Ty Tyson hooked up with "Big Fuzz," after his appearance before the Grand Jury earlier in the day. They met in the back room of a restaurant in Destin and would be joined by Jay Chidister an hour later. Their early meeting would give them a chance to get their heads together about "Odd Job" before Jay arrived. Both had seen the massive news coverage of Leila's arrival and departure, with much less attention being given to Dr. Tyson.

"That bitch is going to destroy me tomorrow," Tyson began.

"Everything has taken off again so fast. I wish we had eliminated her while we had a chance," "Big Fuzz" lamented.

"The rape part of the case is going to come down to her word against mine, and with her looks and popularity you well know who any jury is going to believe. We still need to take her out and do it now," said Dr. Tyson.

"Murder will get you more time in jail than rape--and the charge is not even going to be aggravated rape. I know you are scared shitless, but the smart thing to do may be to just leave her alone. "

"You are not looking up the barrel like 1 am," started Dr. Tyson. "If I get convicted of mass distribution of Rohypnol--and the feds bring in a number of victims--and top it off with Leila's testimony that I personally drugged her, I will likely never get out of prison."

"You know I can get the paperwork if you want to go to Europe or South America?"

"Very funny, you asshole," replied the doctor. "Look, you never touched anything we have done, and you don't really know what they have on you."

"Relax, there is a new development. Guess who Leila hired as her new adoption attorney--my man Rusty Lucas. He has her reporting her whereabouts to him every time she moves. She is lately going back and forth to Aspen, and this is perfect for 'Ace' Tingle to handle. If I pay him the big bucks to plug her, will that make you happy?"

"I am not going to be happy until she is history. Yes, this is great news," responded Dr. Tyson.

"I will take care of it,""Big Fuzz" assured.

*****

"Big Fuzz" and Dr. Tyson welcomed Jay Chidister warmly when he arrived at the restaurant. He had always been a trustworthy and talented handyman for the organization, whether it was simply building barns, or murder. But Jay was not accustomed to such an unusually nice greeting and prepared himself for the next assignment that he knew was forthcoming.

"Is the barn about done?" started "Big Fuzz."

"Yes sir, what's next?"

"We are damn lucky that the search for the forester has not reached across the river to my place, and I have decided exactly what I want you to do about 'Odd Job.' I want you to get him off my property as soon as possible--like tomorrow morning."

"That's it?"

"You know your cousin is a crazy mother-fucker--I know he is family and all, but do you mind making him disappear?" asked "Big Fuzz."

"I told you I would do it if you wanted me to, 'Fuzz.'"

"You have been a good friend, Jay, and I don't mind getting someone else to do it, if his being your cousin bothers you."

"It doesn't, 'Fuzz.' I could probably get my aunts and uncles to chip in some dough for killing him if I asked them. But can I receive any kind of little cash bump?"

"You betcha, Jay."

"Okay," he replied. "It is done."

*****

"Odd Job" was lying in the small trailer next to the dog pens at Tomahawk Ranch, wide awake and thinking about how he was going to snatch his son Luke into his life.

He watched the small television set beside his bunk as Leila ceremoniously arrived and departed the Federal Courthouse building in Pensacola. He admitted to himself she was very good looking, but "I hate every single one of them purty-gals, they never look my way."

"No woman will ever raise my Luke," he thought. "They don't know a damn thing about turning a boy into a man like me. I will kill that rich bitch." The more he thought about being unable to have his son, the madder he got.

"She is the only reason I don't have Luke right now. I am going to beat the living dog-shit out of her for that before I kill her."

He realized it was much too dangerous for the time being to go back over to Leila's estate. He still needed to find the best spot to lie in wait until he could seize the moment he had been waiting on for four years.

"I'm in walking distance from her house after I cross the river. I'm in the perfect place to be," he thought as he drifted into sleep.

Chapter 45

It was a good and bad night for June "Sweet Jaws" Bradley. It was a good night because she had eight different "johns" experience her talented and saucy romance, which gave her plenty of cash to burn. Between client number six and client number seven she sought out her friendly neighborhood drug dealer for a healthy dose of crystal meth, a form of methamphetamine. She loved variety, and the drug increased her sex desire to help her through her workload.

It was a bad night because the combination of the two drug absorptions, by daylight's arrival, had given her a false sense of power that did not complement her increasing level of agitation. She took an Uber ride to a breakfast joint. The morning paper reminded her that Leila would be arriving at the federal building again that day before nine a.m., less than two hours from then.

"I want to face that haughty bitch!" she insanely decided.

She was familiar with Leila's attractive physical appearance and in her stupor did not want to show up looking or smelling like a whore. She stopped by her home and took a shower--and another bump of methamphetamine. She put on a fairly attractive dress that added nothing to her overall presentation.

Then she sat and waited, in confusion and paranoia, until the Uber driver returned at the precise time she had directed.

On the short ride to Pensacola, June had tried to consider exactly what she was going to tell her adversary, but she was having trouble with both focus and recall. She was too impaired and keyed up to do any of the very best things she could have done--that is pass out, go home or go to a hospital. The Uber driver was listening to loud music through his earplugs, so off they went to the federal courthouse.

Upon her arrival, June saw the large crowd assembled near the building's entrance. She approached and stood quietly near the back of the assemblage. Her dark sunglasses concealed her dilated pupils and much of her face. She drew little attention. Unbeknownst to the people around her she was now delusional and dancing in and out of a hallucinatory state. But she knew the person she was after and was bursting at the seams with aggression.

The crowd started to react to the first sight of Leila and Jane as they exited their vehicle over a hundred yards away. Cameras were lifted onto shoulders and pointed toward the oncoming pair. An air of excitement told June the time was near.

June chose not to push herself through the onlookers, but instead to circle around toward the front of the building to the far end of the newsfolks.

Leila and Jane were walking directly toward her. Reporters were moving out of their way as they neared. When they reached about fifteen strides from where June was waiting aside the walkway, all hell broke loose.

June threw off her sunglasses and jumped into the very middle of the sidewalk, screaming at Leila and confronting her head on.

"I WANT MY SONS BACK, YOU CUNT!" she yelled violently.

Leila and Jane stopped in their tracks, totally shocked.

June made a full and fast charge toward Leila, "WHERE ARE MY BOYS? YOU WHORE, WHORE, WHORE!" she repeatedly shrieked as she ran.

Jane was not able to totally cut June off from Leila. June was flailing her arms violently at the woman she had come to harm. Jane was trying desperately to subdue her, but in June's drugged condition she was difficult to restrain. It was a ferocious struggle while it lasted.

Complete bedlam prevailed in front of the federal courthouse. Most of the crowd scattered with June's crazed and animal-like charge, not knowing if she had a gun. But a few cameras continued to roll. Marshals from the building's front door checkpoint, after securing their position, eventually raced toward the action. Jane, with the help of a couple of male volunteers, was able to restrain June at about the time the marshals finally arrived to assist.

There was blood on Leila's face and blouse from where she had been scratched. She was more than shaken by the attack and was in near shock.

Jane's blouse had been completely torn apart and was hanging on one arm. She had been through a number of tough experiences as a policewoman in Atlanta, but was now in mental and physical disarray. Covering herself as best she could, she ushered Leila into the federal building.

June continued to scream and kick even after the marshals wrestled her to the ground. She was handcuffed, arrested and carried to the county jail.

Inside the building twenty minutes later, the federal prosecutors checked on Leila. Because of the attack, she was released from her appearance for the day. She was informed that the Grand Jury would meet again the following Monday, and she would need to be present then.

The events in Pensacola gave rise to what was described across the country as "another huge story out of the Florida Panhandle involving Leila Hewitt." It would not be the last.

Chapter 46

On the ride home from the courthouse with Jane, Leila called John to tell him what had happened minutes before. "Please, please promise me you will not let the boys near a television for the next few days. It would be so horrible if they saw their natural mother attacking me. It was such a nightmare, John."

John could tell from her voice that she was extremely upset by what had occurred. "Why don't you please catch the next plane to Aspen and get yourself away from everything going on down there. You will be safer here."

"I am so exhausted, dear, I need to get home and lie down. I don't know if I have the strength to do anything today. I have been ordered to go back before the Grand Jury this coming Monday. Do I need to send someone up there to sit with the boys until I get back?"

"Don't worry about Luke and Jake. They can ride with me in my jeep everywhere I go, and they'll love it. I enjoy them too. They will be fine until you get back," he replied.

"I am so glad I did not bring them here with me on this trip," she began. "I don't know if they will ever be able to have a normal life in Walton County." It was the first time she had ever admitted this to herself, but much less anyone else. "I miss them and you very much."

"Will you please call me this afternoon after you get some rest?" John asked.

"I promise, John, you don't know how much the sound of your voice helps. Thank you so much for everything."

*****

"Whoa, wait a minute!" Jane said. "That didn't sound like a call to a baby sitter, Leila, it smelled a lot more like romance. What is going on here?"

Leila was still dealing with the aftermath of being attacked and had been oblivious to Jane's keen ear. "I neglected to tell you that John and I have become--close."

"Wow!" Jane was quite surprised to hear of the development so soon after Mark's death. "I expected it would be a long while before you would have an interest in another man," she remarked. "How did this happen so quickly?" she questioned, thinking of one word--rebound.

"I am surprised myself. I have asked myself why. I have even asked God. He didn't give me a clear answer, but he didn't say no either."

"I hope you don't move too quickly. How well do you really know John?"

"The main thing I know about him is that we have a very smooth, natural fit with each other. I feel so comfortable with him. Our dispositions, personalities and wants are remarkably the same."

"It sounds like you have been thinking about it," Jane replied. "I hope you are not unknowingly motivated by your prior loss or a need you might have now."

"You are such a dear friend, Jane. I know you have my best interests at heart. Tell me how you made the decision to marry Bob," Leila cagily answered, shifting the spotlight.

"You hit the key word for us also when you said 'comfortable.' But you are not thinking of marrying him already, are you?"

"I haven't thought about it, and John has not asked. But I have never considered myself particularly fast-acting."

"Good!" replied Jane.

*****

Reverend Tom McGraw and Amanda both called Leila on hearing of the morning donnybrook and asked if they could come over. She told them she was worn out, but it would be all right if they didn't stay too long.

Amanda arrived first and in time to help cleanse the long scratch on Leila's cheek. Jane was still wearing a borrowed shirt given to her by a marshal, and Leila insisted that she go home for the rest of the day. Amanda was determined to spend the night with Leila, who did not put up much resistance.

Leila placed a call to her attorney, Rusty Lucas, to tell him she would be staying in Walton County at least through the next Monday. After she testified she would be returning to Aspen.

The attorney had already seen a news replay of the assault on Leila.

"Based on what I saw this morning, you will not have to worry about losing your boys to June Bradley," Lucas began. "I'll get a copy of all of the news broadcasts, and they will represent evidence against her that she will never be able to overcome."

"That is a great relief," Leila answered.

"What is the address where you stay in Aspen," Lucas asked. "I should have it."

"I don't have the address as I speak, but it is at Powder Mountain on Castle Creek Road. I will text you the numerals on the mailbox when I hang up. Thank you so much for all of your concern, Mr. Lucas. I really appreciate you representing me."

Later in the afternoon, Leila and Amanda closed their eyes as Reverend Tom prayed. The last verse from his prayer was particularly special.

"And finally, I ask You, our Almighty Father, to help Leila not suffer through the long legal process of adopting her two sons, Luke and Jake. Please let justice be ultimately and righteously done to keep all of them together forever. And thank You for guiding her into the hands of her new attorney. Amen!"

Chapter 47

Jay Chidister was up early to take care of his business. He had no particular remorse about killing his first cousin. "After all, he is not a brother or sister," he rationalized. "And he is one sick son-of-a-bitch."

He drove to Tomahawk Ranch thinking how he was going to spend the extra money he was about to make. He decided he would up his membership from a social to an equity member at his high falutin' country club on the beach, figuring he would receive more respect.

No workers had arrived yet to work on "Big Fuzz's" barn. Jay traveled onward to the dog pen area, parked and knocked on the trailer door.

"Who is it?" "Odd Job" barked.

"Jay here, open up, I have some good news."

"Wait a minute."

Scuffling noises could be heard from inside. When the door finally opened, "Odd Job" looked at him through a crack, wide-eyed and cautiously. "Odd Job" was aware that he had been diagnosed as paranoid, but he knew from experience that half the time he was right—and Jay never showed up this early.

"Open the damn door, 'Odd Job,'--I told you I have some good news for you."

No one ever had any good news for him. He never trusted anyone, particularly his relatives. But he opened the door anyway. "What is it?"

"Put your clothes on. "Big Fuzz" is going to do you a favor and let me move you over to a nicer place near Blountstown until things calm down."

"Odd Job" walked outside and down the steps toward Jay. "I like it here, Jay. I am close to my boy, Luke--I want to stay right here until I get him like we talked about."

Jay quickly made up a lie. "We got a tip from the Walton County Sheriff's office that they are about to visit every place on this side of the river still investigating the death of that forester you killed."

"They ain't gonna find shit--he's catfish bait."

"But they are also looking for you as the main suspect in the killing of that lawyer in Destin. You gotta get the hell outa here. Now go inside and get everything you've got in there and come with me." "Odd Job" went inside.

The plan was to drive him a few miles south of Blountstown, then kill and bury him on a remote parcel that was kept for human disposal.

*****

Inside the trailer"Odd Job" rolled all of his belongings up in a sheet. He threw his remaining trash into a garbage can and walked over to the bedside table. On top of the table was a photo, his only photo of his son, Luke. He remembered the promise he had made to himself and Luke while in prison--he would find and raise him when he got out of jail. "Luke is all I have to live for," he told himself.

He bent over and started talking to Luke. "Daddy is not going to you leave you, son, don't you worry. Stay here, I'll be right back." He left Luke's picture where it was.

Before exiting the trailer, "Odd Job" peeked out through the blinds at his cousin Jay. He knew Jay was smarter than he was, and he had to be careful. Jay was acting nervous and fidgety, and when he leaned against his vehicle, "Odd Job" could see the bulge in his back left pocket. "Odd Job" had his own gun but didn't think it would be necessary to use it.

Shutting the trailer door behind him, "Odd Job" started down the steps carrying the sheet full of possessions in front of him. He deftly executed a fake, forward fall onto the ground, scattering everything in his arms toward Jay. "Ah, my back," he wailed loudly as he feigned difficulty in standing back up.

His head was facing downward, and he rubbed his back and continued to moan as Jay approached. When Jay was within three feet of him, "Odd Job" used a powerful kick he had mastered in prison to explode Jay's manhood into mush.

Jay bent forward, grabbing himself and screaming in agony. He was perfectly postured to receive "Odd Job's" next violent and punt-like boot, this time into his face, leaving him completely unconscious.

*****

"Odd Job" removed the gun and keys from his cousin's pockets. He fetched a rope and tied Jay's hands together, then placed him in the trunk of his own car.

Driving first to "Big Fuzz's" lodge, "Odd Job" entered it with the newly possessed keys. He took a Remington automatic rifle with two boxes of ammunition from a gun case. In the kitchen he gathered a cleaver and a couple of sharp knives. He returned to the vehicle and headed back to the dog pen area. He stopped and picked up his possessions from the ground and took them back into the trailer together with the rifle and bullets. He took the sheet with him as he left.

He got into the vehicle and drove it toward the northern end of Tomahawk Ranch. The dirt road ended not far from where he had butchered Josh Snyder. Guiding the car off the road and through the woods, he parked it under the far side of a thick magnolia tree. It was in a location where it would not likely be spotted by overflying aircraft.

He opened the trunk and saw Jay's eyes were open. His nose was broken and blood was all over his face and shirt. ''Don't kill me, 'Odd Job,''' he begged. "I'm family, please."

"Odd Job" pulled Jay out of the trunk and placed him on the ground, with him still pleading and crying.

"I am gonna try not to hurt you, Jay, but I have to kill you," "Odd Job" explained. While face-to-face, he wrapped his powerful hands around his cousin's neck and began to tightly squeeze.

Jay was gurgling and squirming as the two cousins expressed their final farewells to each other with their eyes.

*****

"Odd Job" butchered Jay as cleanly as possible. He deboned him, and chopped the pieces up as small as he could with the cleaver. Then he placed all of his work into the sheet. He carried the remains over to the same small feeder creek of the Choctawhatchee River near the same spot where he had disposed of Josh Snyder.

The automobile was left where he had parked it, and "Odd Job" realized it would have to be fully cleaned up later. "This will soon be me and Luke's getaway car," he mused confidently.

Back at the trailer, the first thing he did was to approach Luke's photo. "I told you I would be right back, son. I will never let you down. I will be coming for you soon."

Almost to Aspen

Chapter 48

The connection between the deaths of private investigator Pearlie Towns and attorney James Watson was finally made. Because Towns had been killed in a very high crime area of Fort Walton Beach, his case had been slowly worked. It was first considered as just another drug-related murder, but when a homicide unit officer eventually interviewed his neighbors there was an immediate new angle. A female neighbor revealed that Towns's main connection in the legal world was James Watson, and that a woman named June "Sweet Jaws" Bradley had hurriedly left the complex immediately before Towns' death. Another resident revealed that June Bradley was a prostitute working with Towns to place her two sons up for adoption though Watson's law office. A hooker working in the same vicinity provided the reason why Bradley had left in such haste. It was because of her great fear of who immediately became the number one suspect in Towns's death--Rufus "Odd Job" Jenkins.

Within twenty-hours, the Walton County Sheriff's office had no choice but to join in a release of an all-points bulletin for "Odd Job's" immediate pick up for questioning as the main suspect in both murders. Loose lips in both jurisdictions quickly informed their favorite reporters that the woman who assaulted

Leila Hewitt at the federal courthouse in Pensacola was running from "Odd Job," a suspected killer with an interest in at least one of the two young boys recently seen with Leila in Aspen. It was assumed that they were in her constant custody wherever she might be.

*****

Rhonda Riveras, the superstar of sensational news broadcasting, watched June "Sweet Jaws" Bradley's crazed attack on Leila and her good friend, Jane, on national television. Knowing also that an employee of Ebenezer Forest had recently disappeared, she placed a call to Jane and left a message for her.

She got right to the point when Jane finally returned her call. "What the hell is going on with your ole friend, Leila?"

"Well, she is more than a friend now--she is my boss," Jane replied.

"That is a surprise. I caught the incident in Pensacola, are you her new bodyguard?"

"No, but I am glad I was with her."

"There has got to be a lot more to this story, Jane. Are you free to talk about it?"

"I really don't feel free to say much now that I am in her employ. But I will tell you there is a lot more to the story."

"If I come down, will you go to lunch with me?"

"Of course, I will, Rhonda. I think you can help the situation, if you promise to stay within certain parameters as you have always been willing to do."

"I will be there in a day or so, and I will call you when I arrive. Thank you, dear."

*****

On Ebenezer Church Road, the press again started to gather daily at their usual spot next to the guinea pens across from Leila's home. They were hoping to get pictures of Leila--and now of her two sons. June Bradley's public assault had catapulted the boys into prime news subjects, and there were no pictures of them yet in the Panhandle.

Jane's defense of Leila at the federal courthouse resulted in her also receiving immense personal attention from the media. Stories were appearing in the local paper about "the beautiful brunette" and her prior work as a sex crimes detective with the Atlanta Police Department. Her engagement to candidate for sheriff, Bob Kirk, was lagniappe locally. The press was very familiar with Leila's blue Oldsmobile and Jane's comings and goings. The entire story was now colossal--and for the time being the press force was going nowhere from dawn to dusk.

"I feel better about the cameras outside than ever before," Jane told Leila. "I think it makes things safer around here until this 'Odd Job' character is located---but only during the daylight hours. I insist you get a home security system that is fully activated at night. You need it now!"

"I am going to take your advice, although I never dreamed I would have to do such a thing here on Ebenezer Church Road.

After I testify Monday, I am returning to Aspen and you will have time to oversee the installation while I am away."

"Great," Jane agreed.

After a long pause Leila asked in a serious tone, "Jane what do you think the chances are that this 'Odd Job' character killed Josh Snyder?"

Jane thoughtfully answered, "Before, I suspected there was a chance Josh's disappearance was caused by someone--anyone--who wanted to hurt you--maybe 'Odd Job.' But with all we now know about him, I would say he is the prime suspect."

"I feel so terrible that Josh may have been killed by ANYONE wanting to kill me," Leila said as tears appeared on her face. "He was so young, such an innocent person to be a victim. I think of him and pray for him and his parents every night."

"Leila, for the time being, you need to be extremely cautious of your own safety while you are here-certainly until this madman is apprehended. Will you please take my advice?"

"Yes," Leila replied solemnly. "I have my shotgun and my pistol. I will try to be vigilant."

Chapter 49

"Odd Job" kicked open a dog pen gate and picked up a young male beagle by the neck. Its bark had been the most irritating of the pack. He began shouting to the other dogs in the pen as he squeezed the puppy's throat harder and harder.

"I told all you little bastards to shut up, but you didn't listen. So watch this!" He finished choking the puppy to death and slammed it to the concrete. He tried to kick another one, but missed. He would have tried again but saw an automobile approaching him from the direction of the lodge.

He quickly threw the dead puppy into a small shelter inside the pen and exited the gate to meet the driver.

The crew boss on the nearly-finished barn construction job parked his car and got out, asking, "Have you seen or talked to Jay? He was supposed to bring us the last paint we need and owes us some money."

"Haven't seen him."

"The front gate was open yesterday morning, and it was still open this morning. Something ain't right around here. Jay is not answering my phone calls." The crew boss was agitated.

"I don't go to the front gate—he probably had to go somewhere else," snarled "Odd Job."

"If he shows up, tell him I'll be back in the morning."

*****

"Odd Job" knew he was running out of time to grab his son Luke. He had watched all the television news and knew Leila was in town. He never considered she might not have Luke with her. He decided to go to her house that night and, if the opportunity presented itself, he would take what was his.

The last few minutes before dark he paddled crossed the river and walked quickly through the woods until he hit the church lane. He turned and walked all the way south until he could see the opening to Ebenezer Church Road. He backtracked about two hundred yards, and then walked due west until he saw the rear lights from Leila's home. By then it was too dark to see well. He sat on the ground, leaning against a large tree, to await daylight. When it began to break, he saw a downed treetop to his right he felt he could advance to without being seen. He relocated very cautiously.

He wore a green shirt and brown hat as camouflage and, from the new vantage point, could see Leila's entire rear home place very well. He had his pistol tucked into his belt and was ready to keep his promise to Luke.

Twenty minutes later, he saw Leila's back porch door open. He recognized her clearly as she stepped into her backyard. She walked directly into a small barn and soon came out with a bucket. Next she walked past a larger barn to an enclosure which he saw her enter to feed her raccoons. "Odd Job" thought he could see a metallic object holstered on her right hip. He was not sure. He would have to approach her across a large open area, and he did not think it gave him the opportunity he wanted. He seethed with frustration but had to wait.

Leila retraced her steps exactly, even replacing the bucket into the small barn. "Odd Job" noticed that the porch door had remained partially open the entire time. Every possible way to accomplish his goal was considered, until one emerged as the best. He sat there over an hour longer until an automobile approached down Ebenezer Church Road. He melted back into the underbrush and returned to Tomahawk Ranch to await the following morning.

*****

Back at the trailer "Odd Job" gathered everything he wanted to take with Luke and himself the next day and walked it all over to Jay's hidden vehicle. He could easily see how much of his cousin's blood had been left in the trunk. He went back to the dog pens and brought a pail of water to clean up the mess as best he could. The Remington rifle and boxes of ammunition stolen from "Big Fuzz's" lodge were wrapped together in a sheet and placed neatly on the back seat. "The pistol is all I will need to kill Leila," he thought.

Arriving back at his trailer, he saw a vehicle parked nearby. A man he did not recognize was sitting at the wheel and another was coming out of his quarters. All three men saw each other at about the same time. "Odd Job" stopped and asked the younger man on the stairway, "Can I help you?"

"We are looking for Jay Chidister--is he around?"

"Who is looking for him?"

The man seated in the vehicle stepped halfway out.

"My name is C.B. Rogers, and I own this place. Have you seen him?" "Big Fuzz" asked. He had already instructed the young man with him that any blowup with "Odd Job" should be avoided if at all possible.

"No, but the workers on your barn are looking for him, too."

"You must be his cousin, right? If you see him, have him give me a call. He has my number," "Big Fuzz" requested as the younger man went back to the vehicle to join him.

As they drove away "Big Fuzz" muttered, "That filthy cock-sucker!" He had already discovered that his rifle was missing and did not want a gunfight on his ranch, particularly while he was there. Jay never failed to return his phone calls, and he expected the worst for him.

Upon leaving his ranch, "Big Fuzz" immediately called and made an appointment with a contact in the mob "cleaning business" to eliminate "Odd Job" the next day.

Chapter 50

Leila had a rare day to herself, she thought, having no idea she had been watched that morning. Business took Jane to Atlanta, and she would not be back until the following afternoon. Other than the presence of a few news reporters across the street until mid-afternoon, Leila enjoyed the most time alone since adopting her two sons. It had been a wild journey since Mark had died less than six weeks before.

After feeding the animals and taking care of some household chores, she settled down into her favorite recliner on the back porch around four in the afternoon. She had turned off the television and computer and unplugged the telephone. It was time to reflect, organize her thoughts and priorities--and talk to Him. She shut her eyes.

Leila felt He had watched over her when she ventured out of the house shortly after dawn that morning. She vowed never to live in fear in her own home or in her beloved Ebenezer Forest.

She revisited the major events of her recent past. "Why would an all-knowing and loving God take the lives of people like Mark or Josh?" she very briefly asked herself before guilt for the thought set in. "I will not question my Creator and Saviour!" she resolved.

Years before, after a philosophy class at Florida State, she had decided not to waste her time seeking answers to life's greatest questions. She had accepted that they are unanswerable. If she were going to find answers to questions such as "What is the meaning of life?" it would be in her afterlife. "I am much too busy," she reminded herself.

She remembered a debate in that same class over whether people have to be able to answer the question "Who am I?" and be content with themselves before they can be happy. The other side of the issue was "Is the real key to happiness simply to help others?"

She decided back then that she was not going to concern herself about who she was, but would rather make sure who she was not.

She would never be ungrateful for everything she had. And she knew that after God took Mark, He had given her Luke and Jake. She would be forever grateful to Him. She would spend her life helping her sons, and others, to know and serve Him.

Life's most important philosophical question to Leila had consciously become, "What am I going to do today?" She recalled with a smile the morning she had decided to try to adopt Luke and Jake into her life. "God gave me the answer that day. It was the best decision I have ever made in my life and now the boys are mine."

She knew that her sons had soothed the pain of loss she had experienced before them, and they gave her life never-imagined meaning and love. Leila decided that without question she would sacrifice herself to protect their safety.

Chapter 51

Leila made another decision that afternoon. Although she was not anxious to direct her thoughts to the dangers that she and her sons were now exposed to, it was a necessity. She decided her sons should never be returned to Walton County until the dangers had been eliminated. She owed that precaution to them, and she owed them complete safety in Aspen. She felt that they were safe while with John and also while they were at Powder Mountain. But she would do whatever more was necessary to tighten their security.

She had worn a gun that morning and would continue to do so. "But I will never be chased off of my own property to the detriment of this estate my parents built or of my Ebenezer Forest," she pledged.

Her daily trip to Ebenezer Church had been almost discontinued. She told herself that if the reporters left early enough, she would make her special walk that afternoon.

"Everything has happened so fast," she lamented. "I know life is short, sweet, fleeting and oftentimes precarious, dear God, but please help us, particularly Luke and Jake, through this storm of danger."

*****

At 4:30 p.m. the news crews packed up and left Ebenezer Road. Leila immediately seized the opportunity to visit Ebenezer Church. She put on her walking shoes, strapped on the holstered pistol and hurried on her way. It was November, her favorite month of the year to walk. The smell of fall was always strongest at that time.

Only a little over an hour of light remained before dark, and she walked briskly until she reached Hominy Creek. She wanted to have ample time to enjoy her most treasured escape and place of worship. But in the bare dirt just before the wooden bridge, she noticed a set of large footprints going in both directions.

Upon closer inspection she could see that the top print was headed to the north, away from Ebenezer Road. It had not rained in a number of days, and it was too dry to really age the prints. She speculated that they could have been left by one of the many volunteers that searched her property looking for Josh. But in case she was wrong, she slowed down her pace and advanced more cautiously. The fact that she had to make the adjustment was disturbing, but she exercised the precaution nonetheless. Her mood was greatly improved when she finally rounded the curve that revealed her lifelong place of worship, shining with its full white splendor in the afternoon sun. Her first priority was to enter the church and pray, and she did for over ten minutes.

Finally back outside, Leila walked around to the crystalline, spring-fed pond nearby. It was bubbling and rippling up from its headwater as usual. It was still blue even as darkness approached. From the moment she decided to make the walk, she had felt a strong desire to ease herself into the clear, cool spring where she had been baptized as a young girl. It made her feel so clean and pure. But the water was just a little too chilly.

Instead she took off her shoes and removed the holster from her waist. Sitting on the baptism dock, she dangled her feet into the swirling, romantic pool. Soon her mind was drifting. She had intentionally put off thinking about John Gillespie in her morning reflections. Hoping she would have this late afternoon chance to visit her favorite sentimental place, she had saved her most intimate thoughts for him. She would not look to the spot where Mark once stood.

Sultry thoughts of arousal were now solely fixed on the long, gentle man from Arkansas. He had with little fanfare and much ease become her partner in every way--but one. "It all happened so quickly, like everything else in my recent life," she thought. "But nothing feels more natural."

She shut her eyes and recalled every detail of his smooth, handsome face. She visualized how his gorgeous, lean, naked body would look without his clothes. She leaned back flat upon the dock and imagined how he would feel atop her, and in her.

Her fantasies took over. Breathing much more heavily, while feeling moist, hot sensations down below, her mind quickly surrendered into a surreal state of explosive bliss. She soon climaxed into a cloud of sweet, quivering fulfillment.

*****

She did not move for nearly five minutes. Still flat on her back, her eyes shut, she savored every second of what she had just experienced. It had been shared with John Gillespie, even though he was over two thousand miles away. "I am in love with a man they call 'No Elk,'" she smiled to herself.

She put her shoes back on where she sat, and then reached over to begin re-strapping her holstered pistol to her waist. But she heard a rather loud cracking sound from about fifty yards away, toward the river. It was from an area of thick vegetation.

Whatever or whoever was coming her way was large and in a hurry.

Crash! Another broken limb snapped loudly as the approach continued.

Leila quickly hid behind a nearby tree that was not nearly large enough to conceal her, but there was no time to run.

Now within fifteen yards, the movement stopped. Had the church been seen—or had I? And then the charge continued straight toward her.

Finally bursting into the open churchyard, a huge, feral boar looked directly at Leila. He apparently felt he had met his match. He spun and escaped the way he had arrived.

Leila had not seen a wild hog in Ebenezer Forest in over five years. They were totally destructive to the trees and vegetation, and she hoped the visitor was not a sign of things to come.

It was almost dark and time for her to head home to check on her boys in Aspen.

Chapter 52

Leila woke up early the next day as usual and was soon on her back porch for coffee. She made an extra-large pot, expecting Amanda later in the morning. She looked out over the backyard very thoroughly as she sipped the dark brew. A smile came to her face as she thought about last night's call to Aspen. After a few minutes of conversation, John had said, "I have a surprise for you, dear." She had then heard, "Hello, mommy, I can talk!" It was little Jake again speaking, this time in a proud voice.

Leila was thrilled. "I am so proud of you, Jake. I love you so much."

"Hello, mommy, I can talk," he spoke again. He had it down pat.

Next, Luke was handed the phone. "When are you coming home, Momma?"

"Next Tuesday, Luke. I love you and miss you very much."

She recalled the last words John had spoken to her. "I cannot wait to hold you again, Leila--please be safe."

And knowing she wanted that more than anything, she strapped on her pistol before going out to feed the raccoons.

*****

The screen door shut itself, but the outside door was left half open. Leila went down the porch steps and walked casually over to the small barn to get a bucket of feed. Afterward she walked directly toward the raccoon pen, passing closely in front of the larger barn. As she reached the far corner, "Odd Job" savagely leaped at her from a hidden, crouched position.

"AAAGGHH," Leila gasped. But, coming from below, he powerfully forced both of her arms upward toward the sky. She had no opportunity at all to reach her pistol.

"AAAAAAAAAAAAAAA," she screamed as loudly as she could, but there was no one to hear her shriek.

In a flash he dropped his right arm and grabbed her pistol, stuffed it in his pocket and then used the same arm to compress her throat. She was unable to make a sound and could not breathe. He dragged her across the yard by her neck, as she hung in a motionless state of shock. "Odd Job" never said a word.

Once inside the house, he threw Leila down on the couch. She was heaving and struggling for air. "Odd Job" wanted to demobilize her but had nothing handy to use to tie her up. He grabbed and turned her head toward him. Then, WHOP, he hit her in the jaw with a violent blow from his closed fist. He stood above her and was satisfied that she would be unconscious for a good while. It was time to find Luke.

"Odd Job" hoped Luke was still asleep. He did not want his son to think he was a violent person. He eased through the main house quietly. When he had completed searching every room and found no Luke, he became very angry.

He quickly returned to what he surmised was Luke's bedroom He pillaged through the dresser drawers and went into the closet. He discovered a dirty clothes hamper, and in it were two sizes of garments. He assumed the larger ones belonged to his son. He picked those out to keep for Luke. He stood in the closet for a while, deeply sniffing each one of Luke's items. "I will have him, and I will have him soon," he thought. "That bitch will tell me where he is."

*****

"Odd Job" returned to the back porch where Leila remained motionless. He needed information from her before he killed her, but there was no point in torturing her until she regained her senses.

Seeing her purse was on the breakfast table, he went through its contents. Inside he found a picture of Luke. He sat down and stared at the photo. Soon he began to talk aloud. "I know you miss me, Luke. I'm coming for you. You know I am. Be strong. I promise--I'm coming."

Five minutes later, he decided it was time to see if he could wake Leila up. He opened the refrigerator door and removed a large pitcher of cold water. There was a dishrag nearby, and he carried both over to the couch. He splashed her face with a quarter of the pitcher's contents. There was no significant response. He noticed that even with the huge welt he had inflicted, she was an extremely pretty woman. "Then definitely a bitch," he thought.

He took the dishrag and placed it over the swollen side of her face. He did not want to have to look at the damage he had caused.

*****

At the same time, Leila was hoping "Odd Job" did not open her eyes with his fingertips. She knew that because she was still alive he had more in store for her. Fully aware that she was half-dazed and likely about to meet her Maker, she needed time to think. And she was having trouble doing it.

Chapter 53

"Odd Job" had never considered that Luke would not be at Leila's home. He had no alternative than to force whatever he could out of her. In his mind he had promised Luke for several years, "I will be coming to git you." He stared at Leila knowing she was his only link to his son, and she was still out cold. He had no other option but to stay put.

Leila, feigning unconsciousness, remembered a woman in Atlanta a number of years ago who had saved herself by talking with her captor about God. Leila concluded that it was her best course of action. She trusted her Lord completely. If she were going to die, she hoped He would forgive her for what she was about to do.

All at one time, she turned her head toward "Odd Job," opened her eyes and said, "You must be Luke's daddy." And before he could respond, added, "I have been praying to find you. Luke asks about you every day."

"He does? Where is Luke?" He barked loudly, totally surprised by her sudden awakening.

"God told me that a man and his son should be together, and he also told me to make sure that YOU get Luke. I am going to do just that."

"Where is my boy?" He demanded in an even louder and angrier voice.

"He is at a police facility that keeps young boys, but I can pick him up anytime I want. But he wants YOU, and I can help YOU get him. I want him to be happy, and he will only be happy with you."

"Don't lie to me you—," he started to curse Leila, but stopped himself. He knew Luke wanted to be with him. "I should not trust this bitch--but I need to use her," he thought.

"Please forgive me for keeping Luke away from you for as long as I have," Leila began. "God tells us we should forgive each other. So please forgive me for that, and I will forgive you for striking me."

"Why should I believe you will help me get Luke?" he asked, still having trouble thinking of anything else he could do but use her.

"Two reasons," Leila replied quickly. "It would be a stupid woman who would try to keep a boy that only wants to be with his daddy. And this is the most important reason for me. I pray to God every night, and like I said before, He told me that Luke should be with you."

There was no reply from "Odd Job." He weighed his choices-- he could torture her, but she had already told him where Luke was. Or he could kill her and lose his last chance to get his son. He was torn with deciding what he should do.

Sensing his indecision, Leila knew she could be murdered at any moment. "Odd Job" was an unhesitant killer, and Amanda was expected to show up soon. She had to do something fast.

She could smell the coffee and knew it would be scorching hot by now. She considered it as a possible weapon and interrupted the silence to try a different ruse.

"Would you like for me to get Luke on the phone?" She didn't know if she would have the opportunity to grab the coffee pot. If not, she could buy a little time by calling Jane's phone number to let her knew she was in trouble.

"Odd Job" still refused to trust Leila but desperately wanted to talk with his son. "Yes, I would like to talk to Luke," spoke "Odd Job" calmly. It was something he certainly wanted to do, whether he killed her or not.

Leila sat up on the couch and realized she was still weak-kneed and unsteady. She rose and walked very slowly toward the table area with "Odd Job" following closely, within arm's reach.

The telephone was on the far side of the table, and she had to first pass the stove top and coffee pot, both on her right. She could see her purse on the table to the left--its contents had been strewn about the table. And she saw that "Odd Job" had left her pistol on the far side of the table. She stopped once, as though she were losing strength.

When she stopped the second time, she was right in front of the coffee pot.

"I am feeling dizzy," she said aloud, as she fake stumbled to her right, shielding "Odd Job's" view of the coffee pot. She flicked the top off and quickly grabbed the handle. Whirling around in high speed, she threw the entire scalding contents at "Odd Job's" face.

"YOU LYING WHORE," "Odd Job" screamed as he raised both hands quickly to his eyes in severe pain.

When he realized Leila was scrambling around the table toward her pistol, he dug into his right rear pocket for his own.

Leila fell halfway to the ground in her frenzied dash. Scrambling to her feet, she reached her weapon at about the exact same time that "Odd Job" raised his to fire.

They were less than eight feet from each other. BAM! BAM! Two shots were fired milliseconds apart. "Odd Job" had shot first. In his haste, and with burned eyes and face, his bullets passed within inches to the right of Leila's head.

BAM! Leila's shot struck "Odd Job" in his upper belly.

"AAWW, YOU CUNT," he yelled. He had dropped his gun. then bent over to pick it up.

As he raised himself with the gun again in his hand--BAM! Leila shot him a second time in his mid-body.

"AAAAAAAAAAWWWWWWWWWW," he moaned loudly, stumbling halfway to his feet, but again dropping his weapon.

Crouching and holding his belly, he charged around the table toward Leila like a wild beast in a bellowing rage. "AAAAAAAAAAWWWWWWWWWW!"

When he was within four feet of where she stood, Leila extended her arm straight out toward him and fired. BAM! BAM! BAM! BAM! She had emptied her gun with four shots to his upper chest. He crashed to the floor.

"Odd Job" would never kill again.

Chapter 54

Shaking and numbed by the violence she had survived, Leila fell to the porch floor, sobbing and thanking God she was still alive. She could see the pool of blood forming on the floor around "Odd Job's" body. She did not have the strength to move.

Eventually she heard a loud rapping coming from the front of her house. She was still afraid and realized she was out of bullets. She rose and circled the table counter-clockwise until she saw "Odd Job's" pistol on the floor. She picked it up and waited silently.

Minutes later, Amanda appeared at the back porch door. When Leila saw her best friend, she walked slowly toward her with "Odd Job's" gun still in her hand.

Amanda was startled at what she saw. "What are you doing with that gun, baby?" And then she saw the motionless body, face down on the bloody floor.

"OH, GGGGGOOOOODDDDDDD," she screamed. And seeing Leila's face, "OOOOOHHH, THAT DIRTY BASTARD BEAT YOU!" Ananda cried. "I'M GLAD YOU KILLED THAT FILTHY SON-OF-A-BITCH!"

She was immediately gasping and could hardly breathe. She grabbed her chest and began to stagger.

"Calm down Amanda. Please sit over here and let me get you some water," Leila said softly. "You are going to be okay, honey. It is over."

*****

Leila called the sheriff's office, identified herself and calmly told the operator, "I shot a man, but don't think you need to call an ambulance. I am certain he is dead."

She had already noted to herself that Amanda was doing better after drinking the water and did not need an ambulance either. She left a message on Jane's phone, "I just killed 'Odd Job.' Please come to my house as soon as you can. Thank you, Jane."

Her last call was to John. She calmly told him what had happened. "Do you want me to come there right now?" He asked, obviously upset.

"No, please stay with the boys—I know they are safe with you."

"Please let me know everything that is happening as soon as you can, Leila. I am so glad you are safe."

"I will, John."

"Will you promise not to keep anything from me," he asked.

"I promise."

*****

The press corps arrived at Ebenezer Road before The Walton County Sheriff's office could respond to Leila's phone call. The crews had no idea what was going on inside Leila's house as they set up their equipment and commenced their vigil.

Photos of Leila and her sons were in ultra-high demand since Leila was brazenly attacked in Pensacola. They were bringing astronomical sums to appease a curious and adoring public that was totally fixed and spellbound on what seemed to be an endless chain of events. The unknowing media was poised to capture another enormous episode.

When sirens could be heard racing toward their location, the cameramen and reporters perked up. The law officers exited their vehicles with drawn guns and surrounded Leila's home. Soon several deputies entered through the rear porch door. Twenty minutes later, one of the officers came out and released the startling news that immediately again made Leila the number one story in America and beyond.

LEILA JANE HEWITT KILLS ANOTHER ATTACKER IN HER HOME!

SERIAL KILLER NO MATCH FOR LEILA HEWITT!

LEGENDARY LEILA LIVES ON!

Other similar headlines immediately mesmerized a world of admirers.

Before "Odd Job's" body was removed from the house, over twenty different news services had arrived at the scene. Two helicopters landed on Ebenezer Road, and pictures were being taken from the air by other aircraft.

The Walton County Sheriff's office was considerate enough to the press to delay the removal of "Odd Job's" body from Leila's home, then later to push his body out near the road without a sheet. Everyone present, and the millions of viewers from around the world who later watched footage of the spectacle, agreed that, even dead, he was "one mean-looking bastard."

*****

In the hours and days that followed, Rufus "Odd Job" Jenkins would be revealed as the killer of Pearlie Towns, attorney James Watson and likely Josh Snyder. But no connection would ever be made between him and the disappearance of his cousin, Jay Chidister. It was simply a family matter that never made the news.

Inside her house, Leila would not discuss any part of how she was able to get the upper hand on "Odd Job" Jenkins. She was not proud of lying to "Odd Job" about God, and under no circumstances was she going to sensationalize that she had misrepresented her Saviour to save her own life. She felt it was a personal matter between herself and God, and there would be no exceptions made. "The Heroine of Ebenezer Forest" wanted no part of any fame or further interruption in the private life she had always cherished.

"He dragged me into my house and hit me in the face. I shot him six times in self-defense," was her simple representation of the facts, and she was sticking to it.

Leila was led out of her home with her face shielded from the press. She was taken to Sacred Lady Hospital in South Walton, where her jaw was x-rayed. One bone was slightly cracked, but surgery did not appear appropriate at the time. She was driven to Amanda's house where she would stay for the next two nights.

With this new act of slaying and survival added to her resume, Leila's universal stardom was now beyond epic. A beautiful woman fending off three separate attackers, ending in the death of each, would never be matched. It might be found somewhere in fiction, but never in real life.

Almost to Aspen

Chapter 55

With Billy Munsey serving as the acting sheriff in Walton County, there was no further criminal investigation whatsoever after the death of "Odd Job" Jenkins. How he had arrived in the back yard of Leila Hewitt was of no moment to Munsey. Under no circumstances would his friend "Big Fuzz's" ranch across the Choctawhatchee River ever be considered as a possible point of embarkation. "Big Fuzz" owned Munsey like a sack of chicken manure and would similarly own his successor--if Tall Tom Hopkins won the coming election.

Leila had saved the evil "Big Fuzz" Rogers' gang some money by killing "Odd Job," but Rogers was an absolute ingrate--without even a tiny morsel of appreciation. Completely embarrassed that an almost fifty-seven-year-old-woman was repeatedly making him look like an inept mobster, Rogers didn't look forward to a previously scheduled breakfast with ex-Colonel Max Barnett and Doctor Ty Tyson. He met them at a Niceville coffee shop to discuss the latest fiasco.

After the preliminary greetings and a brief discussion of "Odd Job's" debacle, the conversation quickly got down to the real stick in their craw. "Boys, Leila Hewitt has dodged another bullet,'"Big Fuzz" began. "We are losing the respect of our peers and it is beginning to really chap my ass."

"I thought you were going to do something about it," replied Doctor Tyson

"Jay Chidister was going to take care of it, but 'Odd Job' killed him before he got his own butt killed by Leila Hewitt," continued "Big Fuzz."

Doctor Tyson interrupted, "I don't give a rat's ass about 'a greater risk' or whether it is a 'dumb thing' or not. With all the time I have facing me, I do not want to go to trial in Pensacola and have Leila Hewitt add ten years to my sentence. Are you going to have the bitch killed or not?"

"I talked to our pals in Tallahassee yesterday afternoon, and they said everyone up there knows if you had kept your dick in your pants we would all be better off," shot back "Big Fuzz."

"Hey, hey, hold on guys," said Max Barnett. "Let's not fight with each other."

"The whole gang is starting to wonder that maybe we should not be the distribution center if we cannot knock off one little ole lady," replied Dr. Tyson.

"The real fact is that Mobile has been trying to steal our action for years. They are the ones stirring the whole damn pot and using this Leila mess to try to make us look like a bunch of clowns," opined Barnett.

"Hopefully it is not as bad as it looks," said "Big Fuzz." "We have a couple of quiet little towns with our own cops and charter boats. We just need to go ahead and take care of our problem, and everything will be fine."

"For you, not us, 'Fuzz,'" snarled Dr. Tyson.

"I will take care of it today," "Big Fuzz" assured.

"Am I getting dementia, or have we been here before?" asked Dr. Tyson.

"Fuck you, Doc," snapped "Big Fuzz" in an aggravated tone. "Don't worry, that lucky, friggin' broad will soon be dead."

Chapter 56

Learning that Leila had a cracked bone in her jaw and was suffering from temporary facial disfiguration, prosecutors in Pensacola canceled her upcoming Grand Jury appearance without scheduling a new date. Leila needed the time to recover from the trauma of the last ten days.

Her greatest desire was to leave immediately for Aspen to rejoin her sons and John. But after looking at her swollen and bruised face the following morning, she decided that she did not want any of them, or anyone else, to see her until she made some substantial improvement.

However, she was not the only one that had been looking at her injuries. A nurse at the hospital had taken a picture of her in the emergency room. She had sold it to National & Global Magazine for worldwide distribution. The buyer then commenced to resell the photo to every other news outlet willing to pay the exorbitant price. Leila certainly did not appreciate that her brutalized and distorted appearance was being universally presented alongside her normal appearance for contrasting effect and shock value. It was of little solace for her to be later called by an apologetic hospital executive to inform her that the employee had been terminated.

Meanwhile, Jane was at Leila's home dealing with worldwide messages and offers that were pouring in at a pace she alone could not handle. Within twenty-four hours, she reported there were five different calls, mostly from California production companies, that had made initial verbal offers of over ten million dollars if Leila would afford them exclusive movie rights to her life.

One opportunistic Rosemary Beach builder and entrepreneur had asked Jane to relay that he would build Leila "a million dollar home" in Ebenezer Forest if she would allow his wife to afterwards conduct tours and sell memorabilia at her estate. He added he would donate a percentage of the sales to her forest operation. When Leila informed Amanda of this offer, her friend commented in her familiar, suspicious way, "This offer was probably the builder's girlfriend's idea, just to get his wife out of town."

Leila was somewhat annoyed when Jane asked if she would allow an exclusive interview with Rhonda Riveras. But after reflecting on the request and realizing that the women were longtime friends, she decided to dismiss her original reaction. As was the case in past incidents, Leila never gave an interview about her showdown with "Odd Job" Jenkins.

*****

The reaction in Aspen to Leila's latest heroic feat and enhanced acclaim was what would normally be expected for only a hometown hero. Everyone in town was fully aware that she had spent a significant amount of her time in their city since she had shot and killed the first two of her would-be killers.

This quaint, world famous resort in Pitkin Valley had been exposed to countless numbers of movie stars and worldwide celebrities for years. But Aspenites had seen more than enough of Leila Jane Hewitt to observe that she was a very special lady. Every single person who had encountered her in Pitkin Valley shared with their friends that not only was she beautiful and classy but also possessed a genuine and loving spirit.

It had not gone without notice that their well-recognized visitor from Florida, known as extremely religious before ever taking her first step in Colorado, had arrived as a guest of Powder White but was now involved with one of his best friends, John "No Elk" Gillespie. Powder was well liked and respected around town as a generous and fun-loving member of the community. But in Aspen, John was a rock, a respected man of God, trust and character. His and Leila's apparent interest in each other was well received.

When Leila was in Florida, John had been observed escorting Luke and Jake around town. Everyone recognized that he seemed happier than usual. When the news of Leila's new escape and survival jolted Aspen, the entire community was in an immediate celebratory mood. Leila and her sons were the new pride of Aspen and enjoyed the goodwill of all.

*****

John was not to be seen in Aspen the evening the news broke, but Powder shared his elation over Leila's escape as publicly as he could. Whether he was cutting his losses for not attracting the affection from Leila that he had originally sought or simply genuinely happy made no difference. There were free drinks for all that night at Jim's Restaurant & Bar. Everyone in the establishment knew that Luke and Jake were still staying at Powder Mountain for safety reasons whenever Leila was in town, and Powder was extremely proud of that fact.

Powder even took the occasion to announce "Ebenezer Forest in Aspen" was a done deal and construction would begin in the coming spring.

"John 'No Elk' Gillespie has agreed to be our manager, and we cannot wait to bring this new attraction to the city we love, ASPEN, COLORADO!" He shouted to the delight of everyone in attendance.

Even Mike "Ace" Tingle, seated alone in a far corner of the bar was pleased by the announcement and also appreciated his free drinks. He wondered if "Big Fuzz," down in Destin, might be more likely now to pay him the fee he had quoted to dispatch Leila. "I hope so," he mused to himself. "It ain't cheap, living up here in Aspen."

Chapter 57

Attorney Rusty Lucas called Leila the day after her shooting of "Odd Job" supposedly to check on her condition and to offer any help that he could. He learned, more importantly, that her Grand Jury appearance had been passed without date and that within the next few days she would rejoin her sons in Aspen for several weeks. He obtained the telephone number from Leila of the investigator who was inquiring into the adoption he was handling and assured her he would give the woman a call so that Leila and the boys would not be subjected to a mandatory early return from Aspen. "I want to help you any way that I can," he assured before he ended the call.

Next, Lucas called "Big Fuzz."

"Hey, Rusty, what's up?"

"Just a quick call to let you know that Leila will be in Aspen no later than this coming Monday, with plans to stay for several weeks."

"Is she going to be staying at that same location you already gave me?" asked "Big Fuzz."

"That is the only address she has ever given me."

"Thanks, buddy, I owe you."

"Just invite me on your pussy boat the next time it goes out."

"You got it, podna. See ya."

The entire conversation was intercepted by an employee of the Federal Bureau of Investigation as part of an order authorized by a federal judge in Pensacola. All phone calls from the law office of Rusty Lucas, including his preceding talk with Leila Hewitt, were being wiretapped as a result of his relationship with four other attorneys in the Florida Panhandle. They were all being investigated for money laundering huge amounts of funds being accumulated by Southern mobsters. The F. B. I. was investigating drugs, illegal alien smuggling and numerous other related crimes including murder which were running rampant along the Gulf coast.

A special officer of the court had been appointed to weed out from prosecutors' view any non-related phone calls that might be protected by attorney-client privileges. And for this last reason, the implications and gravity of the call between Attorney Rusty Lucas and "Big Fuzz" would not be realized until it was too late to avoid what would follow.

*****

Later in the day, "Big Fuzz" contacted Mike "Ace" Tingle in Aspen.

"I was kind of expecting your call," jabbed "Ace."

"Don't get excited--I am not going to let you hike up your fee," replied "Big Fuzz."

"Ain't going down either," he replied.

"You have a deal. And it looks like you are going to have at least a two-week window. And if I were you, I'd assume it is no more than two weeks. I made this call with a throw-away cell phone. When the job is done, call this number back and say, 'the snow is good up here--when are you coming skiing?' Don't say another word. Your money will be delivered to you within a week."

"Don't forget, it's 250 G," replied "Ace."

"YOU don't forget this 'Ace'--you are not targeting some dumb ass dope dealer. Take your time, and don't fuck this up."

"You mean like you guys in Florida have done down there? Don't worry about a thing, 'Big Fuzz'! You are dealing with the 'ACE'!"

Chapter 58

With the Pensacola Grand Jury appearance canceled, Leila returned to Aspen. Her cheek was still discolored from "Odd Job's" punch, but less swollen. She had not wanted her sons to see her in this condition, but yielded to her desire to return to them and John as soon as possible. She would be arriving well after dark, having chosen the previously used commercial flight rather than again imposing herself on Powder. She would regret her decision.

Amanda drove Leila to the Panama City Beach airport. She was recognized by many fellow passengers at the check-in counter and was later besieged for signatures while waiting for her boarding call. The pilot welcomed her on the intercom system shortly after take-off. Arriving for her connecting flight in Dallas, she was greeted with applause by awaiting airline and airport employees, followed by even more fanfare from fellow travelers. It was one of the most miserable experiences of her life, but there was some relief when she was offered an empty first-class seat into Aspen. She was finally able, on this last leg of the trip, to enjoy some brief time for herself.

Leila had total confidence that her sons were being well cared for by John, and this quiet man from Arkansas commanded her thoughts as she rested.

Mark had died on October the 7th, and it was only the 20th day of November. Within that period, she had known John Gillespie for only one month. "Ten days in Aspen, and I was toast," she laughed at herself. She went over and over every possible explanation of how she had fallen for this attractive man. Not one of her explanations could pass any cautious person's usual test of time.

"I have lived most of my life without a man--I never needed one until John," she thought. Recalling that as a young college girl she had decided to adopt as her criteria for a mate what a poetry professor at Florida State said every good poem should have—wholeness, harmony and radiance. That would be the standard she would seek in any relationship. "But John has one more quality I have been foolish to overlook in the past," she realized to herself. "I could see it in his eyes the first moment I met him, and I realize it more every day. His spirituality with God is what we share. Everything begins with God, not ourselves. This is our true, loving connection."

*****

Luke, Jake and John were anxiously waiting for Leila at Sardy Field. Leila hugged and kissed them all.

"What happened to your face, Mommy?" Luke asked concernedly as Leila bent to kiss him.

"Just a bruise that will go away," she assured.

"Did somebody hit you?" he asked

Leila was surprised by the question, and she answered with the only thing she could think of to say, "Why would you think that, son?"

"Our last mommy told me that a mean, fat man used to hit her in the face all the time--and that he was coming back--and that is why we were going to get a new mommy," he disclosed.

Leila was stunned. She paused. "There will never be any other mean men in your life, Luke. You don't have to worry about that ever again. I will always be your mother."

"Good, Mommy. I am so glad you are back home with us."

*****

Later that night John embraced Leila and told her how thankful he was that had she survived her ordeal. He did not ask about details of the horrible event, choosing rather to hold her lovingly in his arms, saying he had prayed for her safe return from the moment she had left.

She told him how much she appreciated his help with the boys, particularly with helping Jake to begin to speak. He looked directly into Leila's eyes and responded, "They have done more for me than I have for them. I always wanted to have children of my own, but it never happened. Being around them has added meaning to my life--and you are the center of it."

Leila was touched and threw her arms around his neck. They kissed each other passionately, deeply inhaling each other's hot breath.

"I crave your taste," he whispered as his tongue eased into her mouth. She sucked it gently and could not suppress a gentle moan. Then she sucked it harder.

She felt her body weakening, and she could smell his masculine scent. It was earthy and aromatic like the northern woods she had recently experienced. She knew he would respect her values, but she wanted to show her intense feelings. She began to kiss his ears, and then his neck. She opened his shirt and sucked his nipples. He too began to moan. His response excited her more. She could feel her growing wetness.

She kissed him even lower, and she could see his enlarged manhood fighting the restraint of his britches. She did not want to unfairly tease him, and reversed direction.

Wanting to share, she gently took hold of his large hand and moved it to her breasts. Her nipples were hard and protruding. She leaned back to let him tease each one, which he did in a slow circular motion inside her winter blouse. "I would never have done this six months ago," she fully realized.

John assessed the situation precisely and guided Leila's head back to rest on his shoulder. "Who is torturing whom?" He asked playfully.

Leila laughed. "You are one smart man, John Gillespie." she began. "I am not very experienced at this, but I know when I am being tortured," she said in silly voice.

"I raised the first flag," he replied tongue-in-cheek. They both laughed.

"I have something serious to say," Leila said in a thoughtful tone.

"Okay," he replied.

"Do you remember the other day when I called to tell you about the shooting?

"Yes.

"You asked me to promise not to keep anything from you--do you remember?"

"I remember."

"John, I take my promises very seriously.   And there is something you need to know."

"Do I need to lie down," he asked.

"Maybe," she answered.

John did not know what to think. Leila seemed sincere.

"I'm ready," he said.

"I don't want to keep this from you." She paused. "I have thought about this and want you to know that--I just want to keep my promise—and you do not owe me a response in any way."

John was more than ready to hear what she did not want to keep from him.

"John-------'No Elk'-------Gillespie-------I am so much in love with you!"

John did not expect what Leila confessed. He reached and took Leila into his arms and kissed her with all of the zest in his body that he could deliver without harm. He pulled away to look deeply and lovingly into her blue eyes and then kissed her again--again--and again.

When he finally stopped, with tears of joy streaming down his face, he spoke the most sensuous and sincere admission she could have ever prayed for.

"Leila--------Jane-------Hewitt, I love YOU with all of my hear!"

Chapter 59

With all of the attention Leila and her family were receiving, John's townhouse on Durant Street in a crowded area of Aspen afforded little privacy or security to Leila and her family. Powder was aware of this and continued to be extremely gracious in making the elaborate guest suite available to Leila. John dropped her and the boys off at Powder Mountain on Tuesday morning, where they would stay for the remainder of the trip. The gated compound took care of most of their major safety concerns.

Before John left he requested that Leila, Powder and he have a brief talk to discuss another aspect of the security situation. His primary concern was not about the lodge, but about Leila and her sons moving about in the Aspen area. It was very obvious from the attention they had received at her airport arrival the night before and at breakfast that Leila and her sons were significantly more celebrated than ever.

After Luke and Jake were settled in the suite, Leila joined John and her host in his kitchen.

"Powder, I want to thank you again for your kind hospitality. Ebenezer Road was bedlam when I left--I had to stay with Amanda and her husband."

"Hopefully, all of that is behind you now. That pretty face of yours is looking a whole lot better this morning than what I saw in the papers. It will not be long before you are completely back to your usual beautiful self," Powder observed.

"Thank you, but it is still quite sore," replied Leila.

"And John," Powder began, "when I told the crowd at Jim's Restaurant the other night you had agreed to manage 'Ebenezer Forest in Aspen,' they were absolutely elated. I have the first appointment with a landscape architect at the end of next week, and I hope you can join me."

"I will, Powder," he replied. "What I wanted to talk with you both about this morning is Leila and the boys traveling around Pitkin Valley without a bodyguard. Now that she is going to be here for at least several weeks, it needs to be discussed. I will be available much of the time. But I do not think it is safe, Leila, for you to leave Powder Mountain without Powder, a bodyguard or me."

"Leila, do you think there is really any danger in you and the boys moving around the valley? What is the real likelihood of those Panhandle gangsters actually trying to hurt you up here in Aspen?" asked Powder.

"I never thought any of the things that have happened to me in the last couple of months would ever have occurred," she replied. "I can't really answer that question, Powder."

"From the celebrity side of this issue alone, I say again you need to have one of us or a bodyguard with you and the boys at all times," said John more emphatically. "I have a trusted friend that is willing to be on call whenever you need him, if you will agree to use him. And I will gladly cover the expense."

"If you think this is necessary, John, I will certainly agree to use your friend. It is probably the smart thing, but I do insist on paying him," Leila replied.

"We can argue about that later," answered John, relieved that she had taken his advice. "I will have my friend, Jim Anders, contact you this afternoon with his phone number."

"Before we break this meeting up, Leila, I have a favor to ask of you," Powder said.

"I will be happy to help you if I can."

"Everywhere I go around here, locals are very excited about 'Ebenezer Forest in Aspen.' Many of the elected officials and business owners are offering to help our project in any way. Everyone feels it can be a real boost to the local economy, particularly in the summer months. Most of the leaders of the community have not met you, Leila, and they would love to have the opportunity. I thought it would be nice to give them that chance by having a private welcoming party in your honor. We could have it here at my place."

"I'm not that much into parties," Leila began. "But you have been so wonderful to me, I guess it would be all right--if I don't have to make a big speech."

"All you have to do, Leila, is just be yourself--and they will love you."

"May I come?" asked John.

"May YOU come?" laughed Powder loudly. "Of course, but you DO have to make a speech--just a short one--about our project."

"I don't know how you are going to go about it," Leila began, "but could you please ask that the guests not question me about what happened back home last week? Even thinking of it is very disturbing to me. I am afraid I could get upset again if I had to answer a bunch of questions."

"I will take care of that. Please don't worry, Leila, I will know every person in attendance. There probably won't be more than a hundred people invited."

Leila looked at John, and he could tell from her expression that the number startled her.

"She would be free to excuse herself if the party became too much for her, or ran too late--wouldn't she?" inquired John.

"I'll have a baby sitter for the boys during the party. Leila can check on them from time to time, call it a night if she gets too tired or just go back and forth to the suite for an occasional shot of fresh air."

"When are you thinking of having the party?" Asked Leila.

"With Thanksgiving in two days, and all of the slopes opening this weekend--how about a week from tonight, next Tuesday night? Does that sound good?"

"Yes," Leila replied.

"We are headed up to my hunting camp to get ready for a Thanksgiving feast. Are you going to be able to join us?' John asked Powder.

"I'm flying up tomorrow to share Thanksgiving with my relatives in Wyoming like I always do and will be back Friday morning. But thank you very much for the invitation."

*****

When the talk ended and Leila had left to check on the boys, John began, "There is another topic I would like to discuss with you, Powder. I didn't want to bring it up in front of Leila."

"Sure, what is it?

"It concerns an extra precaution. It is something that we'll have to discuss with the landscape architect anyway. I am talking about your perimeter fencing.

"The front fence along Castle Creek Road looks like it is in great shape from a security standpoint. But I noticed on the east side of your estate, the fence runs up the hill as far as I could see. How far does it actually extend?"

"Less than two hundred yards on the east side," replied Powder.

"There is no fence at all on the west end of your property?"

"You are correct--there is no fence on the west end or the north side--with it being so steep."

"Would you mind if I initiate some periodic reconnaissance around the perimeter of your property, just as another precautionary measure?"

"Heck no! As a matter of fact, that is a good idea. I would appreciate it, John. I sometimes worry myself about getting robbed. Please let me know if you uncover anything suspicious."

"I will," replied John. "Let's keep this to ourselves. I don't want Leila living in fear.

"Absolutely, I understand."

Chapter 60

Professional assassins enjoy one of the best paid occupations, but believe they do not get the public recognition they deserve. They understand that comes with the job. And hit men prefer high-end addresses. Thus, average middle class people are not likely to have a top-of-the-line killer as their neighbor. High priced neighborhoods in Las Vegas, Miami and Aspen are among their main choices of location.

Rarely do they execute a victim anywhere near the town where they live. Most of their targets live in distant, larger cities. The chance of a professional executioner being caught in a preplanned murder of someone he has no connection with is less than five percent.

Mike "Ace" Tingle made exceptions by agreeing to eliminate Leila Hewitt. Not only was she to be "taken out" near where he lived, but she didn't conform to the usual profile of his quarry. His specialty was the elimination of drug dealers involved in territorial disputes. They hung out in strip joints, road houses and other places easy to access. With Leila staying as a guest behind a private gate on a road with only one way in and out, the job presented a greater challenge.

He considered stationing himself for a couple of days at the loop at the beginning of Castle Creek Road to determine if there was any predictable pattern of her coming and going from Powder's lodge. He knew he could recognize Leila from photos, but did not know if she would be changing vehicles. He decided the idea was fraught with too many potential issues that could either waste valuable time or expose him to unwanted attention.

Ultimately he concluded after careful viewing of Powder Mountain on Google Earth that the lodge was vulnerable to an approach by foot from the western side. There was one problem. His automobile could not be left anywhere down Castle Creek Road during his attack without attracting unacceptable suspicion. He noted there was a difficult, mountainous escape route available by foot to the northeast if necessary. He decided to make a final test run to the "kill site" on a bicycle to fully assess the area.

He needed to determine the best wooded entry point to Powder's estate and to find a suitable place to hide a make-shift cache for the needed items. Later he would have to return by car to construct the hiding place and make sure it was well camouflaged. Another trip to the area would also be by automobile to actually stash away everything required for his assignment.

"Ace" would use a hand-gun, rifle and a number of other accessories, including goggles and binoculars, both of the night-vision variety. None of the necessities could be carried to the site on a bike as they were too cumbersome. His weapons and everything else to be used on the mission were all altered to be made untraceable and would be left behind after the attack. He would wash his hands in the snow and change his shirt and gloves after shooting Leila to eliminate any residual forensic evidence.

He was ready to make his trial run to Powder Mountain. The after-dark trip was a distance of about ten miles from his home in Aspen. "Ace" chose to take with him only his night-vision equipment—no weapons. He knew he could get near the lodge and needed a close view to determine if he could shoot Leila from afar or would have to storm her quarters. He figured if "Big Fuzz" was right about her arrival, Leila would be on the premises by Tuesday night.

The bicycle ride took approximately an hour. Traveling almost a mile past Powder's estate, he took a right turn to the north on a gravel lane. He put on a ski mask to conceal his face. The road was steeply inclined, and "Ace" had to push the bike uphill approximately 400 yards to reach a point he estimated to be at an elevation slightly above Powder's lodge. He looked for cameras on the way up the road and would continue to do so at all times he was in the area. If he found any, he planned to steal them.

The incline had no sign of recent use, which was good news. "Ace" carefully hid the bike about twenty-five feet off the lane. He used a very small flashlight and encountered little trouble walking through shallow snow. Within ten minutes, first illuminations from the lodge could be seen flickering through the aspens and conifers. He turned off his light and strapped the night vision goggles to his forehead. They provided a very clear image of what lay before him.

He walked slowly, with occasional stops. No motion of any kind was detected on the mountainside as he approached the rear of the lodge. Multiple lights were on inside the structure and spotlights were evident on all four corners. The result was that for over a hundred feet the yard was well lit.

The building was not built in a simple rectangular shape. Raised extensions, approximately three feet off the ground, protruded from the two rear corners and appeared to be separate living quarters. The first corner unit had closed drapes, and it was obvious that there were lights on inside.

The far corner was occupied, and the drapes were wide open. "Ace" continued his approach until he was only 125 yards straight uphill from the second corner of the lodge.

He removed his goggles and focused his super-powerful binoculars. Two young boys were sitting on the floor watching television, eating popcorn out of a bag. He could easily discern that they were watching SpongeBob Square Pants.

Suddenly, out of the bathroom into his clear vision, appeared Leila. He recognized her immediately, yet she appeared much younger and more attractive than he had expected. He was dazed by her slender, sexy figure with perfectly-shaped buttocks and breasts. Her long, shapely legs and blonde hair made him hope she would not draw the curtains soon. He watched her walk about the room gracefully and with an air that moved him, as it had many others before.

He reflected on the three men he knew she had killed, knowing full well that he actually admired her courage and heart. "She would make a world class assassin," he thought in a way that only people like he would think.

Still benumbed by his voyeurism, he realized that she was approaching the glass doors. She slid one side open and walked out onto the porch.

"She is looking directly at me"--he was sure.

He dared not move a muscle. His binoculars were pointed squarely at her face, and he could see deeply into her ultra-light, blue eyes. "She is looking at a reflection off my lenses," he seriously believed.

He could see, almost touch, her thick blonde hair and moist, full lips. He was breathing heavily.

On the porch, Leila began to deeply inhale. She held the cold, mountainous air in her chest for a few seconds, and then she exhaled it as warm mist into the evening air. She repeated the process again and again. He could easily see her swelled nipples through her shirt. He was entranced.

Soon, one of the boys called from inside and Leila returned inside, shutting the glass behind her.

"Ace" stayed where he was until Leila closed the drapery almost two hours later. He watched her every move the entire time. When she occasionally left the room, he could hardly wait until she returned.

"She is a national legend, and one of the most attractive women I have ever seen," he admitted to himself. He had killed women before, but never one like her. "I really hate to kill her-- particularly because no one will know it was me," he thought in evil, warped sorrow.

Chapter 61

"Ace" felt comfortable that he had identified the easiest access to the rear of Powder's lodge. However, after the test run from the night before, he realized it would take too much time to backtrack to the gravel road, hide his weapons in the cache, clean up and then peddle past the front of Powder's estate as he returned to Aspen. Although he did not believe there would be a quick law enforcement response to his attack, his getting stopped for questioning was a possibility.

After more thought, he decided that same night to hire a reliable friend he had worked with before to be his driver on the designated night. He called and made the hire. The friend would wait for "Ace's" call after the shooting, behind an abandoned house on a side road less than two miles away from the chosen corner of Castle Creek Road and the gravel lane. His friend owed him a favor, but "Ace" still agreed to pay a $10,000 bonus.

Everything else would continue as planned. On his trial run "Ace" had observed a downed tree wedged against a large rock conveniently close to his access point. The location would serve as the ideal place for his cache. It would be safely out of sight from the gravel road.

He had already constructed a lightweight box at his home that would hold all of the needed items. He delivered it to the chosen site at about nine the next morning after his trial run. There was no indication that the road had been recently traveled. He quickly made sure that the box, even in sunlight, could not be seen from any angle in the unlikely event that someone ambled by it on foot. It had started to snow again and was expected to accumulate heavily as the afternoon went on.

In less than an hour Ace returned to deliver his weapon and other items to his hiding place. He was pleased that the wheel marks from his two trips up the incline would likely be snow covered by nightfall.

He had selected an ACOG-equipped M16 rifle with a M855A1 cartridge for the job. Its precision would allow him to deliver a headshot within a one-to-three inch target range at 300 meters, and with even closer groupings at shorter distances. With its repeating firepower, he felt more than ready for any and all challenges that might arise. He disliked having to leave the weapon behind after his work but had several others back at his residence.

With everything in place, the only remaining decision was to select the night of Leila's execution. The forecast showed that snow would continue to fall for the next couple of days. He chose to wait until the weather cleared to earn his money.

*****

John and "Ace" barely missed running into each other. Just fifteen minutes after "Ace" had left the area after stocking his cache, John showed up to make his first property line inspection on both the east and west side of Powder's estate. He knew that, in addition to making his walk more difficult, any recent marks left by anything or anyone would be erased by the coming snow. He started on the east side by walking from Castle Creek Road to the point where the fence ended, and a short distance beyond. Other than a few tracks in the snow that he easily identified as having been made by deer, he observed nothing unusual at all.

On the west side he turned onto the gravel lane and could not miss the fresh automobile tire marks in the road. He followed them slowly up the incline toward the north. After traveling about 400 yards, he could see from his truck that there were large footprints of some kind going and coming off the road to the east toward Powder's lodge. They were being over-topped with fresh snow yet were obviously not very old.

From prior experience, without the necessity of even exiting his vehicle, John recognized that the tracks were left by either a man or a bear. He knew he could get out of his truck and quickly make the distinction, but what was more significant to him was that he could see no similar tracks on the left side of the road.

Too cautious to stop where he was, John proceeded up the hill. He drove beyond the spot where a prior vehicle had made a U-turn, and then continued around the next curve. He parked and exited his truck, with his pistol in his pocket. He did not yet know for sure if someone had been dropped off, but with the previous vehicle having departed the area, John did not expect to encounter anyone. But if someone was coming and going upon

Powder's property, he wanted to find out without them knowing of his discovery.

He quickly walked about fifty yards into the woods on the eastern side of the gravel road and then south toward the discovered tracks. The walk back down the hill toward Castle Creek Road covered about 200 yards. As he neared where he thought he might intersect the tracks, he was carefully watching the snow ahead of him. Finally he could see the line of tracks, and even from a distance he could tell they did not look as fresh as those near the gravel road. Unknown to John, his cautious procedure had eliminated any chance he may have had to discover "Ace's" cache.

He began to follow the tracks, still from an uphill distance. He saw where the tracks went under an aspen tree and knew they would be better preserved. He walked down to get a closer look. After brushing off an upper layer of fresh snow on the first track he inspected, he could clearly observe the heel print from a boot. John did not have to investigate any further. There was no mistaking it--Powder Mountain had recently had a human visitor.

John broke off a low limb on the far side of the aspen tree and used it to rake away his tracks the best he could for about twenty-five feet. He knew the area still looked disturbed, but his tracks would now be more easily covered by snow.

He then returned to walk approximately fifty feet above the discovered tracks to see where they led. In less than ten minutes he was looking down at the rear of Powder's lodge. The tracks ended there.

John had discovered the intruder's destination, and it was quite disturbing.

Chapter 62

John followed his own tracks back to his truck. He again unknowingly missed any opportunity he may have had to discover "Ace's" cache. By that time he had calmed down enough to realize that he could not tell for certain if the footprints he had followed were left by a wayward daytime visitor or someone with sinister intent. He did not want to overreact, but his first order of business was to find out the answer. Leila and her sons had become the most important persons in his life, maybe the only important persons in his life. "Their safety is my personal charge," he accepted. "I will not allow them to be harmed," he pledged to himself.

He sat in his vehicle for a few minutes to prioritize his course of action. He then hurriedly headed over to Highway 82 and turned to the north, proceeding to the Outdoor Gear Store in Basalt. When he arrived, his good buddy and owner, Doug Laye, saw John approaching across the parking lot in what was high speed for him.

"What are you in such a hurry for, Gillespie? Are you going to finally get yourself an elk this year?"

"They don't call me 'No Elk' for nothing," John replied. "What I am here for is to pick up a couple of those game trail cameras that you 'soup up' to look like wasps' nests. Do you have some, I hope?"

"I only have one left, John. It takes me over an hour to make one up. And then I have to let them get hard before I can paint them. I'm about to walk out the door to get ready for my family's Thanksgiving tomorrow."

"I understand—I will take the one you have."

"Would you also like a regular 'un-doctored' camera?"

"No, thank you. Just please call me when you get another one ready."

"Yes, Sir. It will probably be at least Monday.

John paid and hurried back to Castle Creek Road. He turned onto the gravel lane and stopped his truck. There were no new auto tracks on the road, and it was now snowing harder. He walked about ten yards up the hill and turned left away from the lodge, figuring that if an intruder was looking for a camera, his attention would be more likely fixed upon the lodge side of the road. He hung the camera in a small evergreen bush. Activating it, he returned to his vehicle. He would now be able to check every motion on the road.

John regretted, "I only wish I had thought to do this sooner."

*****

Leila had been shopping in Aspen all afternoon picking up extra food items and decorations to take to John's cabin for Thanksgiving. The driver John had recommended was very helpful in suggesting places to shop and in helping Leila gracefully fend off a number of well-wishers who had recognized her and her family. Aspen was packed with tourists for the opening of ski season, and many of them were taking pictures of the threesome at every location they visited.

She was back at Powder's estate preparing cornmeal dressing and her special sweet potato casserole for the next day when John drove up to the lodge to join her. But before entering, he had walked around to its rear yard and up to the approximate spot where the intruder had stopped. He had not approached it so closely earlier in the day. The visible signs from the unknown visitor were beginning to disappear beneath the ongoing snow.

When he turned to look back toward the lodge, he could easily see into Leila's suite. Extra precautions needed to be immediately put into place. He decided he would insist that Leila keep her curtains closed and that she and the boys stay completely off their porch. He planned on giving the entire situation even more attention upon returning from their planned Thanksgiving trip to his cabin.

John went inside and hugged Leila, and gave both of the boys a cheerful swirl. Leila reached up and ruffled his hair. "Look at the snowflakes all over you, John. You need to wear a big hat in this kind of weather. What on earth have you been doing?"

Not wanting to spoil the holiday weekend with possibly unfounded fear, he made no mention about the details of his afternoon. "I have been taking care of a few things, dear. You and the boys will have a few Thanksgiving surprises tomorrow."

Chapter 63

At ten o'clock on Thanksgiving morning, Luke was shouting, "Look at the deer, look at the deer!"

Two months before, John had hung the largest commercial game feeder he could purchase in a draw below his cabin. It dispersed several pounds of corn twice daily, and the timer had just gone off.

"How many do you see, Luke?" asked Leila.

"Nine, Mommy."

"Jake, can you say 'deer'?"

"Yes," he replied, not feeling overly talkative.

"Okay, a surprise is ready—c'mon, folks," directed John. He carried Jake as the others followed him outside and around through the snow to his storage shed.

A large silver snowmobile made for four persons was already running. "Wow!" Leila exclaimed. The boys ran quickly toward the vehicle, in obvious delight.

John buckled them into the rear two seats, and Leila fastened the hat straps beneath their chins. They took off.

"These heated seats are great," Leila spoke just above the engine noise as they began to climb toward a nearby peak. "How far up are we going?"

"How high does an eagle fly?" He asked with a smile while deftly maneuvering upward along a snow-covered trail at a hasty pace.

Rounding a big bend, John caught a movement in an exposed vista to his right. He brought the snowmobile to a quick halt and directed Leila's and the boys' attention to five elk that were crossing the opening in plain view. They were thrilled.

Continuing another two miles, they arrived at John's selected destination. It was a lookout spot that he called "Weathercock View" because of the rooster-topped weather vane he had mounted on a tall pole near a steep drop-off.

"What a fabulous panorama," exclaimed Leila. "I can see for a hundred miles."

"You are over-looking Kobey Road Park," John replied.

The boys were required to stay in their seats, but they also were astonished by the view. They sat in speechless awe.

"Do you come here often?" Leila asked.

"Only every time I come to the cabin."

"That is the way I feel about Ebenezer Church," she replied as she reached over and squeezed his hand.

"I understand."

*****

Rather than use the more traditional roasting method, John fried the Thanksgiving turkey Arkansas-style. Leila joined the boys at a window to watch his preparation and cooking procedure. It was novel to them all.

When he brought the turkey inside for carving, Leila began to fill the table with all of the trimmings she had prepared. Once everything was ready, the four held hands and John said the blessing. Even the two boys said "amen."

The warm log cabin was an ideal setting for a Thanksgiving gathering. The others were not aware that it was the very first time, since John had purchased the cabin several years before, that he had invited any guests at all to join him there for a holiday meal. He wanted to take a few pictures, and afterwards Leila insisted that she take a few of just him and the boys. She could not help noticing how happy the three males were and realized this was one of the very best holidays of her life.

Pecan pie and ice cream came later. Then John read the boys a story from a book he had read as a child. Leila recalled that she had done the exact same thing when they first came to her home.

Meanwhile, Leila curiously examined the numerous books John had saved over the years. Many of them had to do with wildlife, but several of them dealt with coping with the death of a loved one. After finishing her quick scan of the book titles, she looked at John and thought, "It is a miracle how God brings certain people together." She bowed her head and gave thanks to Him for her wonderful man from Arkansas.

*****

Leila and her sons would sleep in a separate room. She tucked them in and said a prayer. After they were asleep, she rejoined John on the couch in front of the fireplace.

The warm crackling fire in the deep woods on a cold night was more than romantic enough to accelerate their mutual attraction. Which of the two was more anxious to hold and touch the other was indeterminable. They wrapped themselves into each other's arms--it was spontaneous combustion.

Both aroused the other like never before. Soon they were locked together, as though they were one. Only scripture from the Good Book kept them apart--it was God's word.

Leila would have died before she let him enter her, but she desired him more than she could have ever imagined. She knew she was a different person now and felt new yearnings. They were for one man. And he was alternating her nipples into his mouth. She did not want him to stop sucking them--not now, maybe never. "Just a few minutes more," she allowed.

John had loved only one other woman in his life, and she was dead. There had been plentiful sexual overtures from other women--he had avoided them all. But the fire in his heart for Leila was powerfully raging. He knew he was totally stiff and close to sinning. He had promised to honor Leila's wishes and be faithful to his own Christian beliefs. There was still time to pull away, but he was inching forward.

Without warning, the bedroom door opened. Luke loudly said, "Mommy, I need some water."

Everyone needed water. It came just in the knick of God's time--and was a true Thanksgiving blessing.

*****

After things had settled down and cooler heads and bodies had prevailed, they looked at each other without speaking, as though they knew that Luke's interruption had been providential.

Finally breaking the silence, Leila brought up something which had occurred the night before that had really surprised her.

"As I was putting Luke to bed, he said to me, 'Mommy, I wish our little sister could be here with me and Jake.' I had never considered that Luke and Jake might have another sibling."

"What did you tell him?" John asked.

"I asked him a few questions. He referred to her as a baby. He said she has hair the color of mine, and her name is Annette. The last time he saw her she was with his mother."

"She probably gave her up for adoption also," John surmised.

"Their mother was arrested after attacking me, and that is all I know," began Leila. "If she still had the baby when she was arrested, I am sure the state would have intervened. What would you think, John, about getting my lawyer to look into locating the little girl to see if she could possibly be rejoined with Luke and Jake?"

John, hesitating briefly, replied, "Leila, I am totally in love with you. And I love your sons. Whatever you choose to do, I will support. I know you will do what is best for the boys."

"We don't know what the situation is, but I am going to check into it. I want to tell you how much I appreciate what you just said to me, John. It means everything. I love you too. I never dreamed I would feel safer somewhere other than Ebenezer Forest. But I really do--and I think the boys are safer here, too. It has even crossed my mind that Colorado might be a better place for them to grow up than in the Panhandle. I cannot believe I am even thinking such thoughts, but I am."

John recalled what he had discovered the day before, but chose only to say, "I am hopeful there will be a day in the near future when you and the boys can live without fear of anyone. Once the criminal case is over, maybe the bad guys will get their due. I'm praying that will be so."

"What are we going to do with each other, John?"

He was shocked to hear the question and took a long pause before answering.

"Maybe tease each other into legal submission," he said with a wry smile.

She walked over, gave him a huge kiss and whispered, "It has been a wonderful day, and I love you very much."

"I love you, darling--happy Thanksgiving."

Chapter 64

"Ace" had ruled out the holiday weekend because there would likely be more people around Powder Mountain than usual. Monday was his birthday, and he always avoided killing on that special occasion. Thus, he selected Tuesday as "kill night."

On the day of a planned murder he always followed the same ritual. The day would begin with a great lunch at one of the best places in whatever town he was working. Afterwards, he would call his mother. He did this in the event that something might go afoul, preventing him from ever talking with her again. It was all part of his superstitious nature.

With his hired chauffeur already lined up for his evening's work, he selected Element 74 as his special lunch place. The restaurant was named in honor of the element, tungsten. Sometimes, when necessary, "Ace" used special bullets containing this extra-heavy metal. He did not think, however, the easy shot he expected to soon take required the additional firepower. After a delicious meal, he called his mother.

Already dark around six p.m., "Ace" and his driver were on their way to the scene of the anticipated crime. They turned west on Castle Creek Road, driving casually. Nearing the front gate of Powder's estate, they could see the flashing red lights of a sheriff's vehicle parked just before the entrance. There were several other cars backed up, waiting to turn onto Powder's property

"Shit! Slow down. What the hell is going on?" barked "Ace."

A number of cars were already on the premises, and others had their blinkers on to await permission to enter.

"Some kind of damn party," "Ace" growled.

They proceeded around the next curve, where he ordered his driver to use the gravel road to turn around. They returned to Aspen past an even longer line of guests waiting to join the event at Powder Mountain.

"Son-of- a bitch, we will be back tomorrow night," he fumed. "I hate to have to call my fuckin' mother again!"

*****

The arriving guests were greeted by Powder, Leila and John, in that order. Powder had retained one of Aspen's finest professional catering companies. Filet mignon was being served on toothpicks outside the front door as the crowd waited in line to meet the most famous gunslinger of the twenty-first century. The beautiful lady from Red Bay, Florida would soon exceed all of their expectations.

Leila looked every attendee in the eye and shook everyone's hand firmly. Her enchanting blue eyes and soft hands very much contrasted with her legendary feats of fearless courage. The guests did not know what to expect, but they met an elegant lady of apparent humility and sweetness. The line moved slowly with everyone in full awe of Leila as each was introduced.

The high-ceilinged great room was still decorated in Thanksgiving colors. Powder provided his guests with food and liquor of the highest quality, and live music was underway. The fireplace added warmth to the festive scene. Every person in the room was keeping an eye on Leila as people continued to arrive at the entrance. They witnessed her exciting presence and command. She was slender and curvy on the one hand, and larger than life on the other.

After most of the expected guests had arrived, Powder called for everyone's attention. He thanked everyone for attending and gave about a five-minute talk about his planned "Ebenezer Forest in Aspen." He introduced his three friends who accompanied him on the trip south to first meet Leila, and then described the outstanding forested wonderland she had preserved and manicured for the enjoyment and education of thousands of visitors.

John was asked to say a few words, with Powder introducing him as a "master woodsman and outdoorsman," as well as the first curator of "Ebenezer Forest in Aspen." "Let's welcome John 'No Elk' Gillespie!"

John was enthusiastically applauded by the many guests, and smiled at Powder's use of his nickname.

"I accepted this challenge," he began in a less flamboyant voice than Powder's, "partly because of my deep respect for our generous host and for his commitment to the preservation of wildlife and wildlife habitat--also because Leila Jane Hewitt has agreed to assist us by her association with this project and to share her great knowledge and love for our same objectives. I hope that she will consider herself as a permanent part of this community that all of us here tonight so truly love. Thank you, Leila."

Powder shook John's hand after his brief remarks. Then he turned toward Leila.

"Leila, would you like to say a few words?"

His request was unexpected. Even though she had previously been a guest speaker before a number of other wildlife-related groups, she was at a loss for words. She had no place to turn, but to Him.

She slowly walked to a more central place in the room where she could be seen by all.

"There is so much love and warmth in this room, please join me in thanking our Lord for this assemblage tonight and for Powder's project."

Leila bowed her head, praying,

"Dear God, You gave us dominion over this earth and all living things that grow or move upon it. Thank you for bringing all of us here together this evening so that we may unite behind this exciting plan for Powder Mountain. With Your help, projects like this around our wonderful country and the entire world will hopefully pass on to the next generation our duty to protect our environment and habitats, all of which you have blessed us with. Please help us to be better stewards of the forests and animals that You have so graciously entrusted unto us. In Your name, our Heavenly Father, we pray. Amen."

When Leila looked up, every eye in the room was still fixed on her. There was absolute silence. She spoke again, just loudly enough for every person in the room to hear.

"I have never traveled much. In fact this is my first destination west of the Mississippi River. This area is so magnificent and picturesque. I will be forever touched by the kindness and hospitality of the people I've met here in Pitkin Valley. I look forward to speaking to each one of you again before you leave. Thank you all very much."

The guests stood in line over the next ninety minutes for a chance to visit with Leila. She courteously and patiently shared her time with all.

Questions anyone may have had about attending a party for a woman who had killed three people were forever silenced.

She was not a movie star and never would be. But Aspen had a new, real star. And she would be a favorite for as long as she lived.

Chapter 65

"Ace" was totally obsessed with Leila after his surreptitious view of her on his trial run to Powder's lodge. He could not sleep after his plans from the night before had been interrupted by the unexpected party. Every time he tried to drift away, he would think of her. The mere thought of watching her deeply expand her lungs, in and out, gave him sensuous thoughts of what he would prefer doing to her rather than take her life. It made him breathe harder, and he fantasized his forceful thrusts making her gasp. He kept recalling her lovely face as it appeared through his binoculars. Merely remembering Leila tantalized his lustful thirst. She would be his most famous and comely kill. Taking her life would be his greatest moment. He was anxious for nighttime to come again.

Hardly a word was spoken between "Ace" and his driver as they slowly drove to Castle Creek Road for the second night in a row. The plan had been thoroughly discussed, and "Ace" knew he needed to erase Leila's appeal from his mind. He began psyching himself up for the evening's work. "Leila's run of good luck is almost over--she is about to meet the 'Ace,'" he proudly thought to himself. Yet he knew he had better not underestimate her.

He put on his gloves as they approached the drop-off corner. As the vehicle came to a stop, he realized, "Son of a bitch, I forgot to call my mother." He jumped out anyway.

*****

"Ace" chose not to walk the gravel road but instead trekked uphill ten yards on the right side of it. Once hidden in the tree line, he put on his night goggles. It was not overly dark, and the woods opened up into full view before him. He knew he had a significant advantage over anything or anyone he might encounter. He walked cautiously up the hill through the snow to his cache. Upon arriving, he opened its top and uncovered his weapon. He injected a bullet into the chamber of the M-16 and attached a thirty-round magazine. Then he clipped two extra magazines to his belt. After picking up his pistol, a bottle of water and a couple of snack bars, he closed the lid to the cache and briskly headed toward Powder's lodge.

He walked to within 150 yards of the dwelling in less than seven minutes. He came to a complete stop for another five minutes, never moving a muscle. Carefully surveying everything between himself and the lodge, he noticed that lights were visible on both rear sides of the structure. He was aware that he was on the same approximate elevation of his previous visit and was certain he would be able to recognize the tree he had leaned against before. Finally he felt secure in moving forward.

As he drew closer he was able to see the far side of the lodge where Leila and her sons were staying. The drapes were not open. "Dammit to hell!" he thought, "That lucky bitch!"

He recalled that on his first visit it was a good bit later before Leila had walked out on the porch for her breathing exercises. "I hope it is not a long wait," "Ace" thought to himself as he resumed his final approach toward his pre-selected shooting position.

Almost to Aspen

Chapter 66

John had checked out his game camera the day after the party at Powder's lodge. He saw a picture of a dark vehicle that came halfway into the viewing area and apparently stopped. He compared the photo to the automobile tracks still visible in the snow and determined that the car had used the gravel lane to reverse its direction back onto Castle Creek Road. John thought that unless someone knew the narrow drive was there, it likely never would have been seen in the dark because of the angle at which it intersected the main road.

The odds that the gravel lane was used by a party guest were thus very small, John thought. And the huge gathering would have been a certain deterrent to any nefarious plan. He speculated that if the vehicle was in any way related to the danger he had suspected from the week before, there was a high chance it would return again that night. He again made it a point to advise Leila to keep her drapes shut.

But John had never informed Leila or his friend Powder of his strong concern. Right or wrong, it was his decision only. He was going to protect her and her children at all costs. He felt confident he could do so.

He would stand guard that night--and nightfall soon came.

317

*****

John "No Elk" Gillespie was sitting motionless about sixty steps up the hill and thirty steps to the east from where the unknown visitor had positioned himself the previous week. John chose his spot so that if the intruder returned, he would have a better angle from which to view him. He did not want any tree between him and someone who might hurt Leila.

He was hidden on the far side of a medium-sized evergreen tree so that anyone approaching from the west could not see his silhouette. There was good visibility, thanks to the reflection of the moonlight from the calf-deep, powdery snow. The view from where he sat was far better looking downward toward the well-lit home than it would be for someone looking back up in his direction into darkness.

In spite of his readiness, John was nonetheless startled when he first saw the alarming movement of a human approaching below him. The threat had been real.

He soon discerned that the man was carrying in his arms what was surely a weapon. His cautious speculation and preparation had suddenly and shockingly turned into what would certainly soon be an armed confrontation.

John's camouflaged ski mask shielded his face as he peeked around his protective tree, and it was necessary for him to slide back so that his body remained concealed as the intruder neared.

He watched the gunman spread his pouch out on the ground and sit down on top of it. He saw that the weapon in his hand was not an ordinary rifle, but a killing machine.

It hit John, like the bash of a board to his face, that the situation was grave.

"I grossly underestimated this moment," he knew. "I have to be ready to kill him--NOW! Or this situation could explode--and backfire fast—with horrible consequences!"

*****

John rose and eased around to the right side of his tree. He raised his left arm to steady against it and braced his rifle for a steady shot. It was face-off time.

"THROW YOUR GUN DOWN THE HILL, AND DON'T TURN AROUND," John shouted with his finger on the trigger.

The gunman did not move at all. He instantly knew he had somehow screwed up. It was surrender or fight. He was born to fight. "Fuck that bastard," he thought.

"IF YOU MOVE, I WILL SHOOT YOU," shouted John more loudly.

Without standing, the man leaped swiftly to his right to be more shielded by the tree behind him.

POW! John pulled the trigger almost simultaneously. He thought he had hit and rolled the intruder, but he had sprung like a frog--and John was unsure.

A few seconds passed, and he could not see any movement at all. Then the barrel of the gunman's weapon appeared from behind his tree--firing in John's direction.

POP, POP, POP, POP, POP, POP, POP, POP! The assault weapon was firing rapidly and the bullets blasted the evergreen that John was now behind.

When the thunderous volley stopped, John stuck his left arm out, and then pulled it back as fast as he could.

POP, POP, POP, POP!

John knew he was penned down and out-gunned. He had only four remaining bullets in his chamber. There were others in his pocket, but he didn't have time to replace the bullet he had just fired.

He expected to be charged by the shooter at any second.

Chapter 67

Leila and her sons were in their private quarters when the first shot was fired. The barrage of deafening shots that followed threw her into a protective frenzy. The boys started to cry. She hurried them toward the front of the lodge, turning off the lights in the suite as she left. Powder was in the kitchen as they passed. He called 911 and told the operator there was a gun battle underway in his back yard. When he hung up the phone, he ran to his den to grab a rifle and a pistol.

Leila put Luke and Jake in a hallway closet and told them to stay there until she came back for them. She instructed them sternly, "Do not leave this closet, and don't make a sound!"

When Powder returned, he handed Leila the pistol and began, "It is loaded--just pull the trigger if you have to use it." He loaded his rifle, and then added, "I am afraid John may be out there. I know he was going to keep an eye on my property."

There was an eerie silence outside. "Maybe it is over," Powder said. "I am going to see." He left by the side door and hurriedly crept along the side of Leila's suite toward the rear of the lodge.

Leila watched from the doorway as Powder reached the rear corner of the building and stopped.

Uphill, John had no idea Powder was now outside.

Powder was fooled by the silence. "John, are you out here?" he yelled.

When John did not immediately answer, Powder stuck his head and shoulder around the corner of the building.

POP, POP, POP, POP, POP, POP, POP, POP! The shooter razed the corner of the building with multiple shots and hit Powder in his upper-right shoulder and body, nearly tearing off his arm. He fell to the ground with a thud.

From up the hill there was an immediate rifle shot. POW!-- then another--POW! John had realized that the gunman was shooting at someone else, and so he had begun firing to divert his attention.

POP, POP, POP, POP, POP! The intruder was now shooting back in John's direction.

Leila was keenly aware of exactly what was happening and knew the shots that struck Powder had been fired from around the corner. She raced down the side of the lodge to Powder's feet. She dropped the pistol and with an adrenaline rush of profound strength dragged him backwards out of the line of fire. He was moaning in deep agony.

"Go back inside, Powder," she heard John yell.

POP, POP, POP, POP, POP!

Leila knew the shooter was trying to kill her man.

Powder's weapon was lying in clear view. Without a second thought, she raced to the rifle across the open area. She grabbed it and darted toward a small storage building twenty feet away.

POP, POP, POP, POP, POP, POP, POP! The shooter's bullets tore up the snowy ground behind her, narrowly missing a direct hit before she reached cover.

Once behind the structure, Leila quickly made her way to its far side.

There was another period of silence. All Leila could hear were occasional moans from Powder.

Suddenly there was a piercing scream from a child, "Mommmmyy!"

It was Luke. He had left the kitchen and was walking slowly toward Powder, looking for his mother.

He had strong lungs for a not quite five-year-old and was heard halfway up the mountain.

''MOMMMMYY!" he cried out again.

John heard Luke clearly and had already reloaded. POW! He again shot in the intruder's direction to attract the man's attention toward himself.

POP, POP, POP, POP, POP, POP, POP! The intruder returned John's fire.

Leila risked peaking around the far side of the storage building. She could see the profile of the man who was trying to kill John and who would surely shoot Luke next. He was lying on his stomach, firing rapidly.

She took slow, careful aim at his head, and pulled the trigger without flinching.

POW! Leila saw the man's head fly apart at the impact of her bullet.

There was complete silence.

Mike "Ace" Tingle had been trumped by the Queen of Ebenezer Forest.

Chapter 68

"JOHN, IT'S OVER! HELP! POWDER IS SHOT!" Leila finally shouted, breaking the silence. She jumped to her feet and ran back across the opening to Luke.

"I should spank your fanny," she said as she hurriedly hugged and lifted him into her arms--then carried him to the kitchen door.

"Go get Jake out of the closet, and both of you come stay here in the kitchen until I get back--DO YOU UNDERSTAND ME?"

Luke shook his head meekly, still dazed by the gunfire.

Leila raced back outside to Powder. He was lying face down in a pool of blood. She pulled him over on his back and took off her shirt to compress his shoulder's gaping wounds.

Meanwhile, John had carefully approached the shooter to confirm he was down for good. Within ten feet of the motionless body, he could see a large bath of bloody snow. The man's face was still masked but half of it had exploded into plain view.

John wheeled and ran toward Leila. She was still attending Powder's wound but rose up to receive John's hugs. Squeezing him back tightly, she looked lovingly into his eyes, saying, "Thank God you are safe."

"Are the boys okay?" His voice was frantic.

"Yes, but Powder is badly hurt."

Leila's upper body was covered only by a bra. She dropped to the snow-covered ground to again apply pressure to Powder's wound.

"Let me do that," John said, bending down to take over. "Please go call an ambulance and put on a coat before you freeze."

She remembered Powder putting his cell phone in his pocket. Leila dug it out and made the call.

The operator, recognizing the number from Powder's prior call, assured Leila the sheriff's office was on the way.

"We need an ambulance as soon as possible, please," Leila stressed in an excited state.

"I'll take care of it. What is your name please, Ma'am?" asked the operator.

"My name is Leila Jane Hewitt."

"Oh, my gosh," gasped the operator, obviously familiar with the legend.

"I almost forgot--you'll need to send a hearse, too," Leila replied humbly. "I shot a man."

Before Leila could click off the cell phone, she heard the operator yelling to others in the room, "Leila Hewitt plugged another one--right here in Aspen!"

*****

Three sheriff's cars arrived at one time. All the deputies strutted around the scene with drawn weapons which they soon replaced with fountain pens, hoping to obtain Leila's autograph. Of course, she politely declined.

The press was inside Powder's front gate before the ambulance came to take him to the hospital. He was going to survive, but would never deal another poker hand.

The coroner showed up at the scene, probably out of curiosity. But he did later reveal a new fact. It explained why the attempted murderer had not fired his way out of the situation. According to the doctor, John's first shot had "hit him squarely in the butt."

The coroner had added, "The bullet ricocheted off his tailbone. It may or may not have killed him, but he sure as hell wasn't going anywhere. And anything he tried to do after that would surely have been half- assed," he added, tongue-in-cheek.

Both the press and the sheriff's office stayed all night and most of the next day. The tracks left in the snow by the unidentified shooter led back to his cache, then to the road. It was apparent he had been dropped off, but his accomplice was never apprehended.

Another news story related to Leila arose the next day out of Okaloosa County, Florida. Attorney Rusty Lucas, along with several other Panhandle attorneys, was arrested by the federal government for multiple racketeering charges arising from their conspiring with mobsters for money-laundering purposes. Clarence Bectom "Big Fuzz" Rogers was included in the same indictments.

"Big Fuzz" and Rusty Lucas were also arrested on a separate charge and were being held on additional two million dollar bonds for being part of the conspiracy to murder Leila Hewitt. The intercepted telephone conversation between Rogers and

Lucas had been acted upon too late by the F.B I. for them to have prevented Leila from being attacked in Aspen. For their delayed action, the feds were universally crucified by the national media.

*****

Rhonda Riveras, and scores of other top-notch reporters from around the world, raced to Aspen, Colorado to capture the full story. The "Grand Heroine of Ebenezer Forest" had gone northwest for the winter and had taken her invincibility with her. The world was in awe of Leila once again.

U. S. News of Today dubbed her "The Aspen Angel." The article referred to her powers of survival as "supernatural" and also called her a "Good Angel." But for anyone who tried to take her life, she was the "Angel of Death."

With Aspen filling up with skiers, Castle Creek Road was jammed with tourists wanting to get a picture of Powder Mountain. Helicopters hovering overhead, from various television networks, captured footage of the still-bloodied patch of snow where the shooter had died.

The Pitkin County Sheriff's office released Leila's recorded words from her call to their operator the night before. Rhonda Riveras, standing in front of the gates to Powder Mountain, addressed Leila's choice of words.

"Last night, Leila Jane Hewitt ended the life of the fourth person who tried to kill her in the last two months. When she called 911 for an ambulance, she added these words. Listen."

Rhonda played a portion of the tape:

"You'll need to send a hearse, too. I shot a man."

Rhonda continued.

"Was Leila Hewitt being flippant about her killing of a person, as another network has suggested?"

The feisty Latino answered her own question.

"Hell, NO! I was able to get a response from a top employee of Leila this morning. She said Leila was still in an excited state of mind, and doesn't really recall or have an explanation of why she chose the word 'hearse.' After Leila's last good look at her attempted killer, she KNEW an ambulance was NOT needed.

"Let me give you MY opinion:

"IF YOU HAVE PLANS TO KILL LEILA JANE HEWITT, YOU SHOULD GO AHEAD AND RENT YOUR OWN HEARSE! AND HASTA LUEGO----SUCKER!"

*****

It did not go without notice by all of the news services that John "No Elk" Gillespie had drawn first blood from Mike "Ace" Tingle—nor was John's relationship with Leila overlooked. Following every news story of Leila's latest heroics was an article about her involvement with the tall man from Arkansas. He was already beloved in Aspen, but walked even taller afterward.

Nothing is more unpredictable or oftentimes more confounding than who ends up as another's mate. The odds of the girl from Walton County, Florida ending up with John "No Elk" Gillespie were millions to one.

John was finally able to shake the "No Elk" moniker. After the shootout at Powder Mountain, Aspen gave its favorite son a new nickname. Leila was thereafter linked with John "Hit-'Em-In-The-Ass" Gillespie.

She had no intention to ever back off from him, even an inch.

EPILOGUE

Reverend Tom McGraw sat alone in the small room at the rear of Ebenezer Church. In days past he could perform a wedding service from rote memory, but those days were gone. He was going over his notes.

Health problems had required him to surrender his position as pastor of Red Bay Church. And he was choked up that this wedding would surely be the last one he would ever conduct. He had that uncomfortable tight feeling in his throat that people get when they are about to cry. There was even a question in his mind if he could complete his task without breaking down. He remembered how his beloved Leila had lost control of her emotions at Mark Mabry's funeral. "No one will ever forget that day," he thought. He looked at his watch. There was only eight more minutes remaining before he would walk out front to commence the ceremony.

*****

Inside, Jane Anderson Kirk sat on the left-side front row beside her husband, Bob, and their son, Noah. After he had lost the sheriff's race, Leila had appointed Bob co-curator of Ebenezer Forest with his wife. They both agreed it had been one of the best things that ever happened in their lives. Many things had changed over the years. They now lived in their own large home on the Ebenezer Forest estate.

All of the wedding guests had driven their automobiles on the now-paved road across the new Hominy Creek Bridge to Ebenezer Forest Church. Before arriving at their destination, the guests passed the commemorative plaza honoring Josh Snyder, the young forester who had mysteriously vanished while working on the estate. An attached aviary added vitality and music to his memorial.

The outdoor amphitheater, only a hundred yards away from the church, would be the site of the day's reception. Jane was thinking about the enormity of this occasion for her family.

Her husband, Bob, was recalling the staggering events he had witnessed since he had met Jane. The four gangsters who had tried to kill Leila were only a small part of the story. There were many victims of the Panhandle mobsters that he was aware of as a former F.B.I. agent. "No one will ever know how heinous that old crowd of crooks really was. Nor will anyone ever know what happened to so many victims on both sides of the battle."

Bob had never learned if Doctor Ty Tyson was murdered after his indictment or if he were living on an island--or perhaps in South America. "Another unresolved mystery," he thought. "He simply disappeared."

C. B. "Big Fuzz" Rogers, Colonel Max Barnett and Attorney Rusty Lucas had been out of jail for some time. Bob knew from old friends still involved in law enforcement that they were all financially ruined and had lost their seniority with the mob. "More real jobs for the always complaining millennial generation," Bob mulled to himself.

*****

There would be no helicopters flying over the wedding nor were any members of the press invited. The years had relieved the intense pressure from the media. Only a hundred or so close friends were seated for the ceremony. People such as the Branson family, even though Clyde had passed away, were included. Hank Harrison had also died, and Amanda was seated next to Charlie McBride and his wife. There were a number of guests from Aspen who had made the trip.

It was finally time. Sally Whalen's daughter, Sarah, began to play "You are so Beautiful" on the piano.

Reverend McGraw's wife was sitting alone, worrying if her husband had the strength to conduct the ceremony. He soon entered from the rear room into view of the guests. He moved very slowly. Obviously laboring, he made his way to the pulpit.

He looked over to the right-side front row of the church into the aging blue eyes of his prized congregant. Leila was holding her husband's hand tightly.

On the other side of John sat their daughter, Annette Gillespie.

Leila and John had married twenty years before in Aspen, just three months after the Powder Mountain shootout. The reception had been held at the world famous Caribou Club where John was a long-time member. Leila had never dreamed her wedding celebration would be held in an establishment known as a restaurant and bar. Yet she had consented to the venue after John convinced her it was a "western thing."

The first action they had taken after their wedding and honeymoon to Jackson Hole was to file a petition to adopt Luke and Jake's sister, Annette. She was in the custody of the State of Florida at the time. No judge would have ever had the courage to deny the famous couple's desire to reunite the three siblings.

On the far side of Annette sat her brother, Jake Gillespie. He was twenty-two years old, and his girlfriend and several young couples and other friends were down from the University of Colorado for this special occasion.

Sarah Whalen next played "I Can't Take My Eyes Off Of You." Listening to the song, Leila and John's eyes became locked in an inseparable, loving connection--as they had been thousands of times before. Tears of pure joy rolled down their cheeks.

*****

From the entrance of the church, the maid of honor and the best man commenced their slow, slow walk down the aisle. The maid of honor was Bob and Jane Kirk's lovely daughter, eighteen-year-old Haley Kirk. She was the best friend of the bride.

The best man was Powder White. The seventy-eight-year-old Aspen personality was white-headed, white eye-browed and quite heavy. His smile was as wide as Pitkin Valley. When he had selected the groom to become the new permanent manager of Ebenezer Forest at Powder Mountain six months before, he had bartered building the engaged couple their own Swiss chalet atop his mountain if he could be best man. Powder had been his "special uncle" for most of the groom's life.

*****

When the honor attendants were in place, the lucky man entered the church. Luke Gillespie was tall, handsome and smiling ear to ear. He walked straight to his mother and hugged her for a long minute. Leila was again openly crying in her lifelong church, but this time the tears were from absolute happiness. He hugged his dad with similar emotion, then Annette and Jake. He walked up beside his best man and looked back toward the front door of the church.

Sarah began to play "The Wedding March." Everyone stood.

In the doorway appeared one the most striking black-haired beauties that Destin or Aspen had ever seen. She was even more gorgeous than her father, Mark Mabry, had been handsome. She had his strong features and radiant blue eyes. And she had his air of romance.

Moving ever so slowly and gracefully down the aisle, she was fully aware that her father lay just a few yards away. Although having never known him, she could feel his presence.

Ahead to the right, she could see the woman her father was to have married in this same room. She had grown to know Leila and could understand her father's love.

Ahead to the left, she could see her adoptive parents, Jane and Bob Kirk.

Her mother, Mary Kate Nelson, had become terminally ill in New York when her daughter was ten years old. She had called Jane to ask if she and Bob would consider raising her daughter, Charlotte Mabry. She had no relatives to call and knew that Jane was the best friend of her daughter's father.

When Charlotte reached Jane and Bob, she stopped to embrace the parents she had grown to deeply love.

Charlotte then turned her attention to Luke. He was her first and only love, and she was his.

When Charlotte had never wanted to date anyone else, Jane told her, "You will be a one-man woman all of your life, and that man will be Luke Gillespie."

*****

Reverend McGraw was able to get through the ceremony. The only hiccup of the service was when Powder fumbled the wedding ring, his fingers stiff from his old gunshot injury. But he loved his role nonetheless.

After Charlotte Mabry and Luke Gillespie said their final "I do's," but before Reverend Tom declared them man and wife, the aged preacher could not help himself.

"THE MOST IMPORTANT THING WE HAVE IN THIS LIFE IS OUR RELATIONSHIPS WITH EACH OTHER!" he shouted. "ARE YOU LISTENING? DO YOU HEAR ME, EVERYBODY?

"ALL WE HAVE ARE OUR RELATIONSHIPS WITH EACH OTHER!

"ARE YOU LISTENING? DO YOU HEAR ME?

"ARE YOU LISTENING?

ALL WE HAVE ARE OUR RELATIONSHIPS WITH EACH

OTHER!

"DO YOU HEAR ME?"

Made in the USA
Columbia, SC
28 April 2020

93877040R00192